Sondre Lærche

Latin Satins

Latin Satins

Terri de la Peña

Seal Press

Cover and book design by Clare Conrad
Cover art by Nancy Carpenter

Library of Congress Cataloging-in-Publication Data

de la Peña, Terri, 1947–
Latin Satins
1. Hispanic American musicians—California—Santa Monica—Fiction.
2. Hispanic American women—California—Santa Monica—Fiction.
3. Young women—California—Santa Monica—Fiction. 4. Singers—California—Santa Monica—Fiction. 5. Santa Monica (Calif.)—Fiction.
I. Title.
PS3566.E448L37   1994   813'.54—dc20   94-15169
ISBN 1-878067-52-4

First printing, September 1994
10 9 8 7 6 5 4 3 2 1

Distributed to the trade by Publishers Group West
Foreign distribution:
In Canada: Publishers Group West Canada
In the U.K. and Europe: Airlift Book Company, London

Acknowledgments

Extraordinary women inspired and supported me during the writing of this book: Barbara Wilson, amiga y editora, challenged me to transform an unpublished story into a full-length work with lyrics, no less. Willa Sisson, former Personnel Director of the UCLA College of Letters and Science, arranged a job leave so I could expand the manuscript. Nancy Skinner Nordhoff, founder of Cottages at Hedgebrook on Whidbey Island, provided me with seven idyllic weeks of time and space in Fir Cottage. My sister Marguerite and my mother Juanita de la Peña, (who used to complain that I rarely ask for favors) handled my personal finances during my escape to the Pacific Northwest. And Gloria Bando, mi chulita/pajarita partner, phoned, sent love notes, care packages and visited my thoughts as birdwatcher Andrea Romano.

Much of this book's evolution I owe to las hermanas escritoras at Hedgebrook, especially Liz Raptis Picco, Evelyn Livingston, Sherry Witt, Naomi Hirahara and Elana Dykewomon, and to the staff's amazing nurturing abilities. Back home, mis Chicana critics (las criticónas) kept me honest: Professor Sonia Saldivar-Hull, una compañera de primera whose counsel I cherish; Mary Pat Brady whose incisive character analyses made me think; comic Monica Palacios and singer Gina Acuña whose generous comments gave me realistic glimpses into performers' lives. My niece Dané Markoe shared sushi and dreams. My coworkers Barbara Ikuta, Lee Solock, Pat Topper and Kathy Clark "womaned" my desk during my absence. Carolyn Drago, as always, offered friendship and uncommon sense. And a special thanks to the incomparable Sally Seal who first "auditioned" the Latin Satins' lyrics.

In memory of my father
Joaquin P. de la Peña,
February 5, 1903–October 25, 1986,
who loved his familia, his hometown Santa Monica,
y la música Mexicana.
Daddy, no estás lejos. . . .

Contents

Santa Monica, California

Spring 1989

1 Qué Chic

Jessica Tamayo hummed to herself while peering from the yawning door of the girls' restroom at St. Anne's School. Her vantage point in the pale brick building allowed her to gaze without obstruction into the well-lit interior of a red-and-yellow carnival tent across the way. Its sprawling dimensions almost hid the entire parish parking lot.

Through the tent's open flaps, Jessica saw Chicanos and Mexicanos of all ages milling around a crepe-paper-decorated wooden stage at the annual St. Anne's fiesta. Brown-skinned children darted through the friendly crowd, aiming to pelt each other with cascarónes, confetti-filled eggshells. Extended families sat in rusting folding chairs and chattered among themselves between the acts of hourly entertainment. Teenagers at bordering refreshment stands casually scanned the local talent while their parents at nearby picnic tables dined on tacos, tamales and other tasty delights. Some parishioners were too busy playing ring-toss, roulette, or participating in the lotería game, a type of Mexican bingo, to do much more than listen to the ongoing variety show that Sunday evening.

Unlike them, Jessica focused on the stage, watching a smiling troupe of beribboned little girls in lacy Mexican folklórico dresses. The children soon concluded their dance and scrambled offstage to join their proud parents.

"Looks like we're next," Jessica said, turning to the dust-flecked mirror to recheck her appearance. Her skin was a deep cinnamon and her blunt-cut black hair, with thick bangs that almost hid her brown eyes, skimmed her shoulders. The pastel shade of her lavender camisole accentuated the warm tones of her skin and eyes.

"Give or take ten minutes," Chic Lozano replied. Taller and a bit slimmer than Jessica, Chic wielded a tube of red lipstick, the exact color of Serrano chiles, and spoke rapidly while applying it. "When the M.C. does some plugs for the TV raffle and the fiesta sponsors, get ready to hustle, mujeres. Damn stage's halfway 'cross the playground."

"And with that long-winded viejo of an M.C., who knows how long we'll have to wait to make a run for it?" Cindi Carbajal noted with some exasperation while she combed out the edges of her bouncy ponytail. Cindi was Jessica's first cousin and bore some familial resemblance—coppery skin, coarse mestiza hair, dark-brown eyes, ready smile.

"I still can't believe we're singing *here.*" Rita Solís sounded miffed as she glanced at the graffiti-dotted restroom walls. Her black curly hair was cut close to her head, emphasizing her round light-brown eyes and cupid mouth. The manager of the coffeehouse where Rita worked dubbed her "the Chicana Bernadette Peters," a description she no doubt relished. Like Jessica and the others, she wore a lavender cotton camisole, matching satin shorts and high-topped purple sneakers.

"Hey, we have to try our fresh material on a Chicano audience first. If it works, Rita, we'll know Jess is on the right track with the new tunes." Chic finished with the lipstick and proceeded to mousse straying strands of her slick dark hair.

Jessica seized the moment and half-shut the restroom door. "While we're waiting to go on, listen to this." She whirled her agile body into a back-up singer's stance, knees a bit bent, sneakers squeaking on the scuffed linoleum. She snapped her fingers and sang to her friends.

4

I'm a native Californian
Brown-skinned but not an alien
In Spanish I'm not fluent
Is that so incongruent?

I've got the pocha blues
I'm brown, I've paid my dues
I've got the pocha blues
Not white and so I lose

She paused, her eyes searching theirs for feedback. "Do you think I have to define 'pocha/pocho' as a derogatory term for Mexicans born in the U.S.A.?"

Before any of them had a chance to answer, they heard the amplified voice of the paunchy master-of-ceremonies revving up.

"Damas y caballeros, muchachas y muchachos, our next act comes direct from the ever-popular Santa Monica Promenade by way of St. Clement's Parish in Ocean Park." The grey-haired man, more accustomed to ushering at noonday Mass, nonetheless relished his once-a-year role. He tugged at his bolo tie's silver tips and smoothed his embroidered black shirt over his belly. "Welcome these hometown hermositas—the Latin Satins!"

Following Chic's onslaught, Jessica, Cindi and Rita dashed across the schoolyard overflowing with parishioners; they nearly collided with swarms of playful children, grandmothers pushing baby strollers, and teenagers alternately gawking and flirting with one another. The Latin Satins swooped onstage, diverting the attention of obsessive lotería-players and almost toppling the bewildered M.C. Chic pulled the microphone from its flimsy stand and held it trumpet-like to her taunting red lips.

"Hey, Raza—you like the kind of movie roles Hollywood deals us?" she challenged, her dark eyes sweeping over the working-class crowd. "Puro pedo, verdad?"

5

A series of boos and raised fists demonstrated the audience's disdain for film industry portrayals of Chicanos and all other Latinos.

"Pues, here's what the Satins think!" Chic shouted, thrusting her own tawny fist upward. She replaced the microphone while her compañeras surrounded her. Black hair glimmering in the spotlights, the Satins moved in unison with Chic. Their shoulders and arms swung rhythmically while they provided an a capella back-up for her lowdown lead vocals.

Latinos on the silver screen
Dark and greasy, eyes so mean
Gardeners, gangsters, never clean
Stereotyped in every scene

And las mujeres always maids
Or sultry spitfires in the trade
Rounded up in immigration raids
When will injustice fade?

Enough of medium tedium
Who needs that racist helium?
Our turn to grab the spotlight
Take charge 'cause it's our right

Several men in the audience shook their heads, as if wondering what to make of such upfront Chicanas and their confrontational, though indisputable, lyrics. Older women clucked to one another, murmuring "sin vergüenzas," scandalized by the Latin Satins' scanty attire and hip-swinging movements. Most of the younger people in the crowd, however, whooped it up, whistling and catcalling their agreement as the scintillating Latin Satins harmonized into other stanzas.

The studios say we don't have writers
No literary freedom fighters
They close ranks, get even tighter
Won't make our image brighter

Raza, we can't afford to wait
For negativity to abate
We must unite to write, create
Abolish stereotypes, fight hate

Enough of medium tedium
Who needs that racist helium?
Let's put ourselves on the screen
And star in every scene

Amid the waves of applause and yells for more, Chic motioned to Jessica to step closer to the microphone. The group's songwriter and sometime soloist grinned and nudged Chic.

"Turned out to be the perfect audience for 'Medium Tedium.'"

"Yeah, and I thought the tune'd be too political for this bunch," Chic admitted in a whisper.

Jessica glanced at her cousin Cindi and friend Rita, whose beaming faces mirrored their delight.

Chic slipped an arm around Jessica, edging her nearer the microphone. "Ready?"

Nodding, Jessica took Chic's cue. Her full-bodied voice, a distinct contrast to Chic's gritty one, commanded the audience's attention with the first strains of "Hollow Kahlo."

A solid brow, probing eyes
With haunting looks, regal, wise
In love with life, a passionate heart
Communicating through her art

The Satins joined in, their voices matching hers, their expressive hands creating illusionary images of Mexican artist Frida Kahlo.

Frida's face is everywhere
On postcards, T-shirts, and I swear
The hype is hard to swallow
Too much hollow Kahlo

A couple of little girls from the folklórico troupe, their lacy dresses reminiscent of Kahlo's, began to dance at the foot of the stage. They held their wide skirts and pirouetted dizzily. Jessica stood before the microphone, her bare brown legs slightly apart, her arms outstretched.

A woman revolutionary
Her art is evolutionary
Her politics are complicated
For the rich, sophisticated

She looked into the audience, glimpsed her friends Rafael Cortés and Billie Otero, and smiled slightly at them.

Frida transformed her creativity
Into a visual biography
So let her rest, let her be
She's earned her place in history

Read about her, get inspired
By her will, her inner fire
All that hype is hard to swallow
Please, no more hollow Kahlo

The audience jumped to its collective feet, shrieking its approval of the Latin Satins' mixture of music and social commentary. Holding hands, the singers bowed together, enjoying being validated by people who needed no explanation of Jessica's latest compositions. She wished her father and sister would have been present to witness the excitement of that moment.

Known for their parodies of golden oldies and their newer bilingual lyrics, the Latin Satins had acquired a growing local following. They were regular performers on the Promenade in downtown Santa Monica. The outdoor mall a couple of blocks from the Pacific Ocean attracted weekend crowds with its movie theaters, coffeehouses, restaurants, and numerous street performers. The four Chicanas had sung there the previous

Friday night and wherever else opportunities arose.

"Sing some of your oldies stuff," yelled a skinny guy waiting in line at the taco booth.

"We want to hear more corridos," shouted another.

Jessica smiled at hearing that, pleased that somebody had already described "Hollow Kahlo" as a corrido, a folk ballad.

"Muchachas, do you know 'El Paso'?" suggested someone else.

Chic unhooked the microphone and paced the stage with it for a second or so before stopping to face the audience. "Come on, hombres. Do we look like 'muchachas'? We're *mujeres*! And this is *our* version of 'El Paso.'"

She replaced the microphone and shot a quick glance at her back-ups. Jessica wondered if Chic were pushing her luck with this audience, but she fell into place beside her nonetheless. Chic's voice took on a growl as she sang the opening lines of the Marty Robbins' classic, transforming it into the lament of a cowgirl falling "in love with a Mexican girl." She let her sultry eyes drift over the Satins' brown-skinned bodies in their skimpy outfits while she sang. Jessica noticed the uneasiness of the crowd as Chic began ad-libbing additional lyrics.

And she said 'Come a little bit closer
I'm your kind of girl, I'll give you a whirl'

"Those ain't the words," a deep voice complained.

"Un hombre's supposed to sing that," differed another.

Laughing, Chic winked at the Satins, cueing them. Jessica was relieved by her decision to abandon "El Paso" for one of the Satins' originals. Chic skimmed across the stage, not at all chagrined.

"We'd rather sing *this*—about being chic, not in El Paso—on Pico Boulevard!" In constant motion, the Satins' lead singer was stunning, her voice breathy and suggestive.

She passes by here every week
The vatos wait to sneak a peek

At her cuerpo, fine and sleek
And her skin like polished teak

The Satins leaned closer together, singing:

And she's so chic, so chic
Morena y qué chic
Yeah, she's so chic

The momentary tension in the crowd seemed to dissipate as the Satins glided through "Qué Chic," one of their most popular numbers. People began to clap in unison with the beat.

She sashays down the street
Swings her hips, a visual treat
When vatos whistle she ain't meek
She flips them off, her fingers speak

Many in the audience cheered and laughed at Chic's enactment, complete with swivel hips and exaggerated hand gestures. Teenagers emerged from the fringes of the crowd and began to dance, shimmying at the base of the stage.

All the home girls want to be
As cool, as saucy as they see
Her moving, being free
Dicen 'esa vida para mi'

'Cause she's so chic, so chic
Mujer, que chic
Yeah, she's so-o-o chic

"Let's hear it for the very talented, very lovely Latin Satins," the impatient M.C. interrupted the clamoring crowd at the conclusion of the Satins' set. The four Chicanas continued holding hands, smiling and acknowledging the adulation, while the M.C. broadly hinted for them to leave. "Moving right along—we have more música coming up as soon as I make some announcements."

"What a fuckhead," Chic muttered as she leaped off the

stage into the midst of a throng of admirers.

About to follow, Jessica hesitated when the M.C. leaned toward her. "Aren't you Tudy Tamayo's daughter?"

She nodded.

"Shame on you," he scolded, wagging a sausage-like brown finger. "With your pretty voice, you ought to sing with your father instead of with these crazy girls."

"Mr. Garcia, I sing *all* kinds of music," Jessica called over her shoulder. She hurried offstage to meet her waiting friends.

"Ay, mis lindas!" Billie Otero, a poufy-haired Chicana in a zebra-patterned jersey jumpsuit greeted the Satins in a boisterous voice after they had escaped their admirers. Outside the carnival tent, Billie held the hand of Angelita, Rita's six-year-old daughter. The little girl had inherited her mother's large eyes and her father's chocolate skin and tightly curled hair.

"You guys like our new stuff?" Chic hugged Billie's big-boned body and glanced at Rafael Cortés beside her.

Rafael, a wiry Chicano with ebony shoulder-length hair, fingered his pencil-thin mustache. He opened his mouth to speak, but Billie cut him off.

"Muy political, no?"

"I was about to say, the new songs have razor-sharp teeth," Rafael added. "Wasn't sure these gente would like their bite."

"Chic was smart to switch in midstream," Jessica admitted.

"It's all in the timing." Chic grinned, giving Rafael a slow wink and a long hug. "You have to know when to change gears."

"Yeah, there were some weird vibes from this audience," Cindi remarked. "Too many righteous Catholics and macho types."

"We sure shook them up," Rita said with a laugh.

"Marry me, Rafi," Chic joked, grabbing Rafi tighter. "Take me away from these locas."

11

He snuggled against her for a moment before holding her at arms' length and eyeing her moussed hair and slim figure. "You ain't my type, babe. Not quite butch enough."

"Ay, that's cold, Rafi." Rita laughed. "You got her where it hurts."

"Nothin' hurts *me*," Chic disagreed. "The thing is, I'm too much mujer for este maricón."

"Ay, Chiquita. You make me so jealous." Rafi shifted his almost nonexistent hips with an exaggerated swish.

While the bantering continued, Jessica bent to give Angelita a hug. "Did you have fun staying overnight at Billie's?"

The little girl nodded with a giggle.

"I'm surprised you're even here, Rafi," Rita cut in, spreading her hands on her daughter's narrow shoulders. "I thought you'd be busy finishing our jackets."

"Ay, mujer," he answered in mock irritation, his slender hands gesticulating. "You were just in my shop Thursday night getting fitted. I have lots of orders besides yours, honey. At least you Satins aren't as demanding as los cross-dressers and las drag queens." He stroked Rita's cheek. "I'm here to do research, to see you in motion so I could figure out how much sleeve and torso room to allow for your jacket seams."

"La verdad es que I talked him into coming along," Billie differed. "Rafi started going crazy 'cause Angelita was playing with scraps of fabric y todo eso. You know how he gets when he's tailoring."

Rafi chuckled. "Yeah, I'm such a bitch."

Cindi nudged Billie. "What do you think of his bomber-jacket design for us in lavender satin?"

"Maravillosa! Ay, when you mujeres sing in those jackets, you're going to sparkle, eh?"

Chic thrust back her shoulders. "There's going to be lettering on the backs, too."

"Yeah—something bold so everyone can see it says 'Latin Satins.'" Cindi made a sweeping motion with her hands.

"Qué suave. Cindi, I just wish you and Jessie would let me make you up, put some color in those morena cheeks," Billie urged. "Se van a mirar muy drab compared to Chic and Rita."

Cindi was used to Billie's cajoling. "No, we'll just look like ourselves."

"I'm naturally brown," Jessica joined in. "That's the only color I want on *my* face."

"You two are so stubborn."

Jessica shrugged. "Runs in the family."

"These cousins are hard-core dykes, Billie," Chic explained, "from the old school of lesbohood. They don't believe in makeup. It's politically incorrect."

"Pero, mijitas, you're entertainers!"

"Billie, our lyrics matter, our voices matter, and our faces shouldn't matter." Jessica knew she could rely on Cindi and was not disappointed.

"Give up on us, Billie. We're never going to be your customers at the beauty shop."

"I could make you look so natural you wouldn't even think you were wearing makeup."

"Then what would be the point?" Jessica frowned. "You're as bad as my sister. Victoria's always trying to get me into ruffles and lace and all those other cochinadas."

"*You* in ruffles and lace? Chispas!" Chic laughed. "That I would have to see to believe."

Jessica smiled, remembering. "The last time I wore that get-up was at First Communion, twenty-four years ago."

"Maybe you're due for another chance at it," Billie said, batting her artificial lashes.

"No way."

Billie turned to Rafael for moral support. He seemed determined to stay out of that discussion.

Gradually, Chic edged away from her friends and began to stride across the playground to the adjacent parking lot. "So, Rafi," she called while she walked away, "our jackets will be ready by the end of next week?"

"If not sooner."

"Great. Hay te watcho." Without even a backward glance, Chic Lozano took her leave, making her way through the crowds of well-wishers to her tangerine VW bug.

"Where's she going?" Rita let go of Angelita and stood on tiptoe for a parting view of the Satins' lead singer.

"If you don't know, why expect *me* to?" Rafi pinched her smooth cheek.

"You must be slipping, Rafi," Billie cut in. "You mean you don't have *any* gossip about Chic?"

"No chismes yet. Give her a break, huh? At least Chic goes off on her own, instead of sitting around feeling sorry for herself."

Rita sighed. "I won't sleep a wink till I hear her come home."

"Qué metiche. Such a busybody," Jessica said in exasperation. "Rita, if anyone can take care of herself, Chic can. She's probably meeting someone new and doesn't want us to know about it. She's been sensitive these days."

"Sensitive? Not that one," Rita scoffed. "Do you see how she ignores Angelita? Like she can't be bothered with a kid. What's so sensitive about *that*?"

"She just doesn't want to be asked to baby-sit," Jessica suggested softly, mindful of the child next to her.

"Oh, you. You always take Chic's side. If I didn't know better, I'd think you had your eye on her yourself."

Jessica smiled. "Rita, watching you volatile types is fun, but who needs a volcano? I'm too mellow for someone like Chic."

"You're so mellow you'll be sleeping alone for the rest of your life." Rita continued with a snicker, "Rafi, you should see Jessie. She puts seeds in her bird feeder then stays in the attic, singing to herself. No wonder Angelita's crazy about her. She thinks Jessie's a kid, too."

14

"Jessie's my favorite friend," Angelita piped up.

"I'm around kids a lot so I'm used to acting like them." Jessica shrugged while toying with a beaded edge of Angelita's cornrows. "So what?"

"Déjala, Rita." Billie put one plump hand on her hip and gestured with the other. "And Rafi's right. We're standing around talkin' about Chic while all of us are still in a rut. You're not dating anyone in particular, Rita, and neither are any of us."

"Love in the time of AIDS, verdad?" Rafi glanced at them while digging his lean hands into the pockets of his black shorts. "Make chismes, not love. We can bitch all we want, but Chic's got the nerve to go lookin' for—"

"'Love in all the wrong places,'" Rita sang, moving her hips sensuously.

"You don't know that." Rafi brushed aside his long hair, exposing the tiny diamond in his left earlobe. "No wonder Chic doesn't tell you anything. You shoot her down every chance you get."

Rita's usually expressive face turned stolid. "Are you done being a smartass, Rafi? I have things to do." She touched her daughter's shoulder briefly. "You go home with Jessie, Angelita. I'll see you later."

The little girl said nothing, yet reached for Jessica's hand while her mother flounced off. Jessica was unwilling to offer a critical assessment of Rita in the child's presence.

Rafi leaned toward the little girl after Rita's sudden departure. "Honey, how about a snow cone?"

Angelita quickly disengaged herself from Jessica and skipped after Rafi in the direction of a refreshment booth.

Billie wryly surveyed the remaining Satins. "Do you really think it was such a good idea for all four of you, plus Angelita, to live together?"

Cindi shrugged. "Chic and Rita're a couple of scrappin' Satins. We pretty much stay out of their way."

"The two of us get along fine, always have," Jessica added,

watching her cousin with affection. "Rita's a problem whenever she has a hot date and wants us to babysit on short notice—like she did just now. Heck, I'm with kids all day long. Sometimes I'm not in the mood to keep an eye on Angelita, too."

"Right. And Rita gets shook 'cause she thinks Chic has no responsibilities," Cindi continued. "Chic likes to razz her—she likes to give everyone a hard time. It drives Rita crazy. Hey, whose fault is it that Rita's raising Angelita by herself?"

"Not Chic's fault at all," Billie agreed. "Lo sé que la Chic can be temperamental. After a breakup, she's even worse. Whoever figured she'd move in with the rest of you?"

"Billie, Chic doesn't make millions in the music store. She sure didn't have enough for first and last month's rent on her own place." Jessica wrapped her arms around herself in the evening's chill. "That's the downside of moving in with a lover. Chic had to find another hangout when things didn't work out. She wanted to stay on the Westside, and Cindi and I just happened to have that extra room. Bingo—instant housemate."

"Once in a while, it gets tense," Cindi admitted. "Living together makes it easier for rehearsing, though."

"As long as personality conflicts don't affect our performances, fine," Jessica added. "Anyhow, we can't agree on everything—we usually don't. All of us pull together on stage—and that's what counts."

While Angelita sleepily crawled into the back seat, Cindi slid behind the wheel of her ancient Chevy station wagon. "Jess, I didn't expect to hang out with Rafi and Billie that long."

"Me neither." Jessica lay Cindi's Levi's jacket over the already reclining child. She smoothed Angelita's hair momentarily before shutting the car door and leaning against the driver's side. "If it hadn't been for Angelita, I would've walked home so I could think about my review for *La-LA-Lesbian*."

"The streets are too dark for that. Shut up and get inside."
Cindi waited for her cousin to enter the car and snap on her
seatbelt. "What're you reviewing?"

"A new release I got in the mail." Jessica's voice took on an
edge. "Don't ask for details."

"Okay, Ms. Mellow." Cindi eyed her. "What's the matter?"

"Don't feel like doing this review. Guess I'm still unwind-
ing from doing the new songs. We freaked out the conservative
types, including Mr. García."

"Yeah, we did," Cindi said with a laugh.

"Plus," Jessica said in a quieter voice, "I'm bummed that
Rita tries to stir things up by bitching about Chic. I mean, look
at Rafi. *That* man has problems, and he has such a great attitude."

"Oh, he can bitch with the best of 'em." Cindi drove the
wagon slowly out of the parish driveway and headed south on
Twentieth Street. "Billie says he gets real down sometimes."

"He'd have to. Jeez, he doesn't know how long his health
will last, or even if he'll be able to keep supporting himself."

"Has he told you that?"

"Nope. That's reality, Cindi. Sooner or later, his HIV will
turn into full-blown AIDS."

Cindi sighed and made a right turn on Ocean Park Boulevard, heading west. The cousins were silent for several blocks.
Jessica shivered and wished she had brought a sweatshirt. The
temperature grew much cooler nearer the ocean.

Before long, Cindi turned left on Third Street. An eclectic
mix of stately two-story homes, post-World War II apartment
buildings, some California bungalows, St. Clement's Catholic
Church, and an occasional Victorian populated the neighborhood east of Santa Monica's Main Street. Cindi guided the station wagon into a steep driveway before bringing it to a halt
adjacent to a faded yellow Victorian and a narrow flight of
wooden steps.

Other homes in the neighborhood had been renovated by a

17

constant wave of yuppie attorneys, accountants and well-to-do gay men. The Tamayo house was not only one of the oldest houses in the city still owned by its original family, but also the most rundown on Third Street. The cousins, who had jointly inherited it from their maiden aunt, were serious about its upkeep. At present, however, their intentions were greater than their financial means.

Jessica left the car and tentatively touched the bottom step with the toe of her sneaker. "I have to remember to ask Dad to help us fix these steps. They're pretty rickety."

"You seeing him soon?"

"On Saturday." Jessica opened the rear door and carefully lifted the dozing Angelita. "We're having a picnic at Will Rogers. Want to come?"

"Maybe." Cindi took out her housekeys and followed her cousin up the creaky veranda steps.

An hour later, after putting Angelita to bed and comparing notes with Cindi about the Satins' performance, Jessica went to her attic bedroom and plopped into the desk chair beneath the eaves. Methodically, she reached for her headset, turned on her tape player and listened only to the first bars of the new release before slumping into sleep. She did not even hear Rita arguing with Cindi about Angelita nor the clomp-clomp of Chic's cowboy boots on the second-floor stairs long past midnight.

2   Pacific Shores and More

Sometime in the night, Jessica awoke, removed her head-set, inched her way toward her pine futon and undressed. She slept until dawn and awoke to the muted cooing of mourning doves on the attic's roof. She lay on her back, listening to their fluttering sounds, trying to motivate herself to face the damp morning. Humming the fragment of a tune, she rose slowly. Within moments, she pulled on grey sweats, Reeboks, teal windbreaker, and grabbed her fanny pack.

She left the house and headed west through the incoming fog. When she jogged across Third to Hill Street and mentally played with a lyric, she noticed a gentle breeze swaying the neighborhood's abundant bottle-brush shrubs. The red blooms' slight movement brightened the otherwise colorless morning. She walked briskly down Hill Street and passed some of the city's oldest wood-frame homes, the non-denominational Church in Ocean Park and the adjacent women's shelter. Jessica crossed to the south side of the street when she saw a be-draggled white man shuffle out of an alley. She recognized him as one of the neighborhood's homeless and recalled the morning he had spat out "fucking Mexican" when she had ignored his request for "spare change." She clutched her keyring with its dangling police whistle. Shivering, she strode past the Main Street restaurants and trendy boutiques on her way to the ocean.

Used to traveling in a zig-zag pattern, she hurried by concrete-block fences decorated with placas, the stylized markings of local street gangs, and avoided anyone else who seemed suspicious. Her exercise routine kept her on edge, yet she craved seeing the Pacific every day, feeling its wet sand beneath her feet. She needed to remind herself of the familial ties binding her to its shores. Her daily glimpse of the bay offered a temporary antidote to the irony of being a working-class Chicana living in an increasingly gentrified seaside community, among upwardly mobile professionals and destitute beach transients.

Soon she traversed the winding bike path and trudged over the vast expanse of sand. Except for a large flock of gulls staking out their territory by an overturned trash can, the beach seemed deserted. Jessica wished she had brought the birding field guide she had purchased weeks ago to help differentiate between the Western and California gulls. Yet her mind was not on that as much as on the developing lyric. She began to mouth the words while nearing the shore and sidestepping tangled masses of kelp and litter.

> When I was little it used to be
> You'd walk a long way by the sea
> And watch the waves roll in and crash
> Where now there's styrofoam and trash

She repeated the words and wondered about the Satins' reaction to an environmental tune. Pausing, she saw shorebirds, some small and white, others brownish with long black bills, but she could not identify them either. Her interest in ornithology was recent, ever since one of her co-workers at Pacific Palms Playschool had given her a bird feeder for a Christmas gift. She had become not only curious about the local bird population but also about the changing environment of her hometown. She continued to be amazed at the variety of birds in the city and on the beach, especially since she had been unaware of them before. Sometimes she wondered if the coastal fog had penetrated her brain.

Jessica glanced at her watch and decided to go no further. Many homeless people slept nearby, and in early morning remained congregated on the beach. She did not feel safe among them because of neighborhood accounts of assaults and rapes; when alone she knew it was best to be cautious.

The return trip was uphill. She had the habit of stopping at Starbucks on the corner of Main, where Rita worked. Jessica preferred to see her there than first thing in the morning at home. Rita tended to be on better behavior at the coffeehouse.

"Órale, Jessie," she greeted when her housemate ventured through the oak and glass door. Behind the long counter, Rita looked sleepy, her curly hair still damp from her shower. Despite her obvious lack of sleep, she managed a smile. A couple of regular patrons seemed into serious coffee drinking, one immersed in the *Los Angeles Times*, the other in the *L.A. Weekly*.

"Hi," Jessica said as she joined Rita.

"Thanks for taking Angelita home." Rita took a cup from beneath the counter. "Want your usual?"

"Sure." Jessica yawned. "Where'd you go last night?"

"To the Delta to unwind a little." Rita busied herself with pouring the coffee and popping a chocolate croissant into the microwave. "Chic was there, too."

That sparked Jessica's interest. "With anyone special?"

"Couldn't really tell." Rita yawned, not bothering to cover her mouth. "I hung with some people I hadn't seen for a while. Didn't notice when Chic left."

Jessica grabbed a handful of napkins. "Wish you'd told me ahead of time about babysitting."

Rita shrugged and handed her a cup of Costa Rican coffee and the croissant. "No me digas que I'm taking advantage, okay?"

Jessica fished inside her fanny pack for some cash and

21

handed it to her. She kept her voice subdued, but firm. "Rita, I don't mind watching Angelita once in a while. Just don't think I'm going to be there to help *all* the time. That isn't fair to anyone, especially to Angelita."

"At least, you and Cindi are willing to give me a hand." Rita took on an accusatory tone. "Chic *never* offers."

"That wasn't part of the deal when she moved in. Rita, you can't expect that from Chic. Get real."

Rita was about to respond when another customer interrupted. Jessica took the hint, balanced her croissant atop the coffee cup, stooped to grab an *L.A. Weekly* from the pile by the door, and took a seat. She hoped her housemate would be too busy to continue their conversation. Once in a while, Rita glanced her way; however, when business picked up, Jessica ducked out the door with a cluster of other customers. She hurried up the hill toward home.

"Did you see Rita?" Cindi peeked from the kitchen when Jessica entered the front door.

"Looked like she was up half the night."

"Did she talk about it?" In faded jeans and a hot pink T-shirt with "Cindi's Custom Cooking and Cleaning" lettered on its pocket, Jessica's cousin emerged holding a large coffee thermos.

"I didn't really give her a chance." Jessica removed her fanny pack and hung it from her shoulder. "Otherwise I would've been there all morning."

Cindi yawned and put down the thermos. She took her Levi's jacket from the back of one of the mahogany dining room chairs. "Jess, we're going to have to sit down with her and straighten things out. Even though she's paying rent and helping with the utilities, she's taking us for granted when it comes to Angelita."

"I started telling her that a few minutes ago." She helped her cousin into the jacket. "By the way, where's the kid?"

22

"Out in back. She's walking to school with Xochi."

Jessica gave Cindi an exasperated glance. "Rita really thinks she's got it made. We're around in case she needs instant babysitters, and Xochi happens to go to the same school as Angelita."

"Exactly. But we're not mothers, and Xochi isn't obligated either." Cindi grabbed her thermos and strode to the door. "Let's talk later, cuz. Have to run. Two condos to clean, two microwave meals to prepare, and a piano lesson with a bratty kid afterwards. Your turn for dinner, remember? Have a great day."

"You, too."

Despite the independence Cindi's housecleaning/cooking business and piano instructions allowed her, Jessica did not envy her cousin. Cindi seemed to expend enormous amounts of energy maintaining a permanent distance from humdrum office jobs; as a result, she led an even more restricted personal life than Jessica.

Jessica chained her bike to one of the posts of the picket fence surrounding Pacific Palms Playschool. A decade earlier, several local parents had formed a child-care collective that had eventually evolved into the present board-run facility. Taking advantage of a zoning change, the board had raised funds to purchase the one-story brick building bordered by scraggly palms. Once a private residence, it still retained some of its homey charm. The grassy front and back yards served as play areas with sandboxes and swings, and the spacious interior had been renovated into classrooms and small offices.

Toting the navy daypack containing her portable tape player, notebook and lunch, Jessica hurried inside. In the teachers' lounge/kitchen, she stored her lunch in the refrigerator.

Albert Kirby, the only other person of color employed there, put down *The Los Angeles Sentinel*, the African-American newspaper, and toasted her with his TreePeople cof-

23

fee mug. He was a retired public school custodian who had switched careers by earning a credential in early childhood education. His tan skin was dappled with darker freckles, and his greying hair covered his head like a snug fisherman's cap.

"Hey, Jess. How was the beach this morning?"

"Cold and dirty. Lots of gulls. Man, I still can't tell the difference between them. It's embarrassing, you know?" Jessica peeled off her windbreaker. "I was born in this town and can't even distinguish between seagulls."

Albert chuckled. "I bet most native Californians can't. The bigger ones with pink legs are Western gulls."

"And both Westerns and Californias have red dots on their bills. Right?"

He gave her a thumbs-up signal.

"Albert, you'll make me an expert yet." Jessica stored her windbreaker and daypack in the wall cubicle assigned to her. Painted in bright primary colors and hung opposite the kitchen table, the cubicles bulged with teachers' possessions.

Albert laughed again, showing his large teeth. "Get busy with your bird savvy, Jess. I promised Kathleen we'd be in charge of a birding trip for the kids sometime."

"Come on." Jessica washed her hands in the kitchen sink. "A bunch of noisy preschoolers would chase any tweeters away."

"At least we could see gulls, pelicans and cormorants. It'd be good to get the kids on the beach."

"Think I'll write them a song about it first. Well, I have to get my room ready." She waved and headed down the adjacent corridor.

Jessica had decorated the airy classroom with several prints of Chicana artist Carmen Lomas Garza's childhood scenes. One showed two children on a rooftop, wishing on the moon; another had frolicking children trying to break a fish piñata at a birthday party. Bustling about, Jessica arranged tiny red chairs into a semicircle. She left a hand puppet on the chair nearest the entry.

"Good morning, Jessica." Kathleen Scott, the playschool's director, stood in the open doorway. In her late thirties, she was a buxom woman with frosted hair, inclined to favor two-piece pastel outfits with outsized bows at the neck. Between themselves, Jessica and Albert referred to the style as "pseudo-Nancy Reagan."

"Hi, Kathleen."

"I wanted to remind you about your newcomer." She turned toward the corridor. "As a matter of fact, here she is now."

When Jessica approached the doorway, she noticed a well-dressed Latina holding the hand of a little girl. On first glance, the woman reminded Jessica of her sister Victoria: small-boned, brown hair swept into a sleek French twist; café-au-lait skin with a smidgeon of blush, sepia eyes framed by barely perceivable mascara. She looked impeccable in a royal blue suit and cream blouse, a delicate gold chain and thin-looped earrings her only jewelry. Her daughter was adorable in a white ruffled blouse and yellow overalls, her dark pigtails decorated with matching polka-dotted bows.

Kathleen proceeded with the introductions. "Mrs. León, this is Jessica Tamayo. Yolanda will be assigned to her room."

"Pleased to meet you, Mrs. León." With a smile, Jessica took the woman's smooth hand. She squeezed it briefly before squatting beside the child. "Hi, Yolanda. I'm Jessica."

The child kept her head down and did not respond. Jessica could see Yolanda strained to hold back tears. Deciding she needed some assistance, Jessica reached for the hand puppet and slipped it on.

"Aren't you Yolanda?" The seal puppet brought its furry white face close to the little girl's. "I'm Sally. I live here when I'm not in the terrific Pacific. Want to be friends?"

Yolanda began to cry.

"My mother's been caring for her," Mrs. León explained

25

without being asked. "Yolanda's not used to being with people she doesn't know. She's very shy." She bent over and hugged her daughter.

Kathleen Scott patted the little girl's head and gave Jessica a sympathetic look before heading back to her office.

"Don't worry, Mrs. León. Yolanda will be fine here. I was the same way when I was her age." Jessica took the puppet again and made Sally Seal nudge the child's shoulder. She spoke in a breathy voice. "It's easy to cry when you're in a new place. I'll be your friend, Yolanda. Is that okay?"

The little girl peered into the puppet's appealing black eyes, heaved a tremendous sigh, and gave a semblance of a nod.

"Mija, Mommy doesn't want to be late for work. You'll have fun with Ms. Tamayo and the other niños. When I come back, we'll visit Abuelita. I promise." Mrs. León gave her daughter a hasty kiss, Jessica a quick smile, and left, her high heels clicking on the linoleum corridor.

Yolanda bit her lips. She raised long-lashed brown eyes to her new teacher's. Immediately, Jessica was struck by the child's mournful expression. Something besides her mother's departure had caused that sadness, and for a moment, Jessica recalled her own childhood sorrow in being abandoned.

With deft fingers, she changed the seal puppet's expression and made it quizzical. "Yolanda, want to snoop around before the other kids get here?"

The child hesitated and still did not speak.

"I'll show you all the fun things." With the puppet, Jessica took Yolanda's hand and led her inside.

The parking lot was almost empty when Jessica began to unlock her bike. The children assigned to her had left already, yet she remained haunted by Yolanda. In the flurry of the children's departure at the end of the day, Jessica had not had a chance to speak with Mrs. León. She had wanted to assure her that Yolanda would not be overlooked. Although there were few Latino kids at the playschool, Jessica was committed to keeping close ties with each one. She wondered if Mrs. León realized that or if she preferred to keep her distance.

The late afternoon sun was blinding as Jessica aimed her bike west. Even with sunglasses and a visor, she received the spring glare directly. She turned right on Fourteenth Street and headed toward her Montana Avenue destination. Northward, the sun hardly bothered her.

She passed the iron gates of Woodlawn Cemetery and glanced through its once frightening grounds. As children, she, Cindi and Chic had dared each other to enter that forbidding, terrifying place where non-Catholics were buried; Chic had always been the bravest, bounding as far as the stone mauseoleum and screaming all the way back.

Smiling at the memory, Jessica pedaled on, past Chic's old neighborhood, which had become increasingly commercial. When applied to her hometown, the Chicano activists' slogan "urban renewal means Chicano removal," had proven true. During Jessica's childhood, the barrio had been split open by the construction of the Santa Monica Freeway, parts of it rezoned for business use. Many Mexican-American and African-American families had found themselves displaced. Locked out of the city's real estate market by a combination of racial discrimination and economics, they had left Santa Monica for other areas. By the time Jessica had reached adulthood, Santa Monica's stringent rent control law had gone into effect, making vacancies rare. She realized if Tía Irene had not left Cindi and her the house on Third Street, she would have probably wound up in an apartment outside the city limits.

Jessica coasted down the Fourteenth Street hill toward Olympic Boulevard and rode beyond Memorial Park, Fisher Lumber, and across Colorado Avenue, past a slew of auto repair shops, a veterinarian's office, a dry cleaner. Only a few homes remained along Fourteenth Street, like stragglers caught in a time warp. Glancing at her watch, she realized she should have phoned first. She never knew when her sister Victoria would be in her office.

Jessica accelerated her pace. Uphill on Fourteenth, she switched gears and challenged her cardiovascular system. The neighborhood changed north of Wilshire Boulevard, becoming lined with apartment buildings and townhouses, hardly any single-family homes among them. Leaning forward, Jessica pushed ahead. She reached Montana Avenue panting and sweaty, her heart pumping like a hard-driving rock beat. She turned left and whizzed by the Aero Theater, boutique and gourmet shops galore, before coming to a halt on the corner of Montana and Tenth. Hitching her bike to a parking meter, she removed her water bottle from its carrier and drank with gusto. She continued to breathe hard while taking off the sun visor. She shook her damp black hair free, and wiped trickles of perspiration from her brow with the edge of her hand. According to her sister, Jessica never looked presentable enough. On reflex, she adjusted her soggy cotton shirt, tucked it into the loose waistband of her jeans, and caught a glimpse of herself in a store window. Grimacing, she opened the antiqued pink-and-white door labeled "Vestiges by Victoria" in elaborate calligraphy. In smaller lettering below was the notation "Personal Shopping for Today's Committed Women."

Victoria Tamayo was in the midst of a business phone call when Jessica entered the office. She waved while simultaneously giving her sister a disdainful appraisal. With a shrug, Jessica slouched into a velvet chair, doubly mindful of her casual attitude toward clothes in light of her sister's lucrative career.

While waiting, she glanced about the sunlit office, noting Victoria's penchant for neatness, from the alphabetical arrangement of fashion magazines on the end tables, plushy pillows deftly arranged on the chairs, to the pink silk roses in crystal vases on the dust-free window sill. Victoria had chosen antique furniture for her office decor, hints of pink everywhere, in the subdued wallpaper and dusty rose upholstery. Ironically, her sister thought, the soft pastels Victoria found flattering also enhanced her cinnamon skin and ebony hair. Growing up, Victoria had often wished aloud for their mother's lighter skin tone while Jessica had no qualms about inheriting their father's dark shade and proclaiming "brown is beautiful."

"Did you ride your bike up here again?" Victoria put down the phone and fixed her sister with a disapproving stare. "What if I were in the middle of a client consultation? How would I explain *you*?"

"As your sloppy *hermanita* who trips out on wearing wrinkled cotton and jeans. Jeez, Victoria! Not 'How've you been, sis?' but 'You're such a slob!'"

"Jessica, what am I going to do with you?" Victoria rounded her desk and approached her, nevertheless giving her sister an affectionate hug.

Victoria was petite due more to diet than anything else. Six years older than Jessica, she styled her black hair into a loose-waved bob and always wore slim skirts, tailored jackets and co-ordinated silk blouses, tasteful jewelry and, of course, high heels. She looked successful and was, having built her business from word-of-mouth among satisfied Westside clients. Even in recessionary times, Victoria had only lost a client or two; women executives with no time to shop trusted their daily wardrobes to her capable hands.

"Listen, Vickie. I popped in to ask if you'd like to get together with Dad and me for a picnic on Saturday."

Victoria did not reply at first. She returned to her desk and flipped through her burgundy leather appointment book. "I have several prospective clients lined up. Saturday's the only time I can meet them."

"Even if you had time, you wouldn't want to see Dad any

more than you have to. He's always asking about *you*." Jessica studied her. "You're probably more ashamed of him than you are of me."

"You're my baby sister, for heaven's sake. I'm *not* ashamed of you."

"Dad's another story. And you'd rather have me dolled up dressing for success than working with pre-schoolers and singing with the Satins."

Victoria tried to sound flippant. "Oh, my misunderstood little sister."

"Cut it out, Vickie." Jessica turned to gaze out the window at the end-of-the-business-day traffic on Montana Avenue. "I'm tired, all right? Plus I had to deal with a shy kid today. She reminded me so much of myself when I was little. She seemed —lost."

Victoria sighed. "I wonder why you want to work there. Being around kids revives all your issues."

"I should go back to being an insurance company secretary instead? No thanks. I *like* being with kids. I relate to them, and they don't care what I wear."

"Ay!" Victoria was interrupted by the telephone. She reached across the desk to answer it. Her voice changed dramatically, modulating into a professional tone. "Good afternoon. Victoria speaking."

Jessica slung her daypack over one shoulder and opened the door. Putting her hand over the receiver, Victoria spoke softly. "Say hello to him for me."

"Sure."

Jessica walked her bike up the steep driveway and leaned it against the cluttered inside wall of the garage. Fatigued from the bike ride, she opened the ramshackle gate to the backyard and entered the house through the kitchen door. The afternoon sun lit the wide room, creating sunbeams from the crystals she

30

had hung from the window frames. She and Cindi had done their best to brighten the old house, to counteract the inherited mahogany furniture that had been Tía Irene's pride and joy. Throughout the house, they had added their own touches, from Navajo white walls splashed with feminist posters to Oaxacan woven rugs on the hardwood floors.

Jessica threw her daypack on one of the kitchen chairs. She reached into the refrigerator for the bottled water and quenched her thirst. Satisfied, she mustered enough energy to grab a handful of paper towels, and wheeled the second-hand portable barbecue to the open-air back porch. She cleaned off the grill and fired up the coals before going back inside.

House rules called for each housemate to be responsible for dinner once a week; the other three nights were free. If someone did not show up for dinner, the cook saved the leftovers; if the leftovers were not eaten by the next evening, they were up for grabs.

After a shower, Jessica returned to the kitchen refreshed. She removed vegetables from the refrigerator, washed them, and made a large bowl of salad. Finishing that, she went out to check the coals.

"Que tal, Señorita Tamayo."

Jessica stiffened at hearing the baritone voice on the other side of the sprawling backyard sycamore. She was not fond of Efraín Zepeda, a distant relative of the Tamayos and the officious patriarch of the small house at the rear of the property. The Zepedas were immigrants from a village in the Mexican state of Jalisco.

"Hello, Efraín." Since Zepeda expected anyone with a Spanish surname to be fluent, Jessica made a habit of answering him in English. She disliked his proclivity for criticizing her California-flavored Spanish.

"Cómo está tu Papi?" The swarthy man in workingman's khakis stood near the porch's bottom step and gazed at her. Efraín had a balding head of black hair, a bushy mustache, and a beer belly where his waist should have been.

"My Dad's fine. Did Xochi walk Angelita home from school?"

"Pues sí. Angelita está jugando con mi niña. La Rita está trabajando como siempre?"

"Rita will be here in a while. Would you mind sending Angelita home? I'd like to give her dinner soon."

"Bueno." He continued eyeing Jessica. "Me gusta cuando estás cocinando. Así debe ser con las mujeres, verdad?"

"We have to eat and it's my turn to cook. No big deal." Fuming at his traditional attitude toward women, Jessica turned on her bare heel and went inside to get the T-bone steaks. She had remembered to marinate them before leaving for work.

In the kitchen, she waited until Efraín had drifted back to his side of the yard. His meddling nature irritated her and she preferred to shun him. Chic, on the other hand, thrived on provoking the backyard tenant; at times, she wandered outside half dressed in order to tell him to quit staring at her.

Jessica had used such exasperating experiences with Efraín as the basis for one of the stanzas of "Pocha Blues." Taking several ears of corn from the vegetable bin, she began to wrap them in foil while she sang to herself:

I'm not a misfit, crazy pocha
You got a cara de panocha
I'm not fluent with the Spanish
And you wish I would vanish

Chic surprised her by supplying the refrain:

I've got the pocha blues
I'm brown, I've paid my dues
I've got the pocha blues
I'm brown and so I lose

Jessica looked at her with a grin. "I was just thinking about you."

"Por favor, *don't* fall in love with me." Chic clasped her hands imploringly between her breasts. She wore a turquoise tank top, black biking shorts, turquoise slouch slocks and Doc Martens. "Jess, you're my personal songwriter, mi amiga favorita. Being lovers would spoil all that."

"Quit flattering yourself." Jessica laughed. "Listen, I thought of you 'cause Efraín laid it on thick about my cooking tonight. That lard-face macho can't believe I'm actually doing something domestic."

"He has a permanent hard-on knowing there're four dynamic dykes living here, while he has that poor cow he keeps barefoot and pregnant in the back house." Chic opened one of the kitchen cabinets and took out a can of cat food. "Don't know why you and Cindi rent to that loud-mouthed bastard."

"Tía Irene said we had to. It's in her will, mensa." Jessica held her nose at the fishy smell emanating from the tin can Chic held. "Do you have to do that when I'm making dinner?"

"Chill out. I'll put Smudge's food outside. Have you seen her?"

"I bet she's in the sycamore, spying on the bird feeder."

Chic went outside to feed her cat and returned shortly. "Efraín made fast tracks when he saw me. Jess, even if your tía had it in her will about him, *I'd* get rid of him somehow." She peered out the window, watching with satisfaction as her black cat appeared and began to eat. "Don't you think that bastard makes enough from his gardening business to rent a bigger place? The back house is so little his kids are hangin' out the windows. Give him the boot, Jess, so I can take the place over— after it's been fumigated and redecorated, of course."

"Dreamer." Jessica put the steaks on a foil-covered plate and went to the grill, sidestepping the feeding cat in the process. As expected, Chic followed her.

"Rita trailed me to the Delta last night. She was with some black dykes I'd never seen before. She was really checking out *my* action."

"What kind of action?" Jessica lay the steaks on the grill.

33

"I was on a roll after doing the new songs at the fiesta. Was so high I started flirting with the Delta's owner—this Darryl Desmoines chick. I think I can get us a gig there."

"That'd be terrific, Chic." Jessica beamed at her.

"She wanted us to audition. I scratched that idea and—"

"Was that a smart move?" Jessica's smile became a frown.

"Hell, I could tell she dug my spunk. Told her we're on the Promenade every other Friday and she can catch us there next time. We'd better have our jackets ready by then."

"Rafi promised."

"Yeah, but he didn't look too good to me." She paused when Angelita bounded up the porch stairs. "Hi kiddo."

"Hi, Chic. Hi, Jessie." Cindi had combed out Angelita's dark hair and decorated it with fancy barrettes. The little girl held her arms wide for Jessica to embrace her.

Jessica handed Chic the barbecue prongs and caught Angelita in a fervent hug. She gave her a resounding kiss and twirled her around. Undistracted, Smudge finished her meal and proceeded to groom herself. Angelita giggled, shaking her curls when Jessica whirled her again.

Chic put the prongs on the grill's edge and bent to lift her cat. "Give a yell when it's chow time."

3 Sapphic Songbirds and Solo Sex

While Angelita set the dining room table, Jessica busied herself on the back porch, grilling the steaks. Cindi soon arrived and nodded approvingly at the meal in progress.

"I could eat all that myself, cuz." She inhaled the smoky aroma of the sizzling steaks. "Rita's on her way. Saw her heading up Hill."

Jessica tossed her cousin a sly grin. "Why didn't you give her a ride?"

Cindi paused before opening the back door. "I've done her enough favors lately. She can walk herself home." Cindi caught herself when she noticed Angelita searching for napkins in the kitchen.

"Angelita, don't I rate a hug?"

The child immediately darted to her, grabbing Cindi around the waist and clutching her.

Laughing, Cindi reached down and held her closer. "Did you have fun at school today? Was Xochi nice to you?"

Angelita nodded. "She walked me right to my classroom door. She says you owe her a quarter, Cindi."

"No, your Mom does." Cindi tugged one of Angelita's curls. "Be sure to remind her."

At that moment, Rita showed up, breathless from her uphill trek. "Ay, carnalitas, I'm starved."

"Mommy!" Angelita danced over to her.

35

Rita welcomed her daughter with a kiss. "Come with me, baby, while I change my clothes." She took Angelita's hand. "Is dinner almost ready?"

Jessica nodded. "In five minutes. Tell Chic. She's upstairs."

"Who were those fine women you were talkin' to last night, Rita?" Chic dangled a piece of steak off the edge of her fork.

"Javene and Shakinah." Rita had changed into a faux satin dressing gown and wore it loosely, her cleavage visible. "I used to go out with Javene once in a while. In fact, she introduced me to Tremaine."

"My Daddy? Did you see my Daddy?" Angelita's curiosity was piqued. She put down the half-eaten ear of corn and gazed at her mother.

"No, honey," Rita said gently. "I only talked with some women who know him."

"Where *is* my Daddy?"

"That's the question of the year." Chic gave Rita a nudge. "Or maybe the decade."

"Don't say that in front of her," Rita muttered. "Angelita, your Daddy moved away. I told you that, remember?"

The little girl sighed and leaned her head against her mother's torso. Rita gave her a comforting pat.

"Hey—" Jessica thought a change in subject was in order. "Did you know Chic might have a gig lined up for us?"

The other Satins pounced on Chic for details. Jessica leaned back and watched Angelita with concern. She hated to see children with sad faces.

"Weren't we going to talk to Rita about the child care issue?" Cindi backed the station wagon onto Third Street and headed north to Ocean Park Boulevard.

"Why didn't *you* bring it up?" Jessica grinned at her and

36

leaned back. "Listen, we have to do it when Chic isn't around. Otherwise, she'll butt in."

"True." Cindi crossed Ocean Park Boulevard and continued driving north to Pico. "I didn't want to bring it up with Angelita there either. Rita's attitude isn't the kid's fault."

"As much as I was bugged about Rita's coming home late last night, maybe she finally got a lead on Tremaine."

"'Cause she talked to those women who know him?" Cindi seemed unconvinced. "Jess, the dude's flown. Can you blame him for freaking over Rita's 'bi' angle? That's no excuse for bailing out on Angelita, but at least he didn't try to take her with him."

Jessica shuddered. "I don't even want to think about what *that* would be like. I'd go berserk myself."

"You and kids." Cindi made a right turn on Pico. "I wonder if you're planning on having some yourself someday."

"No." Jessica met her cousin's gaze. "Are you kidding? Wouldn't I have to grow up to have them?"

"Rita doesn't seem so grown up to me."

"If I decided to be a mother, Cindi, I'd do it right. Motherhood's too time-consuming, though. I'd rather do a lot of other things instead."

Cindi turned the Chevy into the parking lot of the YWCA on Pico and Fourteenth, stationing it opposite the entrance. "I'm with you."

Most of the thirty members of the Sapphonic Feminist Chorus had already assembled for their twice-weekly rehearsal at the Y. In existence for a dozen years, the Sapphonics performed at pro-choice, civil rights, and anti-war rallies, on college campuses, and for progressive coalitions of all types. Their repertoire consisted of suffragist hymms, peace anthems, feminist standards, women-identified love ballads. Their future plans included performing at a local multicultural faire and at a summer festival of lesbian and gay choruses in the Pacific

Northwest. Jessica and Cindi had been scrupulously saving for that trip for months.

The gregarious altos interrupted their clamorous huddle when they noticed Jessica and Cindi.

"Here come the Latin Satins," a rusty-haired, blue-eyed woman called. "At least two of 'em. When're the other two goin' to join this Chorus?"

"Never." Cindi went over and gave the woman a full-bodied hug. "Jody, can you really see Chic Lozano being part of a group this size? We have enough trouble keeping her in line for the Satins."

Jessica cut in. "And Rita—well, she doesn't even identify as a feminist. Actually, neither does Chic."

At that revelation, the altos booed in unison.

Cindi let go of Jody, grabbed Jessica's hand and raised it triumphantly. "The Sapphonics are lucky enough to have Jess and me—why do you need anyone else?" At her cousin's unexpected action, Jessica felt herself blush.

The altos stomped and whistled their approval.

"Let's settle down." Faye Schneider, a salt-and-pepper-haired woman in navy slacks and a loose pullover, tapped her music stand with the edge of her baton. The Sapphonics' conductor, Faye was a voice instructor at a local community college.

She gazed over her steel-rimmed glasses at the milling singers. "Women, we have a lot of ground to cover tonight and no time to wait for late arrivals. Take your places and let's get started." She flicked the baton. "First off, 'March of the Women.' Some of the harmony is a little shaky, and I'd like to strengthen that."

The women shuffled to their respective sections, a few less willing than others, sopranos and upper second sopranos to Faye's right, lower second sopranos and altos to her left.

Cindi whispered to Jessica. "I swear, Faye reminds me of Sister Robert Michael in fifth grade. Maybe she *is* Robert Michael. Wow, wouldn't that be something?"

"Don't make me laugh." Jessica put her hands on Cindi's shoulders and steered her to a couple of end seats among the second sopranos.

Although the cousins liked the legendary camaraderie of the altos, neither, unfortunately, could sing too long in the lower registers. Jessica's and Cindi's voices were a smooth blend, perhaps due to heredity; Jessica's father, Arturo, was the older brother of Cindi's mother, Anita. The cousins had discovered in childhood that their voices melded well, and had been singing duets ever since, at first merely for fun, then as the kooky Loca Mochas, finally joining Chic and Rita to form the Latin Satins.

At the break, Jody, their alto friend, came over and offered them sips of her large-sized Coke.

"Were you really serious about Chic and Rita being in this group?" Cindi handed the cup back to Jody.

"You've said yourself the Sapphonics need more women of color."

"A feminist chorus is too tame for Chic," Jessica scoffed as she leaned on a window ledge in the small auditorium. "I can't see her getting jazzed about singing 'March of the Women.' She goes marching after women all the time, and feminism has *nothing* to do with it."

Jody raised her brows. "Is she really as wild as they say?"

"You ought to find out for yourself, Jody." Cindi gave her a teasing push. "We've known Chic since we were kids. In more ways than one, if you know what I mean."

Jessica felt her face grow hot.

"No kiddin'?" Jody was intrigued. "She turned you both out?"

"Not just *us*, I'm sure. Chic's kissed and messed around with lots of muchachas. She's always had a way about her." Cindi hoisted herself onto the window ledge. "You notice how Jess is all of a sudden withdrawing from this conversation?"

At times like that, Jessica wished Cindi would keep her mouth shut. "Music's *my* priority, not sex."

"Oh, yeah, that's right," Jody drawled. "I'd never know that by the type of paper you write for, even if you cover music only. *La-LA Lesbian* looks more and more like a tabloid these days 'cause of all the sexy ads."

"At least the new owner kept the music column. That was a surprise since she cut out book reviews and most serious commentary." Jessica heard her own defensiveness. "I'm not crazy about the changes in format either, Jody. Maybe you ought to write a letter to the editor and state your complaints."

"I doubt if it'd be printed. Jess, I don't know anyone who's happy with the new format, except so-called 'gay girls.' Lesbian feminists sure don't like *La-LA Lesbian*."

"Well, Chic does," Cindi added.

Jody grimaced.

"The Chorus is soundin' good." Cindi drove her cousin home shortly after nine o'clock. "I think we're further along than we were at this time last year."

"We'd better be. We're more in demand these days." Jessica sighed. "I really have to write that review tonight. I took some notes during lunch. Haven't looked at them since."

"Did Jody get to you with her comments about *La-LA Lesbian*?"

"That comes with the territory." Jessica sighed. "No one's making me write the column. If I resigned, who's to know if anyone else would get to cover music? I'm the only Latina writing on the staff right now. Even so, it's not like I'm surrounded by those 'gay girls'—I write my column and mail it in. I guess I'll stick it out as long as I can stand it."

"More than I'd do, cuz." Cindi lurched the station wagon into the driveway.

•

Jessica grabbed her tape player, a notepad, a pencil, and settled into her favorite spot on the window seat in the attic bedroom. She flipped on the imitation Tiffany lamp she had found in a second-hand store and gazed out the window for a moment. From the top of the house, she could see the Pacific, the red-violet sunset each evening, the flickering pier lights at night. She turned on the tape player and began listening. Her pencil made quick notes across the page.

She and Cindi had loved playing in this attic years ago, rummaging through their grandmother's trunk for vintage clothes and photographs. When they had inherited the house from the oldest Tamayo sibling, their ever-eccentric Tia Irene, Jessica had claimed the once-musty attic as her own. Cindi had chosen one on the second floor with its eyelid balcony and wrap-around windows, while Chic and Rita had separate rooms down the hall from her.

Jessica worked steadily on her 500-word review. If she had removed her headset, she would have heard the nightly sounds of the big house: Rita singing Angelita to sleep, Cindi and Chic joking on the second-floor landing. And from the backyard, the strains of recorded rancheras, the songs that made Jessica's heart ache even though she wished Efraín Zepeda did not share her fondness for them. Jessica had grown up singing with her father, and every time she heard rancheras, childhood memories flooded her.

She put down the pad and pencil and left them on the window seat beside her. Taking off the headset, she stared into Third Street's shadows. Her neighbors, like many individual homeowners throughout the city, lit their own properties rather than paying exorbitant amounts for street lights; consequently, Santa Monica's residential neighborhoods were often dark and unfriendly.

A furtive movement at the curb across the street caught Jessica's eye. She saw a thin barefoot woman in a straggly dress, wrapped in a torn blanket. The woman bent by the curb's edge to pick up a discarded soft-drink can. She shook it, then immediately put it to her lips and drank whatever trickles remained. She held the can tightly and inched along the curb, searching for another. Jessica shuddered at her desperate condition. Like a wraith, the woman soon disappeared into the night.

Jessica sighed. At the same time, she felt relief that her concerned father had installed extra lights on the front veranda and more on the back porch. As the neighborhood continued to reflect the changing urban scene, such precautions had become necessary. Even so, the wide yard with its twin toyons, fuschia bushes, bottle-brush shrubs and overgrown hedge still seemed ominous after sunset.

During the shifting economics of the 1980s, the city of Santa Monica had taken on more than its share of Los Angeles County's homeless population. The predominantly liberal city government had been reluctant to enforce loitering ordinances and tended to be more lenient than other beach communities especially when dealing with mentally ill transients. As a result, the city's live-and-let-live philosophy attracted hundreds of indigents, the uneducated and unemployed of both sexes and of all colors. Some of the younger men found refuge in the dangerous brotherhood of gangs. Male and female drug addicts and alcoholics wandered through the area, sleeping on the beach, in parks, alleys, even in yards. Jessica and Cindi had often discussed getting a dog for safety's sake. Chic thought a shotgun was more in order.

"Jess, want some company?"

Yawning, Jessica got up, grateful for the distraction.

On the attic stairs, Chic made a shimmying motion. "Qué pasa, muchacha?"

"Finished drafting the review. And, no, you can't look at it yet." Jessica opened the window seat and stored the notepad there atop a pile of tapes.

"You sure overreact." Chic came in and straddled the desk chair. "How was the Sapphic Songbird rehearsal?"

"Went well. Did Cindi tell you Jody asked about you?"

"Yup. Jody has fine gavacha eyes, the kind that switch colores."

"Sounds like you've noticed each other."

"I notice women, period, Jess. You know that." Chic stretched her arms to the ceiling, emphasizing her breasts in their red tank top as she did so. Her arms were shapely, her skin tawny. "The question is, when're *you* going to start noticing them again?"

"Chic, come on." Jessica half-turned toward the window.

"*You* come on." Chic moved beside her. "I've been without a lover for two months and I'm goin' loca. You've been on your own for—how long now?"

"Almost two years."

"How do you do it, huh? A red-blooded señorita like you?" she asked with a fake drawl.

"Why don't you ever ask Cindi these questions? Why's it always *me*?"

"Oh, I bug her about it, too. When we're alone, like we just were in the dimness of her boudoir."

Despite her exasperation, Jessica laughed aloud. "Is it driving you crazy that you're sharing this house with a couple of celibates? I can't speak for Rita."

"Yeah, don't. I think Rita had a quickie last night before she came home. Looked like it was headin' that way."

"Hope she's taking care of herself. You know how it is these days."

"That's everybody's hangup. All we have to do to remember is take a look at Rafi." Chic sighed. "So *what* do you do? Safe solo sex?"

Jessica blushed. "That's my answer—for the time being. I'm in no hurry to find someone."

"I figured that," Chic murmured wryly. "Well, are you into sex toys?"

"Chic, lay off." Jessica stood and moved her windbreaker from the desk chair to the peg behind the door.

"A sensitive topic, so to speak?"

"Don't expect me to throw a sex toys party. I'm not into Tupperware either."

Chic seemed tickled by that comment. Her eyes betrayed her amusement, though she tried not to smile. "Not even into leather or latex?"

Jessica moved near the desk, inches away from her. "Not a chance, Francisca."

Chic did a double take. "Don't start with the nostalgia trip."

"How many people know 'Francisca' is your real name?" Jessica eyed her closely. "Want me to spread it around town to all the dykes I know?"

"All right, Jess. I'll lay off." She studied Jessica. "Never thought you'd resort to blackmail."

"It amazes me how you can dish it out but you can't take it. What's this really about, anyway? Not about how Cindi and I were unlucky in love and now we're celibate, is it? It's really about *you*."

Chic feigned surprise. "*Me?*"

"You're still hurting, Chic. It's only been two months since Roxanne kissed you off."

"The bitch." Chic's face drooped into a morose expression. "Went from living in a high-rise on the outskirts of Beverly Hills to renting a room from my Satins. That's what I get for thinking a gringa in the record business would really care about—" She stopped abruptly.

"You?"

"Yeah, me. And my career. Yours, too. She was supposed to make stars out of the Satins, Jess. That all fizzled out. Doesn't that bother you?"

Jessica shrugged. "I guess I didn't really believe it. Listen, with my track record, I don't set much store in anyone but myself."

"Tough as nails, but adorable dimples."

"Oh, cut it out." Jessica faced her. "I'm trying to be empathetic with you and, of course, *you* don't want to get serious."

"It hurts to get serious, Jess. Besides, I've cried on your shoulder enough."

"You're right on the first point. That's why I avoid it, too. My solution is to live day by day. Write songs about things that matter to me, rehearse and perform them with the Satins. Write reviews for a paper I don't really care about anymore. Don't let the people around here without food or jobs get to me. Go to work and play with kids and try not to think too much about what they're going through at home." She paused and cleared her throat. "Chic, I saw a kid today who made me ache. She had the saddest face. Then I came home and noticed for the millionth time that the place is falling apart and we can't afford to fix it properly, except for some patching up here and there, and—"

"I get the message. We all have our problems." Chic uttered a low moan. "But, Jess, *I'm* horny as hell. It's like, don't give me a microphone or I'm liable to stick it between my legs on stage and go public."

"That won't even get you discovered anymore. Every singer under the sun has done that by now."

"I'm *not* into public sex. You know that. I just want to be with somebody for a night. Entiendes, Mendes?"

Comprehension setting in, Jessica stepped back. "Hey, not *me*."

"Remember when we were kids and—"

"Chic, we've been friends a long time. You've said that yourself. I'm *not* going to mess that up. Think this over."

"I have, Jess," Chic said softly. Looking at Jessica, she wet her lips and uttered a few lines of "Boca Loca" in her gritty voice.

Ay, dáme tu locura
Y tu piel tan oscura
Dáme un beso en mi boca
Y te voy volver más loca

"Be careful," Cindi revealed from the other side of the door. "She's putting the make on all of us."

"Oh, shit." Chic stamped her foot and flipped Cindi off.

Jessica could not help but laugh. "Chic, give it up."

"Try Rita," Cindi muttered through the door. "She's as horny as you are."

They heard Cindi's footsteps going downstairs.

"My cuz watches out for me," Jessica said, still feeling the flush on her face. "Either that or she wanted to make sure I said 'no.'"

"Listen, Jess—"

"Chic, nothing you ever do surprises me."

Chic moved toward her and stood very near. "You *do* have fabulous dimples. And, after me, you're the best singer in the Satins."

"Good night, Chic."

"Your loss, babe." Before leaving the room, she slowly brushed her sinuous body against Jessica's.

Alone in the dark, she curled up on the thick futon pad. She had been tempted to accept Chic's offer. If Cindi had not spoken up, Jessica realized the evening could have ended differently. Not that she would have expected anything else but sex from Chic—merely the thought of lying with another woman, feeling vital brown skin against hers, silky hands and lips ready to pleasure her, had made her want to say "yes." The woman had not mattered as much as the invitation.

Jessica tried to shake the sensual images from her mind. She changed position on the futon, lying on her tummy. That reminded her of how she had used to rub herself against Trish's softness, pressing her body ever closer. She shut her eyes tightly, wanting sleep to overtake her. She lay motionless for several minutes, breathing steadily. Then her left hand crept to her thigh, and she touched herself gently in circular motions.

Her fingers began to drift upwards, finding her moistness. They stayed there, soothing her, exciting her, until she slept.

Jessica left the house earlier than usual. Instead of stopping by Starbucks on her way back, she trekked a couple of blocks over to the Novel Café, the combination bookstore-coffee house Albert Kirby frequented.

"Hey, Albert—I saw Western gulls this morning—pink legs. And they're bigger than California gulls."

"You're something, Jess." He gave her a huge grin. "For that, coffee's on me."

"I won't argue. I'll have a cappucino."

Soon Albert set a steaming cup before her. "How was your new kid yesterday? She seemed timid."

"Yeah. I'm going to try to spend more time with Yolanda today." Jessica sipped the welcome brew. "Thanks, Albert."

"A treat to see you here. Tired of Starbucks?"

"Not exactly. There's been some friction about Rita and the childcare situation. I really didn't want to see her first thing this morning."

Albert frowned at her comment. "That man of hers ever send any child support?"

Jessica shook her head.

"Must be rough. Rita's a pretty little thing and so's her child. She can't make much at that coffeehouse. Hope she finds a more reliable man one of these days."

Jessica decided not to respond to that. She suspected Rita had wound up in Chic's bed last night, and was not about to confide in Albert. Although he was her best friend at the play-school, she had hesitated about coming out to him. He knew she sang with the Latin Satins though he had not seen them perform. Once in a while, Jessica sought his advice about household or other matters. Yet she knew people of color could be as homophobic as anyone else. For that reason, she had not

told Albert anything too personal; she did not want to take a
chance on losing his friendship.

"You okay, honey?"

"Oh, yeah, Albert. Not quite awake, that's all."

"Well, I'm walking to work this morning—decided to get
some exercise. See you there, Jess."

"Later." She raised her cup.

"I knew it was a mistake to have that sin vergüenza under
this roof. See what happens when you feel sorry for someone?"
Cindi grabbed a cereal box out of the cupboard and poured herself a bowlful. "I thought we were doing Chic a favor by renting her the room. What's she do but go after the most vulnerable woman I know—Rita Solís! Just 'cause I made a sarcastic
crack last night didn't mean Chic had to take me up on it."

"So it *really* happened?"

"Cuz, where've you been? At least it wasn't *you*." Cindi
added milk to her cereal. "Chic's still in bed, Rita ran off to
work, and I had to get Angelita ready for school and make sure
Xochi didn't leave without her. Damn it, Jess. We really have to
talk to Rita. What'd she say this morning?"

Jessica shrugged. "I went to the Novel Café—just in case.
Wanted to escape Rita's morning-after theatrics."

"Maybe I should start walking to the beach with you. I'd
like to avoid the drama around here, too." Cindi ate hurriedly,
glancing at the Coca-Cola clock over the kitchen window.
"Gotta go. One condo to clean this morning, two after lunch.
Catch you this afternoon."

48

4 Trace of Race

Jessica surveyed her sleeping preschoolers. She was glad they had finally settled down for their naps. Sometimes she felt out of place among such innocence, though she would rather spend hours with these children than with many people her own age. Among these four year olds, she could sing and play, act silly, simply be herself without being reminded of real-life situations. If the Satins had not scheduled an evening rehearsal, she would have preferred to escape into a movie instead of going home. She dreaded to face the sauciness Chic and Rita would no doubt display.

Yawning, she moved quietly, putting toys on shelves, careful not to disturb the children. She sat at her small desk and removed several music sheets from her knapsack. She bent over another composition, tentatively titled "Brown Lady." Erasing some notes, she jotted in others and mouthed the lyrics as she did so.

> Baby, why'd you leave without a trace
> Were you really hung up by my race?
> Making love in darkness was all right
> But morning showed me in a different light

Jessica concentrated for several minutes until she felt herself being watched. She turned toward the children, expecting to see one of them about to act up. Instead, she noticed Yolanda

León lying sideways on her foam rubber mat, her eyes intent on Jessica.

A cautionary finger to her lips, Jessica beckoned Yolanda to her. A bit hesitantly, the child crept over, pigtails bobbing.

"Not sleepy, Yolanda?"

The little girl shook her head. Her almond-shaped eyes moved over the papers spread on Jessica's desk. "What's that?"

"These squiggly things?" Jessica pointed to the row of notes she had penciled. "Don't they look like tadpoles? Well, they're not—they're musical notes. You know, like 'do-re-mi.'"

Yolanda seemed mystified.

Jessica smiled and hoisted the child to her lap. "That's one of the things I do when I go home. I make up songs and write them on pieces of paper like this."

Yolanda leaned closer and whispered, "Is that why your mouth was moving a little while ago?"

"You caught me in the act, Yolanda," Jessica said, amused. "Sometimes I hear music in my head and my mouth pretends to sing even though no sound comes out. Did I look funny?"

Yolanda nodded.

"Did you think maybe you couldn't hear me? Did you think you had wax in your ears?"

Yolanda giggled, the first time Jessica had heard her utter a mirthful sound. Her brown eyes met Jessica's. "My daddy used to sing—and play his guitar."

"Really?" Taking note of the child's use of the past tense, Jessica wondered if that were intentional. "My Dad plays the guitar, too, and I love to sing with him in Spanish."

At that remark, Yolanda stiffened. As near as she was, Jessica felt a sudden rigidity overtake the child's body. The little girl's eyes swept downward; she seemed to withdraw, almost shrinking before Jessica's eyes. She watched Yolanda with concern, unwilling to question her further.

"My daddy—*doesn't* sing anymore," Yolanda finally murmured. She began to cry, her tiny shoulders sagging.

"Oh, honey. I'm so sorry." Jessica wrapped the child nearer, rocking her gently.

Later, Jessica paused in the threshold of the daycare director's office. "Kathleen, I have to talk with you."

"Oh, hi, Jessica." Kathleen Scott was bent over the wastebasket beside her cluttered desk. "Do you know how to empty this pencil sharpener? I can't even get it open."

Jessica advanced and took it from her. "With those fingernails, no wonder. Let me." She fiddled with the sharpener and soon emptied its contents into the trash. "I love that cedar aroma—the closest I ever get to the woods."

"I think it stinks." Kathleen turned her head in repugnance. "Thanks. You saved the day." She leaned back in her swivel chair. "What can I do for you?"

"Tell me about Yolanda León."

Kathleen seemed surprised by Jessica's request. "There's nothing unusual about her. You know—shy child with a single working mother. Her elderly grandmother used to babysit."

"That's no answer." Jessica heard her own impatience. "Seems to me we're dealing with a little girl who's mourning the death of her father." She revealed the afternoon's occurrences to Kathleen.

"Well, you certainly handled the situation well. Odd that the mother didn't mention anything about this." Kathleen pulled a manila file from the file cabinet next to her desk. "Do you want me to talk to Mrs. León?"

"No, I'll do it." Jessica watched her glance through the little girl's file. "I just wondered if you knew how recently Yolanda's father had died."

"*If* that's the case. It could be a divorce situation. That's a lot more common, Jessica. Or the child can be inventing a story for sympathy's sake."

"She's four years old, Kathleen."

"I've seen it happen." The daycare director put the folder

51

aside and sharpened a pencil; she seemed satisfied with the result. "I'm glad you came to me now, in case this child becomes a problem. Why didn't *you* say anything to her mother?"

"Didn't have a chance." Jessica sighed. "Mrs. Katz started telling me all about the results of Amy's food allergy tests. I couldn't break away when I saw Mrs. León show up."

"I suggest keeping an eye on—what's her name again?"

"Yolanda."

"Yes. It's best to know in advance if there's trouble ahead."

"I can handle things, Kathleen." Jessica turned and hurried out the office door.

Irritated with the daycare director's insensitivity, she pedaled home faster than usual. Would Kathleen have reacted similarly if the child had not been of color? If Yolanda were blonde and blue-eyed, outgoing and vocal, would she have aroused empathetic feelings in Kathleen? Jessica wished she would have spoken with Albert first, but he had already gone. Breathless, she turned onto Third Street, somehow managing to ride halfway up the driveway.

Angelita and ten-year-old Xochi Zepeda, a lanky child in an ill-fitting plaid dress, played tag in the front yard, their sneakers crunching into the gravel around the fuschias and bottlebrush shrubs. Though Jessica waved to the girls, they hardly noticed. She pushed her bike into the garage and returned to the front of the house to catch her breath. She eased herself into the cushioned rattan loveseat she and Cindi had purchased at a local garage sale. Beside the canopied swing seat adjacent to the front door, the worn piece of furniture added a homey look to the veranda. Jessica wondered when, if ever, she and Cindi could afford to buy more outdoor furniture. On warm evenings, they contented themselves with sitting outside, watching the sun set.

Closing her eyes, Jessica relaxed. At least, she did not have to worry about dinner. Tonight was Rita's turn—no doubt the meal would be some kind of takeout.

A high-pitched scream startled her. She sprang to her feet on reflex, in time to see Angelita slide on her knees into the gravel. Jessica leaped off the veranda and darted to the child's side. In panic, Xochi, waist-length ponytail flying, disappeared around the side of the house into the backyard.

"My knees, my knees—" Angelita sobbed against Jessica.

"Shhh, baby. I'll take care of everything." Jessica swept her into her arms. "I'll clean you up and put Band-Aids on. Then you'll be good as new."

"Xochi pushed me," Angelita cried. "Did you see her?"

"Honey, you were playing tag. Xochi didn't mean it."

"She called me 'negrita fea.'" At that, Angelita wailed anew.

Jessica shuddered at hearing that racist epithet. Xochi no doubt had repeated overheard pejorative language; her father seemed the likeliest culprit. Jessica gave serious thought to confronting Efraín about that. At the moment, Angelita mattered more.

"Let me clean you up, Angelita, before your mommy gets home. Then we'll talk about Xochi."

"My knees hurt, Jessie."

"I know, baby." Tenderly holding her, Jessica went up the steps, and unlocked the protective iron screen door. She carried the crying child into the downstairs bathroom and set her on the tiled counter next to the wash basin. Carefully, she dabbed Angelita's scraped knees with soap and water, then alcohol, cleaning the blood and impacted gravel from her skin. The little girl whimpered throughout the procedure.

"Where's Mommy?"

"She'll be here soon. Would you like me to phone her?"

Angelita nodded.

"All right. Stay put. I'll be back to put on the Band-Aids. Don't move, Angelita."

"I won't. Can I have a Kleenex?"

Jessica handed her a box of tissues and went to the tiny alcove by the front door to dial Starbucks. Ernie, the day manager, told her Rita had left a few minutes before on her way to Wildflour Pizza.

Returning to Angelita, Jessica gave her another hug. "Your mom's bringing us dinner."

The child leaned against her and sighed. "Why did Xochi call me names? I thought she was my friend."

Jessica smoothed Angelita's mussed curls. "What else did she call you?"

"Nigger baby. Nigger-toes. Sambo-face." Angelita's features began to contort again.

Jessica lifted the child's face. "When was this, honey? I didn't hear her say anything."

"Right before you got home. Jessie, she wouldn't say those words in front of *you*."

"I'm sorry Xochi hurt you, Angelita. I don't think she meant to be mean. She said things she doesn't understand. I'll tell your mommy so she can talk to Xochi's parents."

Angelita's face became more solemn. "They don't like me."

"What?"

"Efraín and Berta give me dirty looks, and I hear them whispering bad things about Mommy."

Jessica reminded herself to keep her temper in check in front of the child. "We'll take care of that, Angelita. No one has a right to hurt your feelings by calling you names."

"They say black people are ugly, and I'm ugly 'cause my daddy's black. That isn't true, is it, Jessie?"

"Of course not. They don't know what they're talking about." Jessica held Angelita close, and the intimate contact caused the little girl to sob again. Her own emotions on edge, Jessica bit her lip and continued clasping the child to her.

•

"Anybody home?" Chic called from the living room.

"In here." Quickly, Jessica wiped her eyes and helped Angelita blow her nose.

"Catastrophe time?" Chic sneaked a peek and began to back out. Doubtless, she wanted no part of whatever trauma had occurred.

Jessica shot her a warning glance before speaking. "Angelita and Xochi were playing and things got out of hand. Xochi called her names—racist names."

At that, Chic's face lost its ordinarily insouciant expression. "Is that bast—is Efraín home?"

"I don't know." Jessica kept her voice at an even tone. "Chic, Rita's on her way. Don't handle this yourself. It could get messy."

Jessica noticed her friend did not hide her anger. Chic Lozano, who had had lovers of every ethnic group imaginable, was no racist and would not tolerate bigotry in anyone else.

Her voice sounded tight. "I'll wait for Rita out front and let her know the score."

"Then would you tell her to come inside?" Jessica opened the medicine cabinet and removed a Band-Aid box. "Angelita needs to see her mommy."

Sniffling, the little girl nodded. "Yes, I do."

When she had patched Angelita's knees, Jessica carried her into the living room. She knew she was pampering the child, yet she felt the need to keep Angelita safely near. "Let's see if your mommy's coming up the street."

"Can I look?" Angelita sounded eager.

"I'll go with you. Chic's already standing on the sidewalk." Jessica lowered Angelita and unlatched the front door.

Angelita became distracted when she observed her reflection in the full-length mirror adjacent to the door. Sticking out her lower lip, she patted her patched knees gingerly.

Jessica paused for a moment before stepping to the veranda.

55

She viewed Rita crossing Third Street diagonally at mid-block. Balancing two boxes of pizza, she trotted toward Chic, cheeks flushed, eyes radiant. Even from a distance, Jessica recognized Rita's infatuated expression.

"Angelita, wait a second." She touched the child's shoulder. "Your mommy might get upset when she sees your knees. Let Chic tell her first. And be careful going down the steps."

"I'm going to be all right, Jessie." Angelita gazed up at her. "You fixed me up good."

"It was the least I could do, honey." Jessica watched her slowly negotiate the steps and head down the driveway to her mother.

Noticing her daughter, Rita flung the pizza boxes at Chic. She gathered Angelita into her arms and held her tightly.

"She was my hero," Angelita said when Jessica came closer. The little girl sighed and lay her head on her mother's shoulder.

"Oh, Jessie." Rita grabbed her with one arm and squeezed. "Gracias a Dios you were here."

"Angelita's very brave." Jessica managed to release herself. "Chic filled you in on the details?"

Rita nodded, seeming bewildered.

"I'm goin' back there to knock some sense into that racist S.O.B." Chic clenched her fists at her sides. "Where else do you think his skinny brat picked up her foul mouth?"

Jessica put a placating hand on her arm. "There has to be a better way to handle this, Chic. We have to think it over."

Exchanging glances, the three women stood in the driveway, while Cindi manuevered her station wagon toward them. She honked at her housemates, and they moved aside dazedly.

"Hey, what's up? You guys looked spaced."

"Look, we *can't* tell Efraín to move. As much as I hate the thought, he can stay here as long as he wants," Cindi said while they shared the pizza on the front steps. "Tía Irene specified that in her will."

"What'd he have on the old lady?" Chic grumbled. "Don't tell me he was screwing her?"

Cindi tossed Jessica an amused glance. "I really doubt that. Tía Irene helped Efraín with his immigration papers, like she did with half the Mexicanos on the Westside. Her loyalities were stronger toward him, though, 'cause he's a relative. I have to admit Efraín was wonderful to our tía, helping her keep up the property by doing chores and yardwork. She was very fond of him."

"Sentimental old—"

"Don't say it, Chic," Jessica cautioned. "Our tía had a big heart. Otherwise, why would she've left this house to Cindi and me? She had her idiosyncracies, that's for sure, but she was well loved in this town—still is."

"Yeah, yeah, yeah. Even so, she stuck you and Cindi—all of us—with this racist asshole in the backyard. We can't let this slide, mujeres."

"What do *you* think, Rita?" Cindi gazed at her, while chewing a piece of pepperoni pizza.

"I'm upset my baby was hurt." Rita sat on one of the steps, keeping a protective eye on her daughter. Angelita, butterfly net in tow, prowled through the front yard intent on her chase. "Like you said, Efraín's going to be around, whether we like it or not. We're going to have to learn to live together."

"Try tellin' *him* that. He's grossed out 'cause he wound up with four dykes living here and two of 'em are his landladies." Chic bit into the thick pizza crust. "Chispas! If you think about it, that's really cool. We could make *his* life miserable so he'll *want* to get the hell out."

Jessica shook her head. "I can't stand him either, Chic, but who has time for games like that? With Efraín, it's a cultural thing. He's like those hombres at the parish fiesta who got freaked over our lyrics. Efraín isn't used to being around all types of people. In Mexico, he must've known everyone in his village. He's probably been in culture shock as long as he's been in California, trying to sort out all the racial and ethnic groups, not to mention *us.*"

"Right. That's why I think it'd be a better idea if we start working on his kids—Xochi, in particular, since she's the oldest," Cindi stated. "We could invite her over for ice cream. Get her alone and hand her some anti-racism clues."

Rita looked pensive. "Do you think that would work?"

"It's worth a try," Jessica said quietly.

"I'd rather get physical with her butt-faced old man. If he doesn't like the U.S.A., what's he doin' here? I'd like to beat in his pinche cara de nalga." Chic swung an imaginary punch.

Rita rubbed Chic's knee. "You can get physical with *me* instead, baby. We'll forget all about Efraín tonight."

Chic leaned toward her, slipping a hand behind Rita's neck, pulling her closer. They kissed lingeringly.

Cindi cleared her throat and picked up the empty pizza boxes. Jessica gathered the soft drink cans and followed her cousin inside.

"Lovebirds and racists on the same plot of land. Híjole! I can't cope." Cindi tossed the pizza boxes into the trash bin.

Jessica smiled at her cousin's assessment. "Those two won't last. Are you kidding, Cindi? Chic wants what I want—a warm body—that's all."

Cindi whirled to face her. "Is that *my* cuz talking? I can't believe you said that."

Jessica pretended to be engrossed in stuffing the soda cans into the recycling container. "I *was* tempted last night. For the sensation, mind you."

"With Chic? Dios mio." Cindi shook her head unbelievingly.

"Don't tell me you don't even feel a twinge when she starts

58

teasing." Jessica stepped closer to her cousin. "She was in your room last night, too. What went on, huh?"

"Nada. The sad part is Rita thinks she was the only one Chic came on to."

"I'm staying out of *that*." Jessica slammed the top of the recycling bin. "My concern right now is Angelita."

"Switching the subject back to racism? That's safer?"

Jessica nodded. "For once, yes. I think inviting Xochi is a good idea, Cindi. The thing is, will Efraín agree to it? He might think we're trying to 'corrupt' her by luring her into our house."

"I'll tell him we want to let Xochi know how much we appreciate her walking Angelita to school."

"Brilliant, C.C."

Cindi shrugged. "Have to talk to him tomorrow, anyway. He's supposed to trim the hedges."

"Notice how you and me are the ones planning this?" Jessica leaned against the sink. "Rita's got other things on her mind."

"I think she's scared, Jess. Whenever that happens, she does everything she can to avoid her fear. She probably figured Angelita would be really safe here. Turns out she isn't."

"At least Chic's in her corner on this. If it were some other childcare issue, Chic wouldn't give a damn."

"And how could someone like *that* tempt you, cuz?"

"Cindi, at least I'm willing to admit she does—sometimes."

Angelita wandered into the kitchen and stashed her butterfly net on the hook behind the door. "Chic said to tell you it's rehearsal time."

"We'll be right there." Cindi opened the refrigerator and removed a popsicle from the freezer. "This is the last one, Angelita."

"I'll save it for a hotter day. Any cookies left?"

Jessica moved to help Angelita. She lifted her to reach for the teddy bear jar on the pantry shelf.

"Oh, goodie. Chocolate chip!" Angelita grabbed a handful and Jessica closed the lid. "I'm going upstairs to watch TV in my room."

Surprised by her comment, Jessica set her down. "You aren't going to tell us what you think of the new song?"

The child shook her head. "I'm too tired."

"All right, honey. See you tomorrow."

Angelita blew kisses and rounded the corner to the stairs.

Later that night, Jessica perched on her window seat, knees drawn to her chin, gazing into the darkness. She had finished typing her music review and would mail it in the morning. Exhausted from the day's events, she mulled over the evening's rehearsal.

She had introduced the completed "Pocha Blues" to the Satins, hoping its hints of anger about racism would be cathartic. However, their rehearsal had been unproductive, off-kilter. They were too demoralized over Angelita's afternoon experience to concentrate on learning a new tune. Though the four Chicanas dealt with racism daily, this time reality had struck them harder than usual. How could they help Rita prepare Angelita for a lifetime of racist encounters? What could they do to prevent further bigotry from the backyard tenants? Before calling it quits for the night, even Chic grudgingly agreed that Cindi's idea seemed the most logical. Confronting Xochi with kindness might work.

Jessica's thoughts wandered to Yolanda León; evidently, she, like Angelita, had been traumatized in some way. She wore the same world-weary though innocent expression Angelita had shown earlier.

"Damn adults," Jessica muttered.

60

Rita's voice interrupted her reverie. "Jessie, are you working on your review? I'd like to talk."

"I'm through. Come on in."

Rita pushed open the bedroom door. "At first, I thought I heard you say something. Were you writing lyrics?"

"Just talking to myself. Is Angelita asleep?"

Rita nodded. "Look, Jessie. I—" She broke off, seeming embarrassed. "I really owe you for today. Angelita says you're a hero. I think so, too."

Jessica leaned against the window and rested her chin on her upright knees. "Anyone would've done the same. And if Xochi hadn't run away, I would've talked to her myself." Jessica smiled slowly, hoping to deflect the conversation. "So— what's the deal with you and Chic?"

Rita's brown eyes turned dreamy. "She told you?"

"She didn't have to. I saw how she kissed you."

"Me vuelve loca, pero I've always thought she's muy sexy, muy suavecita." Rita studied her lacquered fingernails. "I never figured she'd like *me*, too—like *that*."

"What about Angelita?"

"Ay, we didn't do *anything* in front of her!" Rita grew flustered at the question. "I know you think I'm a horrible mother, but I would never do anything that crazy. We were in Chic's room all night."

"You're *not* a horrible mother," Jessica said quietly. "I've never said that."

Close to tears, Rita moved nearer. She sank beside her friend on the window seat. "Ay, Jessie. I hate when people say awful things to Angelita. It's so hard explaining to her that some people hate her only because of her color. You know how to deal with kids much better than me. And Angelita trusts you."

"I think the world of her, too." Jessica awkwardly stroked Rita's back.

"When I was with Tremaine," Rita continued, her voice

61

becoming choked, "I just wanted to have a good time. I was trying to make up my mind if I wanted to be con hombres o mujeres. Tre's so handsome, verdad? Macho, pero sweet. I *never* thought I'd get pregnant. I made a stupid mistake, Jessie." Rita started to sob. "When I found out I was going to have a baby, I thought—well, maybe *this* is what I'm supposed to do. Tre wanted to do the right thing, too. He said he loved me. Later he even tried to understand how I feel about women. I guess it finally got to him, you know? When he had the chance, he went on the road with his rappers. Quién sabe if he'll ever come back."

Jessica continued to stroke her friend's heaving back. "No matter what happened between you and Tremaine, your daughter's *not* a mistake. Angelita's an incredible child, Rita, and we all love her. We don't want anything else to happen to her. Please *tell* us when you need our help."

"Sí, mi amigita." Rita sniffled, touching the ends of Jessica's blunt-cut hair. "Tomorrow I'm going to take her to school myself. I already phoned Ernie to tell him I'll be a little late. I hope I won't have to change my work hours, but till we get a chance to talk to Xochi—"

Jessica nodded in agreement.

Rita started to rise. "Anyway, you and Cindi have been fabulosas. If you hadn't rented us the room, we'd be in the Valley living con toda la familia. I don't want to be dependent on my parents anymore, Jessie. And even if ese cabrón Efraín lives in back, I love this place. It's the happiest home I've had in a long time."

"That's true for all of us, Rita."

5 Pocha Blues

"What're you still doin' here?" Entering the kitchen, Chic squinted at Jessica.

"Overslept," she explained, yawning. "Took me a while to conk off last night. Too much happening around here."

Chic grunted and poured herself a cup of coffee from the potful Jessica had made. Eyes drowsy, she sat opposite.

"Everything okay, Chic?"

"Top of the world, babe. Rehearsal went like shit, right? And all I wanted after that was a little action. Wound up with a cryin' mujer in my bed. Chispas!"

Jessica stuck a sliced English muffin into the toaster. "You were sympathetic to Rita, I hope."

"Don't like racism anymore than you do. What else *could* I do?" Chic downed a huge swallow of the brew. "I'm just pissed 'cause Rita didn't feel like playin'. Kept tryin' to give her somethin' else to think about, but no dice. Then she got up a couple of times to be sure the kid was all right. I'm outa here tonight—even if it's solo for *me*. No wonder you play with yourself."

Jessica turned her back while slathering the muffin with orange marmalade. Chic's frankness was much too challenging before breakfast.

"I see you're not denying it." Chic grinned when Jessica returned to the table.

"Mind your own business and drink your coffee."

"Ay, carnala. You're makin' me ache."

"You're making *me* sick."

Chic laughed. She leaned back in her chair and crossed her legs, left ankle to right kneecap. "Want to go to the Delta tonight?"

Jessica shook her head. She took a big bite of the muffin.

"Why not, loca?"

Jessica took her time answering. "If we're not going to rehearse tonight, I have other plans."

"Like?"

Jessica glared. "Look, most of the time—not counting last night's rehearsal—we groove together with the Satins. Our personal lives are our own business. I don't have to tell you everything I do."

"Never mind then—girl *friend*." Chic got up abruptly and stomped out the back door.

On her way to work, Jessica hardly noticed the sunshine peering through the clouds. She pedaled quickly, trying to make up for her usual morning exercise. She knew she had not handled Chic well, yet she was not in the mood for joking around with her. Maybe that was the problem. Had Chic been teasing or not? Jessica preferred to evade that question herself.

When she rode into the Pacific Palms parking lot, she noticed Mrs. León had just driven in, too. Jessica pedaled close to her car.

"Hi," she greeted as the mother and daughter got out.

The woman smiled and glanced at her daughter. "Mira, Yolanda. Ms. Tamayo has a bicycle."

Yolanda stood by to her mother. She offered Jessica a tiny smile.

Jessica walked beside them with her bike. "Mrs. León, do you have a minute?"

The woman checked her watch. "A few."

Jessica leaned her bike against the fence. "Let me take Yolanda in first. I'll be right back." She reached for the child's hand. "Come on, honey. Say 'bye to your mom."

Yolanda clung to her mother for a moment before dutifully going inside with Jessica. The little girl seemed content to sit by herself with a picture book, unmindful of the other children already gathered there. Jessica gave a cursory glance over the room before leaving.

She thought Mrs. León looked somewhat uneasy while waiting by the car. Approaching, Jessica decided to get to the point. "I've been wondering about Yolanda—and excuse me if it seems like I'm prying. Has there been a death in the family?"

Mrs. León blinked and looked away, as if she needed to compose herself before answering. "Her father—passed on a few months ago. My ex-husband."

"I'm sorry," Jessica said quietly.

"I am, too." Yet Mrs. León's eyes did not match the mournfulness of her daughter's.

"Yolanda told me he doesn't sing to her anymore. Then she cried." Jessica continued in a soft tone, "I grew up without my mother, Mrs. León. I thought it best to ask for details because I need to know how to deal with Yolanda."

"Thank you. It—hasn't been an easy time."

"I understand—and I care about your daughter. I'll do everything I can to make her feel at home." She pushed sweaty bangs off her forehead. "And, please, call me Jessica."

"Gracias—Jessica." Mrs. León moved briskly into her car.

"Music might be the link," Albert remarked when Jessica sat on the bench beside him. The children in their play groups scampered around them in the fenced yard, some at the swings, riding tricycles or attempting to climb the jungle gym. Yolanda sat alone in the sandbox, making flat-topped structures and humming to herself.

"Whenever we sing, Yolanda perks up." Jessica chewed on

a slice of apple. "I'm glad we talked, Albert. Kathleen wasn't any help."

"Did that surprise you?" He shook his greying head. "You know, if I had the bread, I'd open my own daycare center, take in black kids, brown kids, all the ones who don't get enough attention. You'd be the first teacher I'd hire."

Jessica smiled. Without Albert, she would be at a loss on a daily basis. "Win the lottery, man."

"No other which way I could do it." He kept his eyes on the frolicking children. "This Mrs. León—she didn't offer any explanation of how Yolanda's father died?"

"No. I could tell she was uncomfortable. I didn't ask any more questions."

"Maybe that's the core of it. If *she's* uncomfortable, how can her little girl cope?"

"And that's where *I* come in." Jessica sighed. "Gosh, Albert. I'm not a shrink."

"You don't have to be. Look at you and Angelita. That child's crazy about you. I think Yolanda needs you, too."

Rafael plucked yellow roses off the fragrant bush below his tailor shop window. He offered one to Jessica when she rode up.

"Isn't something wrong with this picture? The hombre's supposed to be riding up on a white caballo, no? And la mujer's supposed to be plucking roses?"

"Not in *our* world, man." Jessica put down the bike's kickstand and went to hug Rafi. She lay the rose on the rack situated over the bicycle's back tire. "You ready?"

"Let me just grab my wrap, darlin'." He darted inside for his pullover. In the meantime, Jessica locked her bike to his wrought iron stair railing. Rafi soon returned, knotting his sweater jauntily around his neck.

"Mr. Snazzy." Jessica grinned while he insisted on pinning the errant rose to her shirt pocket. She allowed him to fuss over her. "Thanks, Rafi. You in a sushi mood?"

"No argument." He took her arm in his thin one. "I'm glad you're alone, Jess. I saw Rita today when I went to stock up on coffee. Potential soap opera brewing en la casa amarilla."

"Yeah. I needed a break from it tonight."

"Anytime you want to crash in my spare bedroom, let me know. I could use the company."

The friends began walking west along Pico Boulevard. They sidestepped to allow a shabby woman with an overladen shopping cart to pass them on the narrow sidewalk.

Jessica kept her attention on Rafi. "I thought Billie always came by."

Rafi shrugged. "Haven't seen much of her this week. Billie's been busy with the Casillas family. Carmelita's about to turn fifteen." He made an extravagant gesture with his out-stretched hands. "That whole family's in a whirl, getting their hair permed, faces and nails done and what not for the quin-ceañera. Gracias a Dios, I have Carmelita's party dress finished. That Casillas bunch was about to drive me loquito."

"So some people really are worse than the Satins when it comes to fittings?"

Rafael chuckled. "You chicks were a breeze. I'm almost done with the jackets." They paused on the corner of Pico and Lincoln for the traffic light to change. "Dígame, Jess. When did Chic decide to take care of the itch in Rita's chones?"

"Oh, Rafi," Jessica groaned. "Do we have to talk about *that*?"

"Not if you don't want to, honey." He stepped off the curb, cupping her elbow with his palm. They walked on the north side of the street, past Santa Monica High School toward Main Street. "Rough day at the old schoolhouse?"

She did not answer right away. They continued for almost a full block before she decided to be open. "Remember when my parents split up?"

He nodded, tightening his clasp on her while they strolled past the Santa Monica Civic Auditorium. "You were about Angelita's age. And your sister was in my grade. Vickie had to become your mother, more or less."

"*More*, not less." Jessica gazed at him, grateful she did not have to launch into a detailed explanation of her family history. "In some ways, I feel I'm in that position with Angelita."

"That brings back memories, I take it."

"Yeah. And I get this whole protective attitude—like I'm Mother Earth. In some ways, it feels out of sync, Rafi—and in others, it feels just right."

"All of us have mixed emotions at one time or another. Don't be so hard on yourself."

Rafi led her across Pico to Main. Before long, he held open the door of a recently opened sushi bar and restaurant off Main Street.

While they waited to be seated, Jessica continued talking. "Besides all that about Angelita, there's a Chicanita in daycare who's dealing with her father's death. Maybe there's too much going on emotionally this week, Rafi. It's gotten to me—big time."

Rafi nodded as they followed the kimono-clad hostess to a small table overlooking Main Street.

"At the risk of slipping into psychobabble," Rafi said when they were alone, "maybe it's time to deal with some of your inner child stuff."

She gave him a withering look.

"I'm serious, mija. You mother little girls instead of mothering yourself. Sounds pat, I know, pero I tend to do the same. I fuss around trying to make everyone else look sensational." Rafi's brown hands made sweeping gestures, combining Chicano emphasis with a gay flair. "But look at *me*—I'm a haggard wreck."

She laughed and sang, "'You're so vain.'"

"Your sister acts the same." Rafi swung into full high camp mode, his eyebrows, shoulders and wrists fluttering. "Vickie dresses all those gavachas for success, and when does she have time for herself? When was the last time *she* had a date?"

"Who knows?" Jessica took a sip of lemon-flavored ice water. "Do you ever see her?"

"Matter of fact, I ran into her at Nordstrom's not long ago. I was trying to snag a quick sketch of a cocktail dress a customer wanted me to copy. Vickie was putting together a bitch exec wardrobe for one of *her* clients."

Jessica tried not to laugh. "Was she friendly?"

"Not too. She *hates* when I camp it up. If I'm in a low-key mood, she's simpática."

"Of course, you camped it up."

"Could I help it, darlin'? She's so stuffy, your sister."

"Not anything like me, huh?" Jessica watched him with amusement.

"Ni modo." Rafael flicked his wrist again and picked up the menu. "Not like your dad either. How is Tudy, anyway, Jess? Been a while since I've seen him."

"Still working at Will Rogers, his home away from home. I'm going out there Saturday."

"One of the chirinoleras down the block told me Tudy wows las viejitas at the Senior Center when he whips out his guitar."

"Oh, yeah," Jessica agreed. "Dad's a regular heartthrob."

"Like his daughter." Rafael winked and scanned the menu. Jessica felt herself blush.

Rafi peered over the top of the menu. "Do you want to talk about Chic *now*?"

"Nope."

"Did she hit on you, honey?"

"On Rita, man."

"Yeah, I *know* about Rita. Ay, that mujer gave me todo los details. Like a gay boy really wants to hear all about pussies y chichis."

Jessica laughed outright.

He leaned toward her. "Did you hear them doing it?"

She shook her head. "I sleep in the attic, remember?"

"Out of sight, out of mind?" He signalled for the waiter.

"Any possibilities in that Chorus?" He arched a brow as he picked up his chopsticks.

Jessica frowned. "What do you mean?"

"Ay, cabezona." Rafi nibbled a clump of rice from the edges of his chopsticks. "*Women!* Any possible girl friends in that Chorus?"

Jessica sampled one of the California rolls on the sushi platter. "Do you grill the other Satins like this?"

"Whenever I have the chance." He served himself more white rice. "Tell me, Jess. Do you think you've gotten over your break-up with Trish?"

She sighed. "When a woman says she'll never come out of the closet 'cause she could lose her job, then packs up and leaves, there's no choice *but* to get over her. Rafi, Trish was running scared. Haven't seen or heard from her since." Jessica took another California roll and dipped it in soy sauce. "She didn't really mind when the Satins sang on the Promenade, but she flipped out when we started getting dyke gigs."

"I wonder if she'll *ever* come out," Rafi said with annoyance.

"She teaches child development at a community college." Jessica gave him a skeptical look. "A Chinese-Chicana lesbian with a full course load. According to her, she can't afford to come out."

"*You* work with kids."

"That's different. I keep my music separate."

He poked her arm with a chopstick. "And your sexuality?"

"Nowadays that isn't even an issue. Rafi, what you see is what you get," she said, spreading her arms, palms upward. "I'm a celibate lesbian. No need to go around flaunting *that*."

"In some ways," he retorted, "you're as closeted as Trish."

She frowned. "Aim your guns at someone else. I don't need this."

He peeled a piece of shrimp off a sushi roll. "Sometimes I'm jealous."

She did not say anything, letting him continue.

"*You* know all about safe sex. You can go out and *still* have fun. And you're not even doing anything about it, Jess. You're wasting time. It makes me crazy."

Jessica sensed his frustration and kept that in mind. "Rafi, that's *my* choice. Anyway, to me, it's time out." She poured them both tiny cups of jasmine tea. "Maybe next week I'll change my mind and start climbing the walls. Right now, I like being by myself. I'll admit, sometimes I'm lonesome. But, then, I could be that way in a relationship, too."

He took the cup and walked his fingers around its rim. "That's for sure. I know about *that*, too." He drank a bit of tea. "Even if Billie and I have our little therapy sessions now and then, that never takes the ache away."

She sighed. "I guess time's the only thing that does that."

"The point is, Jess, I don't know how much time I have."

Jessica rode through unlit residential streets on her way home. Being with Rafi had both soothed and disturbed her. She liked the way she could be alternately serious and frivolous with him, yet he had a knack of focusing on her loneliness while only hinting at his own. Jessica had wanted to concentrate on him tonight; as usual, he had eluded her.

She walked her bike up the driveway, relieved to see only Cindi's station wagon parked there. She found her cousin at the kitchen table with utility bills in a neat pile before her.

"Has everyone paid up?"

In a sleeveless cotton nightgown, her long hair cascading over her shoulders, Cindi glanced up from their household account checkbook. "I made sure of that before they split."

"They're together?" Jessica paused before opening the re-frigerator.

"Naaa. Rita went to her mom's and took Angelita. Who knows where Chic was off to." Cindi continued writing the check. "There's herbal iced tea if you want some."

"Thanks." Jessica poured a glass and pulled up a chair. "Any fireworks around here tonight?"

"Everything went fine." Cindi sealed the envelope ad-dressed to the Southern California Gas Company and affixed a stamp to its front. "Rita had Xochi over for ice cream. Efraín didn't make a fuss, probably 'cause Chic was nowhere in sight."

"Good. Do you think Rita got through to Xochi?"

Cindi shrugged. "I was doing laundry, trying to eavesdrop. Didn't hear very much of it. Rita must've thought about it all day, 'cause she went right into it. Xochi cried a little, then apol-ogized. She wants to keep walking Angelita to school. She doesn't get an allowance, you see, and likes getting paid."

"A quarter each way isn't much," Jessica remarked.

"Hey, when you're ten years old and don't have any-thing," Cindi reminded her, "it's a lot."

"I suppose." Jessica stirred the iced tea. "Hope Xochi got the *real* message."

"We'll see." Cindi stuffed the Southern California Edison bill into its envelope and licked a stamp for it. "Rita seemed sat-isfied."

"Hmmm. Did she see Chic before she left?"

"I'm not even sure when Chic got home. She didn't stay long." Cindi gave her a penetrating look. "Cuz, do *you* know something I don't?"

Jessica put down her glass and crossed one leg. "This morn-ing Chic gave me the impression Rita's a temp."

"No surprise to me." Cindi began writing another check. "Don't be next."

"What's the matter?" Jessica grinned. "Don't you think I could handle her?"

Pen in hand, Cindi paused. "You're blood, Jess. You can do better than Chic Lozano."

Jessica reached over and squeezed her cousin's shoulder. "I think you like playin' big sister."

"We *practically* are sisters, and you know it," Cindi responded firmly. "By the way, Tío Tudy phoned. Wanted to know what time he'll see you Saturday. As long as I had him on the phone, I asked him about the steps. He can work on them after your picnic."

"Great. He left some extra planks in the garage last time he was here."

"He mentioned that." Cindi's voice was affectionate. "He makes me laugh, Jess. Said my mom's trying to be a matchmaker. She knows a widow who has her eye on him."

"I hope that works." Jessica leaned back, musing. "I'd really like my dad to get married."

Cindi was skeptical. "You'd *want* a stepmother?"

"He's been alone for years, Cindi. He's not getting any younger."

"Look who's talking."

Jessica got up. "I could say the same thing about you."

After phoning her father, Jessica lay on the sofa, reading the rest of the morning newspaper. Cindi had gone upstairs to soak in the bathtub. Without the other Satins, the big house was quiet, echoing with creaks and memories. Yawning, Jessica folded the *Times*, and sat up. Singing "Pocha Blues" to herself, she wandered into the kitchen, rummaged through a cabinet, and pulled a large sack of birdseed from the bottom shelf. She scooped a hefty amount into a plastic container, turned on the porch light, and went outside, still singing softly.

She took the stepladder and approached the redwood bird feeder hanging from one of the sycamore's lower branches. She stopped in mid-refrain on glimpsing Efraín in the shadows, the glow of his cigarette pinpointing his position.

"Ten cuidado, hijita." He came closer. "Yo puedo hacerlo."

"No thanks. I can do it." Jessica carefully stood on the step-ladder. She scooped birdseed into the redwood and plexiglass canister.

Efraín paused beside the ladder. "Hoy día los chamacos estában tirando piedras a los pajaritos."

She shot him a disgusted look. "I hope you told your kids to stop throwing rocks at the birds."

He shrugged his shoulders. "Así son los niños."

"Efraín, I don't attract birds to this yard to make them targets. Tell the kids to quit—or *I'll* tell them myself."

"Como la Rita le dijó a Xochi que no le gusta oír palabras como 'negrita'?" He watched her leave the bottom step.

"Yeah, just like Rita told Xochi." Jessica folded the ladder and leaned it against her hip. "Efraín, maybe where you lived in Mexico you didn't see black people or people of other races— but you aren't *there* anymore. In this country, we make an effort to get along with everyone."

Efraín flicked cigarette ashes toward the gravel surrounding the tree. "Me parece que eso no es verdad."

"I never said the U.S. is perfect. It definitely isn't. Look, Cindi and I like to think of *this* piece of property as our own little country. We don't want problems with anyone who lives here. That means no name-calling, no bird killing. Do you understand what I'm saying, Efraín?"

"Pues, sí, Señorita Tamayo." He let his slitty eyes roam over her before strolling away.

She glared at his departing figure.

Saturday morning, she sat with her coffee mug on the front steps, alternately scanning the newspaper and watching hummingbirds flitting from one fuschia bush to the next. Her Peterson's *Field Guide to Western Birds* lay beside her, yet the tiny birds moved so rapidly she could only catch flashes of their iridescent plumage. She wondered if she would ever be able to properly identify them.

Jessica had risen early to pack a picnic lunch. She had enough steak left over for sandwiches, and tossed some carrot sticks, nectarines, peaches and oranges into her daypack as well. For good measure, she added a few oatmeal cookies. She had moved stealthily through the kitchen, not wanting to awaken anyone. Then she had grabbed her coffee mug, a bowlful of granola, and headed outside. She liked being the first one up on weekends. That allowed her the chance to choose the coffee flavor, gave her dibs on the *Times*, and offered fleeting moments of privacy.

From her perch on the top step, she gazed at the patchy lawn. The long-term drought had turned the grass dry and sparse; it had never looked like that during her grandparents' lifetime. Jessica recalled Sunday morning brunches at her grandparents' home, long before Tía Irene had inherited the Victorian. The extended Tamayo clan had congregated after Mass and feasted on fresh-squeezed jugo de naranja, chorizo con huevos o huevos rancheros, a variety of pan dulce, café o chocolate. Afterwards while the grown-ups visited, the children—Jessica and Cindi included—had played on the sloping front lawn.

Sighing, Jessica finished the last of her coffee, folded the newspaper, stuck the field guide in her daypack and rose. Within moments, she was on her way to the Main Street bus stop.

About an hour later, she disembarked from the RTD bus on Sunset Boulevard in Pacific Palisades. Slinging her daypack over her shoulder, Jessica hiked up the winding paved road leading to Will Rogers State Park. She trudged along, passing sprawling hilltop homes trimmed with blooming bougainvillea and groves of towering eucalyptus trees on her way to the park entrance. Situated in the Santa Monica Mountains, the 144-

acre ranch, polo field, and wooded surroundings once owned by the late Oklahoma-born humorist had been donated by the Rogers family to the State of California. Jessica's heart always beat a bit faster when she approached those well-tended grounds. Much of her family history remained entangled and enmeshed among the eucalyptus-lined paths and trodden turf of the polo field. No wonder, she thought, her sister Victoria seldom visited the site.

"Hey, Jess." The woman in the khaki ranger uniform leaned out of her kiosk at the park entrance when Jessica advanced. Tall, blonde and blue-eyed, she seemed the epitome of the so-called "California girl."

"Hi, Kyla." Jessica smiled. "Pretty day."

"Going to be a warm one." Kyla Sherman grinned. "Saw you dynamite Satins at the DeLovely DeDykeful Show last month. My friends and I went ga-ga over your lead singer."

"Chic *does* have that effect." Jessica took a breather beside Kyla's booth. "We'll be on the Promenade next Friday, in our usual spot by the Midnight Special. And at the multicultural faire Saturday."

"I'll see if I can catch ya." Kyla waved Jessica through as cars began to approach. "Your dad's at the corrals."

"Thanks." Jessica nodded and walked on.

To her right lay the broad expanse of the polo field, while to her left another grass carpet unfurled alongside the two-story ranch house. Picnickers lounged and children scampered, playing Frisbee. In her formative years, these grounds once belonging to a local folk hero had seemed a magical place, high above the city, its hiking trails offering a breath-taking view of the Pacific and the Westside. Jessica had been known, on particularly nostalgic days, to take the house tour, listening to the commentary about the Remington sculptures and other Western art objects within the historic residence. She still enjoyed going into the Visitors' Center to view the documentary footage about Will Rogers's life and tragic death in a 1935 plane crash. Today, however, she did not stop and continued toward the path leading to the corrals.

A brown-skinned man not much taller than Jessica stood within one of the white-fenced enclosures. In dusty jeans, scuffed tooled boots, a faded cotton shirt open at the neck, and a battered straw cowboy hat, he moved with an easy grace, his skilled hands guiding a sorrel gelding through its paces with only a flicker of his lariat.

"Ay, qué guapo eres, caballito," Arturo Tamayo said admiringly. Without turning his head, he addressed his daughter. "Órale, muchacha."

"Hi, Dad. Wow, your new friend's quite a beauty." Jessica stopped at the corral.

"His name is Redwing." Arturo began drawing in the lariat. Eventually, the gelding slowed its pace and with a snort came to a halt. "Ven, mijo. Come meet my baby girl."

Jessica sat on the top rung of the corral and watched them approach.

"Stay there, Jessie," her father warned. "He's a little skittish." He led the gelding to her. The horse shook its rusty mane, snorting again. "Behave yourself, son."

Jessica leaned forward and patted the gelding's sleek neck. He relaxed a bit at her touch.

"Did you bring apples?"

"Carrot sticks."

"Pues, give him what you have," her father urged.

While Jessica reached into her daypack, Redwing began to nuzzle her leg. Giggling, she soon held out two carrot sticks. He took them within his large teeth and chewed loudly.

Arturo and Jessica laughed. Her father rested against the gelding's bowed neck. "Te miras bien, hija."

"You, too." She gazed at him with affection. "Dad, I hear Tía Anita has a widow lined up for you."

77

Arturo kept his grin. "What do I want with an old woman?"

"As if you weren't nearly sixty yourself."

"Mira, muchacha." He patted his trim torso. "I stay in shape. You probably have more grey hair than I do, eh?"

"I think you're right."

He smiled and tugged at the lariat. "Stay put while I hand this boy over to Pedro."

On his return, Arturo brought a faded serape from his late 1970s El Camino truck. He spread it on the grass beneath a canopy of eucalyptus. Jessica inhaled their fragrance. She always associated their pungent scent, along with the horsey smell, with her father; both seemed elemental to his presence. Side by side, father and daughter shared the noonday meal.

"Good steak. You make it, mija?"

She nodded. "It's not quite carne asada."

"It's your version. Cómo están tus amigas?"

She sighed and told him about her housemates' latest exploits. He chuckled about Chic and Rita, yet turned sober when the talk turned to Angelita and Xochi.

"Ese Efraín—I don't know what my sister Irene saw in that hombre. He's trouble, no?"

"I'll say." She took the bottle of Corona he offered. "Dad, we can talk about Efraín any time. Are you ever going to tell me anything about this widow woman?"

6 Every Rock, Every Sunset

"Ay, mija." Arturo removed his hat and ran a strong brown hand through his thick hair. "You want to marry me off so you won't have to worry about me anymore?"

Jessica took a sip of the Corona and handed it back to him. "You know me better than that."

"Verdad. You're Jessie, *not* Vickie." He drank the beer slowly. "Tu hermana thinks I'm crazy to stay here."

"Vickie thinks you're wallowing in the past." Jessica leaned on his firm shoulder. "You do what you have to, Dad."

When Jessica mentioned his older daughter's assessment, Arturo shook his head. "I've worked for the Sinclairs since I was fifteen—for three generations of them. Son como familia, sabes? They board their polo ponies here, so why shouldn't I stay on? Why should that matter to Vickie?"

Jessica was familiar with his loyalty to the wealthy Sinclairs. "I don't think she would argue about your keeping your job. Vickie just doesn't like where you happen to work."

"It reminds her of—" He gazed far beyond the eucalyptus grove. "—your mother. Se acabó aquí. Hace tanto tiempo."

Jessica nodded. "It *was* a long time ago, Dad. And how can any of us forget that her life with us ended here? Sometimes I ask myself why I've never looked for her."

He brought his dark eyes to hers. "You have that right."

She shrugged. "I wonder how a woman could do that—she

didn't only walk out on *you*, Dad. On Vickie and me, too."

He drank more beer. "You still think about this, hija?"

"I have this week." Her voice was quiet. "Probably 'cause of Angelita and that little girl I mentioned. Kids are so vulnerable."

"Jessie, if I could change things—"

"It *wasn't* your fault, Dad," Jessica said gently. "My mother wanted another life."

For the first time, bitterness crept into Arturo's voice. "Some life, eh? With a polo player who rode for los Sinclairs." He sighed. "I used to think about following the polo circuit, trying to find her. I heard they went to Houston, but I don't even know if that's true. Los Sinclairs were ready to hire a detective. I told them no. If Carolina wanted to leave—"

Jessica dug into her daypack for a couple of peaches. "How did we get on this, huh?"

His roughened fingers traced the contours of hers when he took the peach. "Vickie blames *me*. I hope *you* don't."

She reached over to kiss his unshaven cheek. "No, Daddy, no." She clenched her teeth. "Damn, I don't want to cry."

"Maybe you have to, mija." He held her closer, caressing her smooth black hair, so like his own.

"Let's walk," he suggested when her tears stopped.

Jessica heaved a deep sigh. She knew crying had been cathartic, the result of an emotional week; nevertheless she felt embarrassed. She took his hand and they rose together. "I'm sorry, Dad."

"Memorias. Mija, you wouldn't be human without them. And this place has memories around every tree, every rock, every sunset. It makes sense, no? Tenemos raíces aquí." He pointed northeast. "Right over that ridge was where my great-grandfather had his ranchito. Ahora it's where los ricos live. At least this ranch belongs to the state now. These acres won't be developed, gracias a Dios."

They carried the serape to his truck and left it on the seat. Rounding the corrals, they chose the Bone Canyon Trail into the Santa Monica Mountains dotted with sagebrush and California buckwheat.

She swung her hand in his, eager to veer the subject away from the past. "What're you doing on Cinco de Mayo?"

"Hay un baile at the Senior Center."

"Can you come to my daycare room that morning? I'd love to sing with you for the kids."

Arturo squeezed her hand. "I'd like that, hija."

"Great. I'm teaching them 'Cielito Lindo' 'cause it's simple. When you come by, we could sing some rancheras. Dad, that'd be fabulous." Jessica suddenly felt carefree. "Cindi said you'll fix the steps today?"

He nodded. "Later. I have chores before I leave here."

"Fine. Can I borrow your truck in the meantime? I'd like to swing by the Malibu Lagoon for a while." She knew he rarely refused her anything. "Then I'll come back and get you. Have dinner with us, Dad. And stay overnight?"

"You sure the other muchachas won't mind?"

"Why should they? You can sleep in my room," she urged, "and I'll take the sofa bed."

Arturo smiled and hugged her to him. "You've sold me."

Jessica left him by the corrals. Tossing her daypack inside the El Camino, she sat in the driver's seat and began backing out. She had learned to drive in that old truck, and enjoyed being behind its wheel again. She wondered when she would ever be able to afford her own car.

Driving out, she waved to Kyla, feeling somewhat self-conscious in her father's truck. As a child, Jessica had been proud to say her daddy was a cowboy; however, by adolescence, she had realized he was merely a hired hand for a rich Pacific Palisades family. Through adult eyes, she acknowledged that a Chicano of his generation had not had many career options.

She only wished her mother had recognized that.

But no, Carolina Tamayo had seen a glimpse of "the good life" during the weekly Will Rogers Park polo matches. The Sinclairs had often encouraged Arturo to invite his family to watch the competitions while he worked among the horsemen. Fair-skinned, with enormous brown eyes, dressed in Sunday finery, Carolina would pack a tasty lunch, spread a hand-made quilt on the lawn, and sit with her two beribboned daughters to view the polo games.

Preoccupied with the past, Jessica drove along Sunset toward Chautauqua Boulevard. She veered the truck into the left-turn lane, recalling the glint in her mother's lovely eyes when a tow-haired polo player named Keith had become attentive one Sunday afternoon.

"Keith." Jessica said that despised name aloud. To her six-year-old ears, the name had sounded foreign, unlike Arturo or the names of her Tíos Gustavo y Leobardo. Perhaps it had seemed so to Carolina as well—an Anglo name that promised glamor, adventure, romance. Jessica wondered if Keith had ever lived up to that.

At the end of Chautauqua, she turned right onto the Pacific Coast Highway. The afternoon sun heightened the blueness of the ocean, causing it to shimmer. She spotted squadrons of brown pelicans flying low over the water, searching for fish. Further along, bolder cormorants circled the parking lots of seafood restaurants. She had no trouble identifying those birds, even at a distance, by their distinctive silhouettes. Albert would have been proud of her.

Though beach traffic had begun to build in the southbound lanes, Jessica whizzed past toward Malibu, keeping in mind she would have to limit her stay at the Lagoon. Otherwise, she could get caught in a traffic jam later and leave her father temporarily stranded.

She turned right into the Cross Creek Shopping Center parking lot within a quarter hour. To remind herself to buy birdseed, she stationed the truck near the pet store. She glanced around, hoping the old vehicle would not arouse suspicion; it seemed to mock the upscale cars stationed beside it. Usually, the only Chicanas and Chicanos near that Malibu shopping center were domestic workers waiting for the RTD bus or groups of grizzled, sometimes homeless, men looking for manual labor jobs; their trucks, if they were fortunate to own any, were not unlike Arturo Tamayo's. She relied on the Will Rogers State Park sticker in the back window to keep the El Camino from being towed. Locking the truck, she checked to make sure her binoculars were in her daypack and headed to the crosswalk.

When the traffic light changed, Jessica hurried across the highway. A weather-beaten brown and yellow sign announced "Malibu Lagoon State Beach." Like many Mexican-Americans native to southern California, Jessica had never paid much attention to this locale. Instead her family had frequented the beach not far from the Third Street house. Pacific Palisades, Malibu and beyond were areas where Chicanas and Chicanos went to work as domestics, gardeners, babysitters or busboys, rarely to enjoy themselves.

During her relationship with Trish Beltrán, Jessica had more or less stumbled upon the Lagoon. The women had gone to an arts and crafts fair at the Malibu Civic Center. Parking had been a nightmare, and by sheer luck, they had managed to squeeze Trish's Subaru into a spot near the Lagoon's entry gates. Afterwards, while Trish hemmed and hawed over buying a seascape, Jessica had trekked back to the Lagoon for a needed respite. Hooked by its windswept beauty, its ever-changing tides, she had borrowed her father's truck or Cindi's car to come back often, especially after the breakup with Trish. Sitting on a rock, surrounded by the Pacific's undulating waves and by shorebirds, ducks and other waterfowl, Jessica felt soothed and mesmerized.

One wintry Saturday, chilled to the bone, she had left the Lagoon and jogged across the highway bridge to the Adamson House. Another historical home turned over to the state of

California, it boasted original tileworks, lovely gardens and a museum on its grounds. She had sought refuge from the cold weather in the tiny gift shop and found herself fascinated by its collection of local history books.

Jessica had squatted by a display case and paged through a booklet written by a member of the pioneering Rindge family. The author proposed Malibu Lagoon as the site of the Chumash village where Juan Rodríguez Cabrillo had landed on October 10, 1542. The explorer, sailing the California coast and claiming it for Spain, had named the village by the lagoon "Pueblo de las Canoas" because the Chumash had possessed numerous canoes. While most historians fixed the village's location further north at Point Mugu, the author claimed Malibu seemed the more logical site. He reasoned that, while sailing northward around the Palos Verdes Peninsula, the first large Indian village one would encounter on a lagoon would be Malibu. Whether true or not, the proposition had intrigued Jessica, and learning of the lagoon's history had increased her fondness for the locale.

This spring afternoon, she approached the first plank bridge over the inlets branching from the lagoon. On a wooden fence post, she spotted a chunky black bird with white on its belly and outer tail feathers. It scanned the area above its dark head, searching for insects. Before owning the field guide, Jessica had seen a similar bird. She paused to retrieve the book from the daypack and quickly flipped through its pages.

"A Black Phoebe," she whispered. "Are you going to sing for me? Fee-bee! Fee-bee!" She smiled, knowing she sounded silly. She studied the appropriate page of the field guide. "Wow, you range from the Southwest all the way to Argentina. I'm impressed."

The bird apparently did not feel likewise. It flew to a clump of coastal sage. Jessica did not take the rebuff personally. At the next bridge, she tiptoed on the creaky planks and leaned over the wooden railing. She hoped to see the swallows nesting there. As she did so, one sailed under the bridge. Jessica could not tell whether it had continued through or darted into its mud nest. She would have had to dangle upside down to be sure. Sighing, she paged through her field guide again. Birds moved much too fast.

As she approached the ocean, she noticed some beachgoers surfing while others napped on the toasty sand. A homeless man lived nearby, his sleeping bag and piled possessions evident against the chainlink fence separating the lagoon from Malibu Colony. Everyone, particularly families with small children, tended to avoid him. A golden retriever sniffed its way along the shoreline, while a flock of little birds competed for tiny crabs and insects.

Jessica passed these and went to one edge of the lagoon. She plopped down, setting her daypack beside her. She took out her binoculars and aimed them toward the sandy island in the midst of the inlets. Pelicans and a variety of gulls congregated at the base of a jagged dead tree. A few creamy-breasted cormorants lingered on the lower branches. According to the field guide description, they were Brandt's cormorants. The two with yellow bills were double-crested cormorants. Jessica enjoyed the small victory of being able to identify them.

During the afternoon, sea and shore birds were not very active. She trained her binoculars across the lagoon in the direction of the Adamson house. Sometimes, she had seen an American kestrel among the trees there. She scanned that verdant area, before focusing on the viewing outlook built along the bank.

An olive-skinned woman occupied that space, standing motionless, overlooking the water. The sun shone on her wavy brown hair, creating a gilt glow. From the distance, Jessica could not be sure of the woman's height. She wore tan hiking shorts and an azure T-shirt with a purple silhouette of two wolves silk-screened on it. Around her neck was a camera with a zoom lens. She seemed to be scoping the large, dark bird below her. Jessica could not identify it, and she could barely glimpse the woman's face. Yet she was intrigued by her concentration.

With a sigh, Jessica put down the binoculars. She had kept a few scraps of sandwich bread in her daypack and tossed them to the mallard and its mate swimming toward her. They quacked their appreciation and gobbled the bread. Jessica was amused at their greediness, but ignored their incessant quacking for more. She retrieved her binoculars and gazed at the woman on the oppposite shore. Jessica wished she could see her more clearly. Changing camera lenses, the woman sat on the viewing bench, her attention on the nearby bird. She continued studying its sleek black crown and back, its greyish wings and white underparts while her fingers deftly clicked the other lens into place. The woman's face looked gentle, her eyes unwavering. Her movements deliberate, she inched to the railing, careful not to disturb the elegant bird, and took aim. She leaned forward, her shorts accentuating the slight curve of her hip, a hint of a round buttock, strong thigh and calf muscles.

Jessica admonished herself for being a voyeur. Aside from the fleeting temptation of Chic Lozano, she had not felt an attraction toward another woman since Trish had left. No question about it, this bird photographer had caught her eye. Jessica did not like the implications. She got up suddenly, deciding to stretch her legs.

She returned to the bridges and veered off one of the inlets where coastal sage lined the banks. She paused to watch a couple of hummingbirds' aerial display. They buzzed around her like scarlet and green miniature jets and whizzed off again. She laughed, frightening a cottontail into the underbrush. Unable to avoid glancing at the photographer, she noticed the woman leaned against the railing, scanning with her own binoculars. Jessica's heart quickened. Was the woman watching *her*?

On a large rock, Jessica rested, her face glowing hot; she knew the sunshine was not fully responsible. "This is crazy," she told herself. "I'm imagining things."

Yet when she looked at the opposite shore, she again glimpsed the woman viewing her. No shorebirds nor ducks were in the immediate vicinity, and only coots and mallards in the inlet behind her. An experienced birdwatcher would not be distracted by such common waterfowl. The woman could only be contemplating Jessica.

She took a peek at her watch. To beat the traffic, she would have to leave in order to get to Will Rogers at a reasonable time. She rose and took her time dusting off her jeans. Might as well let the woman get a good look, she thought whimsically. Such long-distance flirtation seemed safe, especially with the wide lagoon between them.

Slinging the daypack, Jessica began to trek through the sagebrush. She took the shortcut under the highway bridge, hurrying through its damp, though convenient, shelter where homeless people often stashed belongings. She had never encountered anyone below the bridge, but did not want to take any chances. She emerged at the spot where the chainlink fence had been unfurled, winding up in the Cross Creek Shopping Center parking lot. She found a pay phone and made a quick call to Cindi to let her know Arturo would be a dinner guest; Cindi had figured that. Pleased, Jessica gave the El Camino's hood a welcome pat and dashed into the pet shop.

A litter of playful cocker spaniels yapped at her entry. Jessica reached into their open pen and petted their silky coats. The puppies squirmed at her touch, trying to nip her hands. She crooned to them, giggling at their clumsiness, before going to the rear of the store. She bought two large sacks of wild bird seed and carried them to the El Camino.

Taking a cigarette break, a couple of Latino busboys from the nearby Italian restaurant made flirting comments in Spanish and loud kissy sounds while Jessica loaded her purchase into the truck. The two seemed coltish, feeling their oats at noticing her own brown skin and black hair. Although she felt a pang at realizing their future employment was limited, she decided to mind her own business and not comment on their sexist behavior. She only hoped they would not be foolish enough to react to Malibu blondes in such a carefree manner.

She eased the El Camino southbound onto the Pacific Coast Highway. Crossing the bridge, she saw no further trace of the bird photographer along the lagoon's shore.

"Hope you weren't waiting long, Dad. Traffic was bad most of the way, even on Sunset." Jessica found him at the ranch house, shooting the breeze with some of the Visitors' Center volunteers. The middle-aged women seemed charmed by Arturo's courtliness. When he tipped his cowboy hat to join his daughter in the truck, they waved their good-byes.

"Your fan club?" she teased.

"Como eres. I've known Tilly and Norma por años." He had shaved and changed into a plaid shirt and clean work pants, his black hair slicked back. Jessica doubted he knew "the wet look" was back in style.

"You're in luck, Dad. Cindi's making beef enchiladas to-night."

"Qué bueno. Want me to drive, Jessie?"

"Relax. I'll have us home in no time."

Arturo Tamayo pressed the aged wooden step with the edge of his boot. When it creaked and almost gave way, he uttered a low whistle and gestured for Jessica to follow. She helped him remove the stacked planks from the garage.

"Aquí viene Efraín," Arturo murmured when they had set the wood between two sawhorses. "If he hangs around, I'll put him to work, eh?"

"In that case, I'm going inside. I'll fix the bedroom for you in the meantime."

"All right, hija."

She brushed past Efraín, who nodded in greeting.

"Where's Tío Tudy?" Cindi chopped onions and olives on the cutting board in the kitchen.

"Already getting to work. He said he wanted to build up an appetite." Jessica rolled her eyes. "Efraín's buzzing around out there."

"Wouldn't you know it?" Cindi wiped her hands on a paper towel. "Well, looks like it's only you, me and Tío Tudy for dinner. Rita went to her mom's this morning, and Chic's AWOL."

Jessica was relieved. "Need any help?"

"Check the crockpot. The frijoles have been cooking most of the day."

Jessica lifted the lid and poked at the pinto beans with a fork. They were almost soft, and the aroma of cilantro, oregano and scallions filled the air. She closed the lid with a satisfied smile.

"Cindi, I'm going to change the sheets on the futon. I'll sleep on the sofa bed 'cause I'd rather have Dad away from the noise if Chic comes in late. She always makes a racket."

"No lie."

"Aren't you going to tell us about this widow, Tío Tudy?" Cindi served her uncle another enchilada and smothered it with beans and grated cheese.

Arturo waved away her question. "Ay, you girls sure like to rub it in. Jessie's already tried to find out about her."

"Any luck, cuz?"

Jessica shook her head. "Ni modo. Maybe he'll be more polite where you're concerned."

Arturo gave his daughter an affectionate grin. "All right. Might as well say something. If I don't, Cindi's mamá will." He downed some of his Corona. "Se llama Emilia Salcido. I knew her husband Luís. He had diabetes, died about four years ago.

Emilia took it muy hard."

"And now she's coming out of her grief and has her ojos on you, Tío?" Cindi giggled. "Tell us more. What's her age?"

"Como cinco años younger than me."

"So she's around fifty-three," Jessica remarked. "Hmm. That's not old, Dad. She may be menopausal, though."

"Ay, Dios." Arturo slapped his forehead, making both women laugh. "Anita didn't say anything about *that*." With his fork, he swirled his beans and rice together. "Mira, muchachas. I've been solito por años. I wouldn't know what to do with a mujer going through that."

"Good point, Dad," Jessica admitted.

"Carolina was thirty-one when she left, and I was a year older. What do I know about mujeres in their fifties?"

"Dad, I doubt if you're inocente when it comes to women." Jessica felt herself blush at the audacity of her comment.

Arturo looked a bit sheepish. "Pues, I've never gone around telling my daughters my personal business, Jessie. Don't expect me to do that now. Your sister would really throw a fit about that, verdad?"

Jessica and Cindi nodded, both trying to keep from giggling.

Arturo continued. "No soy inocente, pero fifty-three years old—"

"I catch your drift, Dad." Jessica squeezed more lime into her Corona. "You'd prefer a younger woman."

Arturo's dark skin showed a perceptible flush. "Tú sabes." He shrugged, gazing at them both. "You both like women yourselves. I don't think I have to explain, eh?"

"Ay, Tío." Cindi lay a soothing hand on his shoulder. "Sounds like we're all in the same boat."

Jessica dozed off, her head against Arturo, while he watched Lucha Libre on the Spanish-language television channel. As she drifted into sleep, she recalled how Trish had been embarrassed by Arturo's penchant for wrestling and boxing matches. Until Trish had voiced that opinion, Jessica had been in agreement; since then, she had reversed her position. A working-class Chicano who had raised two daughters after his wife had deserted them had a right to watch anything he damn well pleased.

Eventually, Jessica heard him whisper to her. "Mija, it's late. I'm going to bed."

She opened her sleepy eyes. "Everything's ready upstairs."

He nodded and gestured toward the front bedroom. "I opened the sofa bed for you, pero I couldn't find the sheets."

"Thanks, Dad." She gave him a drowsy hug.

"Good night, honey," he said, kissing her forehead.

7 Salsa Sex

Jessica lay on her side to catch the tiny lamp's glow. Listening to Ottmar Liebert's *Nouveau Flamenco* tape on her headset, she skimmed through the thin volume of lesbian erotica she had discovered in the living room's bookcase after her father had gone upstairs. The book's purple paper-bound spine was bent, the pages dog-eared and musky; apparently all the housemates except Jessica had taken pleasure from the book's allure. She wondered if any of the printed fantasies involved an olive-skinned woman, reclining invitingly beside a reed-lined lagoon.

She glanced toward the window. Its dusty panes offered a murky view of Third Street. When no one had wanted this room, she and Cindi had left Tía Irene's massive couch in the sala, dragged the smaller sofa bed into the front bedroom and made it available for guests. However, the constant street noise from Ocean Park Boulevard rattled the panes and kept the room inhospitable. Jessica did not mind; she liked to open its windows to the coastal fog and sleep on the sofa bed on warm nights like this one.

She fluffed the rather flat pillows and let herself be transported into the sexual fantasies of the collection's contributors. Lying still, she read about tropical moonlit nights, passionate sex among Mayan ruins, and began to feel herself respond to the erotic stories. Her nipples became tight nubs and her bare legs moved restlessly between the patterned sheets. She held the book with one hand and let the other slide gradually beneath her cotton T-shirt. She began to touch herself, imagining the woman at the lagoon abandoning her camera, striding forward to fondle Jessica instead. Slowly, she allowed lazy fingers to inch upward to her breasts.

"Hot night, huh?"

Startled, Jessica looked up. Chic stood in the doorway. Hair freshly trimmed and moussed, she wore white cut-offs and a red bandana-style sleeveless shirt.

"I didn't even hear you." Jessica sat up quickly. She let her hands busy themselves with removing the headset, coiling its wire and setting it beside her. With the edge of her elbow, she slid the book beneath the sheets.

"Didn't think so." Chic's teasing eyes glinted in the lamp's glow. "Saw your light from the driveway and popped in to investigate."

Jessica felt her color rising. "You got your hair cut."

Chic eased herself on the bed's edge, keeping her long legs slightly apart. "Yeah. Afterwards, Billie and I went to *Out on the Screen* to see the dyke film."

"Any good?" Jessica crossed her arms over her breasts. She knew they had caught Chic's attention.

"One of those foreign jobs with subtitles." She grinned. "Hell, I didn't need to read anything to figure out what those chicks were doin'."

Jessica smiled on reflex. Knowing she behaved defensively, she explained her reason for being in the front room.

"You wanted to protect your daddy from big bad Chic, huh?"

"Oh, please." Jessica reached for the headset again. "Since when are you interested in men, much less one his age?"

"You're right. There. Lookin' real fine." She leaned toward Jessica. "Didn't you *really* want to check if I came home or not?"

"Chic, you're so confused. I'm *not* Rita. And, in case you're

93

wondering, she's at her mom's." Jessica moved one pillow behind her. "She and Angelita are spending the weekend there."

"Fine with me." Chic gestured to the bunched-up edge of the sheet. "What were you reading?"

"Can't you ever mind your own business?"

"Me? Since when isn't mi amiga favorita my business?" She reached for the buried book.

Jessica pushed it further beneath the sheet. With a provocative laugh, Chic pulled back the sheet and tried to grab the book. In the process, her arm brushed against her friend's bare leg. Jessica tried to ignore the sensuous charge she experienced from that sudden touch. Wresting the book from Chic, who gave in far too easily, she rolled to the other side of the bed. Jessica lay atop the book, giggling, knowing her rumpled T-shirt had risen above her bikini panties.

Not one to refuse a challenge, Chic leaped on top of her. She pushed her breasts into the middle of Jessica's back, her hips pressing against Jessica's buttocks.

"Híjole. Forget the damn book. I'd rather do this." Chic undulated her hips once. "I like the feel of you, loca."

Jessica heard her own voice grow sharp. "Get off."

"Isn't that the point? Hey, Jess, we can both get off if we put a little effort into it."

Unwilling to admit her increasing arousal, Jessica knew her heart betrayed her. It pounded beneath Chic's weight, and she felt Chic's thumping, too. "I want to get up. Now."

Sliding off, Chic lay beside her, eyes amused. "I got carried away, okay? All of a sudden I got a flash of us as kids at one of Priscilla Montelongo's slumber parties. We'd pull our sleeping bags next to each other, remember? Feel each other up when everyone else was out cold."

Jessica sat up and adjusted her T-shirt to cover as much of her as possible. "We're not twelve anymore."

Chic took the book, smoothing its bent exterior. "And now we read stuff like this. Imaginary sex instead of the real thing. Pretty sad, if you ask me."

"For God's sake, Chic, my father's in the house," Jessica said spontaneously. She blushed on realizing she had uttered her thought aloud.

Chic gazed at her with renewed interest. "You'd consider fooling around if Tudy wasn't here?"

"I never said *that*." Jessica wanted to open another window; she was sweating.

"I heard the implication, loquita. Hell, Tudy's snoring away. The man works hard, sleeps good. You want to be like him—without anybody?"

Jessica glared at her. She let her eyes flicker beyond Chic's cajoling face to the darkness outside. Recalling the afternoon's long-distance flirtation with the bird photographer, she could not deny her eagerness to pleasure herself as soon as she had been alone. Her body seemed to yearn for sensual expression more than her mind—or her emotions—did.

Chic lay there, watching her. "Tell me what you're thinking."

Jessica shook her head.

"Knowing you, you're weighin' the pros and cons. Mira, sometimes you just have to go with the flow. I don't want to mess up anything between us either, Jess. Are you kidding? You write songs for me. Besides, you stood by me when that damn Roxanne thing went up in smoke. I won't forget that. Why don't you let me pay you back the best way I know how?"

"Do you realize you're sexually harassing me?" Jessica tried to sound annoyed. She wished Chic would sit up, too, instead of lying still, her elongated ebony eyes relentless. She seemed like a modern-day Chac-mool, offering herself. The tempting outlines of her breasts were visible in the flimsy bandana shirt, and her slim legs were stretched invitingly over the side of the bed.

"I'm here, I'm queer, I'm fabulous—and I won't tell anybody. What more can you ask for?"

"What about—Rita?"

"Ay, reality—Jessica Tamayo's middle name." Chic toyed

with the buttons on her shirt. She undid the one above her breasts. "One of those R-words. Roxanne. Rita. Reality."

"Recapitulation."

"Huh?" Chic frowned. "What's that?"

Jessica relished upstaging her. "The title of a terrific jazz tune by Kenny Burrell. It means 'a summary or concise review.' In other words, from listening to you tonight, I gather you're up to your old tricks again."

"Is that a tune we could scat to?"

"See what I mean about tricks? Now we're on a music track."

Chic gave her a sly grin. "We could work on a sexy, collaborative arrangement. Lozano y Tamayo. Tonight."

Jessica sighed. Her willpower, her customary barriers, were eroding.

After a momentary silence, Chic spoke. "You look triste, Jess. Am I making you sad, or getting on your nerves?"

Jessica gazed at her. "At least you haven't said we could 'make beautiful music together.' *That* would've gotten on my nerves."

Chic laughed, causing the bed to shake, her breasts to bounce.

Against her better judgment, Jessica began to move next to her. Chic continued smiling, and Jessica was glad she did not say anything else. Reclining beside her, she observed her friend at a wholly different angle, noticing how Chic's angular facial contours softened with amusement. Her black eyebrows and dark eyes tilted in unison, and her wide mouth, which she often kept in a smirk, actually seemed inviting.

"Tell me what you want," Chic whispered.

Jessica kept her eyes on Chic's, noticing how steadily they stared back. She questioned her sanity, but opted for impetuousness. "First close the door. And lock it."

·

Jessica set the glass lamp on the floor; its pleated shade dimmed the light, allowing them enough to see each other.

Chic kicked off her high-topped Reeboks and slouch socks. Next to Jessica, she sat and began unbuttoning the rest of her shirt. For a second, Jessica hesitated, before reaching over to stop her. She kept her hands on Chic's, and swung her legs over to straddle her. Chic looked at her with some surprise, but did not seem to mind.

"You're makin' the right moves." She smiled again, slipping tawny arms around Jessica.

She liked feeling Chic's smooth legs beneath hers. Her thighs were warm, and the thought of lying against them excited her. "Let's make this like a fantasy."

"Like the ones in the book," Chic agreed. Licking her lips, she watched Jessica undo the three buttons.

Jessica opened the shirt. "You've grown since we were twelve." She stared at Chic's darker nipples against golden skin, delicious chocolate-dipped fruit.

"We never did it by lamplight. We were always in the dark."

"In more ways than one." Jessica raised her arms to let Chic take off the T-shirt.

"Ay, Jess. Piel canela. Cinnamon-girl." Languorously, Chic rubbed her breasts against Jessica's, their nipples perking at the reunion.

Lying back, she guided Jessica down with her. They shed the rest of their clothes, kicking panties and shorts off the bed.

"Tell me what you want," Chic murmured, the tip of her tongue gliding along Jessica's neck.

She sighed, luxuriating in the tingling sensation. "I want to touch you. And then you—oh, don't talk, Chic."

Chic did not argue. Hands surrounding her breasts, she lifted them slightly, offering them to Jessica. Her compañera bent over them, her blue-black hair falling over her face, tickling Chic's receptive skin. Wanting the visual sensation, too,

Jessica drew the edges of her blunt hair over each of Chic's brown nipples; Chic's half-closed eyes revealed her enjoyment of the coarse mestiza strands' provocation. Jessica repeated the motion several times before twirling and tucking her thick hair behind her ears, out of her way. She brought her yearning mouth along the same path, swirling her tongue into leisurely licks, tasting Chic's sweaty saltiness.

Chic was leaner than Trish, but that did not matter as Jessica noisily sucked those chocolate nipples, sensuously stroked her slender body, pressed that dark bush tantalizingly against her own. Eventually, she felt Chic's hands on her shoulders, as if encouraging her to lift her head. And, on doing so, she opened her mouth unhesitantly when Chic's wet lips found hers.

As adolescents, they had practiced kissing together; since then, they both had learned much with other women lovers. Teasing, playing, their tongues curled around each other's, showing off, bragging, wanting. With Chic, Jessica was free to say anything, do anything, without hangups, without fear. Chic thrived on pleasure, rarely withheld it. To her, sex was like chips and salsa; once you had tasted that potent spiciness, you could not get enough. Jessica remembered Trish had not shared that philosophy; Trish had never wanted either of them to lose control.

"Oh, you've been missing it, huh, baby? Yeah, you've been wanting it," Chic whispered.

Jessica could only moan in response while Chic continued kissing her, their mouths clinging hungrily. She slid her greedy fingers lower along Chic's damp body, wanting to touch her deeper. But Chic prevented her by firmly taking hold of Jessica's hands.

"Let me see them." Breathless, Chic raised her head a bit. "No nicks or cuts?"

"I'm clean." Jessica stared at her, panting. "Isn't this safe?"

"Just know I ain't going down on you. Wasn't ready for this, and—"

Jessica leaned toward her. "Touch me, Chic. I don't like that—other—anyhow."

"You *don't*?"

"Damn it!" Jessica became impatient. "Who needs a discussion of preferences right now?"

"Okay, okay. I just didn't expect you to say that. Baby, don't you know you need to talk about sex while you're doin' it?" Chic murmured. "How else are you going to know what women like?"

Jessica glared. "You're starting to get on my nerves."

"Didn't mean to." Chic outlined Jessica's lips with her tongue. "Mmmm, carnalita. You taste like tomato sauce."

"We had enchiladas for dinner."

"Make me some salsa, Jess. Ojos color de mocha. Dáme tu locura, amor es la cura. Dáme tus labios sabrosos."

Her words aroused Jessica further; Chic had chosen bits and pieces of "Boca Loca" to incite her. Their lips became inseparable again, congealing crazily. Jessica created ever diminishing caressing circles with her hands, culminating in her fingers' becoming entranced with Chic's black pubic triangle, its tempting secrets.

"Yeah, baby."

Jessica probed further, her thumb and fingers becoming drenched and sticky amidst Chic's labia. She let her fingers stop for a moment while she paused to view Chic's face.

She lay facing Jessica, eyes sultry, lush lips beckoning.

"Do me like you used to."

Jessica pressed the palm of her hand against her. Chic groaned sensually, wrapping one tawny leg around Jessica's hip.

"Do me, too."

Chic licked Jessica's mouth, her tongue teasing as she brought both hands to her compañera's longing vulva. With a slow, sweeping motion, Chic slid her hands back and forth, along Jessica's aching clitoris, slipping teasing fingers into her and out again. Jessica thought she would swoon.

The women continued stimulating each other, rubbing, stroking, licking, sucking, brown hands continually pleasuring brown bodies.

With a low moan, Chic came. She lay in silence for a long moment, then chuckled and opened her gleaming eyes.

Jessica hesitated before raising herself on one elbow and edging even closer. "I want to get on top of you."

"And that, folks, is why we'll never be a couple. Side by side is fine with me, but who gets to be on top is another story." Chic grinned. "Only kidding, loca."

Jessica smiled before leaning forward, allowing her breasts to skim Chic's mouth. Chic held them, licking and suckling each alternately while Jessica moved over her. She grew even more excited, watching Chic's lips surround her nipples. She continued rubbing herself against Chic before raising herself a bit.

Her compañera knew what Jessica wanted. Her strong hands found Jessica's wetness. She tiptoed her provoking fingers to Jessica's clitoris, inciting it repeatedly. Moaning, Jessica undulated against Chic's stimulating hand, feeling it within, around, all over. Repeatedly, they continued the sensuous motions until Jessica came, dizzy and out of breath. Still throbbing, she lay immobile over Chic, every pore of her body deliciously alive.

"How long did you say?"

"Two years." Slowly, Jessica rolled off her and lay back. She felt glorious.

"Solitaire isn't the same as this." Chic stayed near, their heads touching.

"Don't make me think right now. For a change, I did something impulsive. That's all there is to this."

"Like I said the other day—'baby, don't get hooked on me,'" Chic sang, relaxing against the pillow.

"Please. Like you're the only lesbian in town, verdad?" Jessica sighed, waiting for her heartbeat to subside. "Besides, I saw the woman of my dreams today."

"Now she tells me," Chic muttered. "Who, where—todo eso?"

"At the Malibu Lagoon."

"I might've known." She arched a brow. "Why weren't you with her tonight?"

"Mensa, I didn't *meet* her. She was on the other shore."

"Couldn't you communicate somehow—like send up flags, carrier pigeons or somethin'?"

Jessica giggled.

"Wait a minute. All of a sudden it's gettin' clear. I was a substitute for this mujer?"

"Well—"

"You're lowdown, Jess."

Jessica nudged her. "You caught me reading erotica and touching myself. You could've put two and two together." ·

"Chispas! You were thinking about *her* while we—"

"You're the one who always says 'no strings.'"

"Well, yeah." Chic raised herself and leaned against the back of the sofa. "But—"

"Chic, I started off thinking about her—then it changed. For one thing, you two don't look a bit alike. It was hard to focus on her, when I'm not even sure what she looks like."

"I'm sexier, verdad?"

Jessica ignored that. "I don't even know if she's Latina. She might be. At least, she's olive-skinned." Jessica met Chic's quizzical expression. "We looked at each other through binoculars. I couldn't even tell what color her eyes are."

"*I* would've swum the lagoon to meet this chick. But—don't tell me—you're not *that* impulsive. Hell, at least I filled in for your fantasy." Chic swung her legs over the side of the bed and searched for her clothes. "Better that than being your worst nightmare. You wouldn't be the first to say so."

Jessica touched Chic's shoulder. "I wouldn't say that about you."

"Ditto, J.T. You don't mind if I go, huh?" Chic zipped her shorts and started to button her shirt. "No point in startin' rumors."

"That makes sense. Listen—thanks." Jessica leaned toward her for a final hug. They held each other for an extended moment before Chic let go.

"Hey, air this place out, Jess. It smells like sex in here."

Jessica lay awake a while longer. Off-shore fog drifted through Third Street, cooling the temperature, passing ghost-like by the open windows. She pulled the blanket over her and smiled, thinking of Chic. They had fallen into bed so easily, so naturally. She did not want to make sex with Chic a habit, but she did not regret their interlude either. In bed, they had seemed to fuse as easily as they did as songwriter and singer, creating for and leading the Satins. Yet Jessica knew of Chic's self-centeredness, her restlessness, her yearning for attention, especially recognition of her singing talent.

She also remembered how emotionally wrenched Chic had been after the Roxanne fiasco. On many a night, when everyone else had gone to bed, Jessica had sat with her on the veranda, listening to her curse Roxanne, plotting revenge scenarios. Jessica had held her while she cried—something Chic rarely allowed anyone else to witness. She trusted Jessica, and oddly enough, the feeling was mutual.

For all her impetuousness, her callejera ways, Chic had always been loyal to her. She had even told off Trish after the breakup, showing up at the apartment one evening to distinctly express her unflattering opinions. She had left only when Trish threatened to phone the police. Though Jessica had been unaware until later of Chic's visit to Trish, she knew such fealty was rare. In their own ways, she and Chic loved each other, and always would.

•

In the morning, Jessica took over the kitchen, making coffee, flipping over bacon strips, scrambling eggs. Cindi had risen early and bought a large bagful of pan dulce from the tortillería on Broadway. While Jessica cooked, she arranged the sweet bread on a platter and set the dining room table. Whenever Arturo visited, the cousins did their best to recreate their grandmother's elaborate brunches.

"You muchachas didn't invite Emilia Salcido, I hope," Arturo remarked as he entered the kitchen. Holding two fuschia branches and some fern fronds, he bent to remove a vase from beneath the sink.

"We wouldn't do that to you, Dad." Jessica smiled and turned the bacon. "Sleep well?"

"Cómo no? Maybe I should get one of those little beds."

"It's a futon," his daughter supplied.

"Another Japanese invention, eh?" He ran the tap water to fill the vase.

Jessica nodded. "And cheaper than a mattress and box springs."

"Hi, Tío Tudy." Cindi came in and pecked his cheek. "Any signs of life from Chic's room?"

He shook his head. "She came in late. Déjala dormir."

"She'll be lucky if there's anything left over," Cindi said.

"Save something for her, eh?" Arturo carried the vase and one of the plates into the dining room.

Jessica smiled at his generosity, took a seat beside him, but decided not to comment. "Are you bringing the coffee, C.C.?"

"Coming up." Cindi returned with the pot and served them. "Too bad you're missing Angelita, Tío."

"Tan linda muchachita." He dug into his bacon and eggs. "I told Efraín yesterday to keep his kids in line. He said you'd already warned him, Jessie."

She shrugged. "He'll listen more to you than to me— 'cause I'm a woman,'" Jessica finished in song. "I think Rita was smart to take off this weekend. She was stressed out."

"It's a big responsibility, raising kids alone." Arturo

103

reached for a pan dulce. "Tell her she can talk to me about it any time."

"She'd like that, Dad." Jessica sipped her coffee. "Hey, Cindi, this man's agreed to sing with me on Cinco. We're rehearsing after breakfast."

"She gave me short notice, eh?" Arturo smiled fondly. "She knew I wouldn't say 'no.'"

Cindi offered him more coffee. "Mind if I listen in?"

"Pues, sobrina, how can we sing if we don't have an audience?"

Arturo carried two mahogany dining room chairs into the living room, setting them next to each other, while Jessica went upstairs to get her guitar. Although she was careful to be quiet on the attic stairs, she realized Chic would no doubt awaken once she and her father started to sing. That thought amused her.

"Cuando estás lista, mija." Arturo sat tuning his old guitar. "Have you thought about what songs?"

"Well, we need to keep things lively for the little kids. How about 'La Mariquita,' 'El Toro Relajo,' 'Palomita de Ojos Negros,' and 'El Gustito.' We'll finish up with 'Cielito Lindo.' If you feel like it, I'd love to sing with you all afternoon, Dad."

Arturo blew her a kiss and helped arrange her chair. Drying her hands on a checked dishtowel, Cindi set three glasses and a pitcher of ice water seasoned with slices of lime on the glass-topped mahogany coffee table. She seated herself across from them on Tia Irene's massive couch, with its matching, curved mahogany legs.

When the guitars were tuned, Jessica and Arturo warmed up by strumming and humming. Soon they launched into "La Mariquita," her lower soprano complementing his husky baritone.

At no other time did Jessica feel such emotion in her voice as when she sang with her father; even ballads with the Satins were no competition for the feelings aroused by Mexican music. Throughout childhood, he had taught her to sing with him in Spanish, to play on the guitar the often heart-rending songs which soothed him and, consequently, bound them ever closer. Victoria, who would have none of such musical therapy, did not share the same relationship with Arturo as did her younger sister. She remained ill at ease when her father and Jessica entertained at family gatherings. Older, more aware of the troubled relationship between their parents, Victoria had opted for other pastimes, other ways to forget Carolina Tamayo.

"'Mariquita dáme un beso/tu mamá me lo mandó,'" they sang, dark eyes mirroring an identical sparkle.

"Ajua, Mariquita!" From atop the second-floor landing, Chic uttered a guttural grito. She stamped a pseudo-folkórico step with her leather sandals and danced her way downstairs.

Laughing, Arturo, Jessica and Cindi watched her whirling at the foot of the staircase, a Chicana dervish in orange tank top and tropical print shorts. "Ay, yi-yi!"

"All this before her morning coffee," Cindi marvelled.

Chic danced her way into the living room, pausing to give Arturo and Jessica wet kisses before disappearing into the kitchen. Immediately, Jessica felt herself blush.

"Que loquita," Arturo chuckled when they brought 'Mariquita' to an end.

Chic reappeared in the archway of the dining room, coffee cup in one hand, pan dulce in the other, and took a deep bow. They cheered her raucously.

"Hey, Tudy. Mi baile was all for you." She advanced and affectionately patted his back. "What a voice this man has, huh? Let's dump Rita and have Tudy join the Satins instead. What do you say, mujeres?"

Giggling, Jessica and Cindi clapped their hands.

Arturo shook his head abashedly. "I don't even know how to sing your kinds of songs, Chica. I'd rather teach you some of mine."

"Jess has the voice for those. It's probably in her genes—

g-e-n-e-s." She gave Jessica an easy grin. "She can do that Mexicana contralto stuff. It's too dramatic for me, but I love to hear it, man."

"Porque eres Mexicana, Chic. It's in your blood, mujer."

"All I know is, I'd rather wake up to Mexican music than to traffic noise." She sat cross-legged on the woven carpet at their feet. "At first, I thought I'd gone haywire last night and somehow wound up in Tijuana. All of a sudden I recognized your voices." She munched the pan dulce. "Hey, don't let me stop you. Let's hear more of los Tamayos. Verdad, Cindi?"

"Que vivan los Tamayos!" Cindi shouted, waving the dishtowel over her head as if it were an impromptu Mexican flag.

8 Hard to Swallow

"You look like a contented woman." Jody sidled up to her in the YWCA auditorium.

Jessica let the lemon-spice tea bag dangle from the side of her cup and decided not to ask for specifics. "Maybe 'cause I've been singing all afternoon. Thought I better have some tea before I get hoarse."

"Since when do the Satins rehearse on Sundays?" Jody leaned against the rough stucco wall beside her.

"Not the Satins, Jody. My dad and I jammed for hours."

"You singing demon, you." Jody's eyes roamed the room, keeping tabs on the comings and goings of other chorus members.

Jessica smiled. "What's new?"

"Not much." Jody focused on her again. "Went hiking with a friend this morning all the way out to Sycamore Canyon. She's one of those outdoor dykes, had me huffing and puffing up and down hills. Made me feel really out of shape. It was pretty out there, though. Lots of wild flowers."

"Did you see any birds?"

"Andrea had her eye out for them." Jody chuckled. "I was too busy panting like a hound dog most of the time."

Their conversation was interrupted when Faye Schneider beckoned the Sapphonics to take their places while the chorus accompanist awaited instructions from the piano bench. Jessica left Jody to join her cousin among the second sopranos, and set the cup of tea on the hardwood floor beside her folding chair. Soon, the chorus began its customary warm-up exercises.

"Tío Tudy was really grooving today." Cindi whispered. "Reminded me of old times."

"Yeah." Jessica cleared her throat. "Cinco's going to be fun."

"Quite a musical lineup: you and Tío Tudy on Wednesday, the Satins on the Promenade on Friday, the Satins and the Sapphonics at the multicultural faire on Saturday." Cindi's tone turned serious. "Don't lose your voice, cuz."

"I'm trying not to."

When Faye Schneider heaved them a reprimanding glance over her half-glasses, the cousins quit whispering and started vocalizing.

"'Many mumbling mice/are making merry music in the moonlight/mighty nice.'" They tried not to giggle while repeating the silly lyrics into higher and higher octaves.

"All right, women." Faye Schneider surveyed the assembled chorus. "I think we're ready to try 'Beautiful Soul.'"

"Buena suerte, Jess," Cindi murmured.

Nervously, Jessica stepped forward for her solo. She had competed with half a dozen Sapphonics for the chance to sing the Margie Adam composition.

"Two, three four." Faye nodded to the accompanist and gave Jessica her cue.

Taking a deep breath, Jessica kept her eyes on Faye and launched into the ballad.

She sang the lesbian standard in a bluesy voice. She knew the lyrics by heart and addressed them directly to Faye, watching for intonation signals.

Faye moved her baton rhythmically, at times easing Jessica into softer tones. After the first stanza, the Chorus joined Jessica. She thrilled at hearing the twenty-nine women's voices backing hers.

"Well, quite an improvement for everyone," Faye remarked at the song's conclusion. "And you're sounding more passionate tonight, Jessica. Hmmm." She gave the soloist a knowing wink and the whole Chorus broke up.

Jessica relished the compliment, though she was abashed by its insinuation. She turned and grinned sheepishly at the other Sapphonics.

"All right, all right." Faye tapped her music stand. "I said 'an improvement,' not perfection. Let's work on this line by line. We're doing it for real Saturday night."

The Sapphonics rehearsed the song strenuously for the next hour. At the break, Jessica was about to make a beeline for the refreshment table when Faye waved her over.

"Careful with your voice, Jessica." The conductor stuck her baton between songbook pages. "Even though your delivery sounds better, you seem a little strained tonight. I know the 'Beautiful Soul' lyrics can be personal—"

"I was singing rancheras with my dad earlier," Jessica said, realizing Faye alluded to the breakup with Trish.

Faye pursed her lips. "Well, no wonder. You've been singing some heavy duty music. Lots of tea with honey and lemon won't hurt. We're counting on you, Jessica. You're a very focused singer with a gorgeous voice."

"Thanks, Faye." Jessica walked with her toward the hot-water dispenser.

"In case you haven't heard," Faye continued, refilling Jessica's cup with hot water and pouring one for herself. "Trish's transfer went through."

Jessica slid the lemon-spice tea bag into the cup while Faye chose a cinnamon-apple flavor. "When?"

"In mid-semester, which is unusual. Trish pushed for it. She couldn't wait to relocate to northern California. Last fall, the faculty formed a lesbian/gay coalition with student groups. Trish felt things were closing in on her. She decided to go away." Faye studied Jessica. "Sounds familiar, doesn't it?"

"She ought to realize she can't run forever," Jessica said. She noticed her matter-of-fact tone, as if she were discussing a stranger—a point she could not dispute.

"Obviously, I had zilch effect on her," Faye remarked. "She didn't even say good-bye when she left last week. She's one of the most stubborn women I've ever met."

"I won't argue with you on that. Thanks for bringing me up to date, Faye."

The conductor nodded and moved on.

"Did I hear Trish's name mentioned?" Cindi came by, munching an oatmeal cookie. When Jessica informed her of the details, Cindi looked concerned. "You okay, cuz? First you're nervous about the solo and now you hear this."

"I'm fine." Jessica blew on the tea, not wanting to burn her tongue. "Cindi, I'm doing what I want to do—working with kids, making music. And Trish's doing what she wants to do—whatever that is."

"Women are weird." Cindi swallowed the rest of the cookie. "On the other hand—*you're* sensational. You sure breathed life into that schmaltzy 'Beautiful Soul.' Did us proud."

"Thanks. Like Chic said, it's in my genes."

Jessica poured water into the tea kettle as soon as she and Cindi arrived home. Hearing them enter, Rita wandered into the kitchen. She and Angelita had been watching TV in the living room.

"Hi, carnalitas. Where's Chic?"

"She was here when we went to rehearsal." Cindi opened the refrigerator, searching for munchies. "How's your family, Rita?"

She leaned over Cindi's shoulder, helping in the quest for a snack. "My sister was there with her kids, so Angelita had her cousins to play with. Pero, ay, estába muy caliente in the Valley."

"You've gotten used to the ocean breezes." Jessica leaned against the sink. She caught Angelita as she bounded into the kitchen. "Hey, little girl. Did you miss me?"

Angelita had an impish expression. "Maybe."

Jessica laughed. "Well, *I* missed you. And my dad was disappointed he didn't get to see you."

Angelita's mouth turned downwards. "I like Tío Tudy."

"You can see him next time, honey. I notice he fixed the steps." Rita emerged from the huddle around the refrigerator with a wide wedge of apple pie. "Do you think this is big enough to share?"

"You better believe it is," Cindi responded. "Want any, Jess?"

"No. Just tea for me."

"Then we'll split it in three, Rita."

Though Rita did not seem thrilled with that prospect, she let Cindi cut the pie in thirds.

"No tienes hambre, Jessie?"

"Nope. And my throat's a little scratchy. Have to be careful this week." She carried her mug toward the staircase. "See you tomorrow. I'm off to bed."

On the window seat, she sipped the tea, letting the hot liquid slide down her increasingly raspy throat. A greyish layer of spring clouds hovered over the night sky, making it opalescent. Jessica studied the drifting clouds while her thoughts centered on Faye Schneider's revelation.

Trish was really gone, from her life, even from southern California. Often, she had spoken of wanting to leave city life behind. That isolated kind of existence had not appealed to Jessica. Like the other Satins, she wanted to remain close to the Los Angeles music scene, not stagnant in a small town. Since the break-up, Jessica had become more her own person. Why, then, did she feel depressed on hearing Trish had gone?

"'Cause I overdid it today and I'm tired," she said aloud. Putting down the mug, she opened the window seat and flipped through her tape collection. She searched for Aretha Franklin's

"I Never Loved a Man the Way I Loved You" cassette, popped it into her tape player, and fast-forwarded to the last track on the second side: Sam Cooke's "A Change is Gonna Come." To combat melancholia, Jessica had a habit of playing that song, infusing her feelings into Aretha's soulful rendition. The lyrics usually proved an effective antidote to the blues.

She leaned against the window panes, mouthing the familiar words, unwilling to strain her voice further by belting them out. She sighed and took another sip of tea.

Along Third Street, she noticed a tangerine VW chugging toward the house. Chic parked her car across the street and strode up the driveway, swinging her hips and car keys in unison. Jessica liked her don't-give-a-damn-about-the-rest-of-the-world stride. She wondered if she would soon have company.

"How's your throat?" Chic peered into the dimly-lit room a few minutes later. "How about another cup of tea?"

Jessica turned from the window. "Thanks. I suppose I don't know when to quit, huh?"

"What're you referrin' to, loca?" Chic entered and handed her a steaming cup. "Let it go down r-e-a-l slow. Chispas, mujer! Don't get laryngitis, at least not this week."

"I don't want it any more than you do." Jessica carefully drank from the hot cup. "You even put lemon and honey in it."

"Do I take care of my Satins or what? Want you to be tip-top this weekend." Chic grinned, straddling Jessica's desk chair. "Cindi says you soared tonight. Trying to steal my thunder?"

"You don't even like to sing ballads." Jessica left the cup on the window sill. "Don't worry. I'm not sick. Just overused my vocal instrument."

"Famous last words." Chic yawned. "I was kissin' up—so to speak—to Darryl Desmoines again. She's going to take some time off Friday to catch us on the Promenade."

"That's definite?" Jessica asked quickly.

"Yeah. Last time we talked, she wouldn't commit. So don't let us down, Jess."

"Believe me, I get the message." Jessica surveyed her, unable to forget the previous night. Chic had reverted to her easy-come, easy-go self.

"Good. Get some sleep, huh? Want me to tuck you in?"

"No." Jessica half-smiled at that. "Rita was asking about you."

"Hell, don't I know it? Got the third degree soon as I walked in." Chic got up. "Sleep tight, loca."

In the morning, Jessica skipped her usual routine. Her throat had gone from raspy to sore, and she decided not to tempt fate further. Cindi gave her a ride to work.

"You probably caught a cold from one of the kids. You know how it goes. The virus incubates and before you know it—you have it, too. Don't panic, Jess."

"I'm trying not to." Jessica sighed. "What worries me is, if I'm sick, the whole classroom'll be infected by the end of the week."

She kept the children occupied by having them make red-white-and-green decorations for Cinco de Mayo. She recounted to them the Aztecs' purported exodus from the territory which became the U.S. Southwest to the valley beyond present-day Mexico City. According to legend, on observing a cactus where an eagle perched with a writhing serpent in its beak, the Aztecs recognized they had arrived in the land of their destiny. Though that Aztec myth had nothing to do with Cinco de Mayo, Jessica knew its simplicity had more appeal to these pre-schoolers than did an involved tale of Mexican political struggle. While she played recorded Mexican music for them, the children cut out eagles and cactus from construction paper. Some of the more creative ones even drew their own concepts of the Aztecs. Jessica moved from child to child, admiring their handiwork.

"My Daddy looked like this," Yolanda said when Jessica came by. "He would sing and jump around and shake a rattle thing." The little girl had drawn a burnt sienna man in a golden loincloth and an elaborate feathered headdress. Yolanda's spontaneous version seemed a cross between Aztec mural figures and Hollywood's take on Native Americans.

"The colors are very pretty, Yolanda."

Because of the details in the drawing, Jessica wondered if the child's father had belonged to a folklórico troupe. Several local ones sang and performed Aztec as well as traditional Mexican dances. Somehow, she could not imagine the business-suited Helen León married to a singer-dancer, yet stranger events had been known to happen.

Yolanda began to cut out a plump cactus. "Are we going to sing today?"

"With the record, honey." Jessica stood up and clapped her hands for attention. "Children, on Wednesday we're going to have a guest at our Cinco de Mayo party. My father is going to bring his guitar and we'll both sing for you. You'll hear what Mexican music really sounds like."

The children looked at her expectantly as she selected another recording. "In the meantime, let's practice 'Cielito Lindo.' I want you all to sound wonderful on Wednesday."

"Mrs. León," Jessica called as the woman escorted her daughter out of the playschool at the end of the day.

"Yes?" She whirled, stylish in a red linen suit.

"If you can get away at noon Wednesday, we're having a Cinco de Mayo party. The flyers went out before Yolanda started here, and I'm sorry I didn't mention it sooner. Some mothers are planning to come."

"Was this your idea?"

Jessica detected a suspicious tone in Mrs. León's voice.

"The party? Well, I try to be as inclusive as possible. We celebrate Martin Luther King's birthday and Chinese New Year, too. I only wish there were more Latino kids enrolled."

Mrs. León came closer. "Forgive me. It's not that I don't appreciate what you're doing."

Jessica followed her instincts. "Yolanda, why don't you take your drawings and wait for your mommy in the car?"

"Sí, mija." Her mother gave Yolanda an encouraging nudge. "Do what Ms. Tamayo says."

When Yolanda skipped away, Jessica observed the child's mother. "I'm only trying to be friendly, Mrs. León. Yolanda's a new student, and I thought you might like to see how I'm incorporating music into the children's time here. I'll admit, I'd like you to see Wednesday's program because it's more than an amateur attempt. My father's coming to sing música Mexicana with me."

Mrs. León's eyes narrowed a bit. "And you thought since my ex-husband used to—"

"Please—if it'd bother you, I understand. I'm hoping Yolanda will enjoy it, anyway."

"I'm sure she will." Mrs. León started to move toward her car. "I may not be able to make it."

Jessica watched her go. She recognized the woman's aloof exterior as camouflage for something more deep-seated. Jessica herself was no stranger to that tactic.

She took the Pico bus into downtown Santa Monica to stock up on vitamin C and herbal throat lozenges at the health food store on the Promenade. Purchases in tow, she strolled beneath blooming jacaranda trees along the brick-paved outdoor mall and noticed a few transients panhandling near one of the topiary dinosaurs. She chose to give her spare change to the elderly African-American woman who regularly sat on a wrought-iron bench next to a neat flowerbed. Chic had dubbed her "Mabel" and often bought her lunch.

"God bless you, miss," she murmured, reaching for the quarters with a shaky hand.

Jessica nodded and hurried a few doors down to Urban Madness, the music-video store where Chic worked as the day manager. Inside the store, the "graffiti wall" was the focal point. There customers could scribble their frustrations, create an art piece, or comment on life in general. Surrounding it were life-sized cut-outs of current pop stars and promotional posters of films to rent. Racks of audio and video cassettes and compact discs filled the rest of the store. Clusters of teenagers congregated throughout, and, as a rule, Chic kept an eagle eye on them all.

When Jessica entered, Chic was on the phone and seemed surprised to see her.

"Shoppin' around, loca?" Chic greeted when she finished her call. Since she knew the inventory inside out, she was eager to be of service.

"Just browsing." Jessica surveyed a dizzying wall of cassettes. "I saw 'Mabel' out there."

"She's back already?" Chic smirked. "The cops rousted a bunch of folks a little while ago. You know, hide the homeless, keep the tourists comin'. Shit, wouldn't be the Promenade without 'Mabel.'"

Jessica came closer to the counter. "Really bothers me to see more women on the street these days."

"As long as it's not you and me." Chic shuffled some paperwork. "Hey, times are tough all around. We're sure keepin' our day jobs and we're better than most acts outside on Friday nights. We're not rip-off artists and we have more vocal range than the rappers. Can you believe no hotshot record producers have been tryin' to sign us for a contract?" She met her friend's gaze. "You know, Jess, I think it's time for us to record our stuff and get it out there."

Jessica stared back. "Didn't I say that months ago? *You* said we weren't ready yet. Chic, those Andean guys who perform down the street from us sell tons of tapes and we have more

116

material than they do. And ours is *original*."

Chic shrugged elaborately. "Okay—I'm a little cabezona at times."

"A little?" Jessica raised a teasing brow. "At times?"

Chic laughed. "I'll look into finding a low-cost way to record." She watched one of the stock boys carrying an armload of new releases toward the shelves. "Larry, C&W tapes go to your left."

The Latino teenager nodded and changed position. Chic looked satisfied as he began stacking the tapes in their proper slots.

"You like being jefa, don't you?"

"Don't give me a hard time, Jess. How're you feeling?"

"Sort of better. Now my throat's only sore on one side. I think it's more strained than anything."

"Are you up to rehearsing tonight? We have to, you know."

"I can handle it. If I hang around, can I catch a ride with you?"

Chic winked. "I'll take you for a s-l-o-w ride."

"You expectin' me to talk about the other night or what?" Chic glanced at her across the VW.

"Not really." Jessica smiled. "I know how you operate."

"Been thinkin' about it, though?"

Jessica kept her eyes on the rush-hour traffic southbound past City Hall. "Chic, I'm only human."

"That's for sure. So am I."

"What's *that* mean?" Jessica turned to gaze at her.

"Go find your dream dyke, and I'll keep lookin' for mine. That's what it means." She drove across Pico Boulevard.

"Chic, I'm *not* falling for you. Being with you really reminded me of how I'm so used to being alone."

"Sure. And Cindi told me Trish split L.A." Chic hung a left on Main and Ocean Park Boulevard. "Forget her, Jess. She didn't deserve you in the first place."

"I didn't expect to get the blues when I heard she'd gone," Jessica said quietly.

"She's l-o-n-g gone." Chic found a snug parking spot in front of the house. "Work it out in a song, baby. The Satins can always use more tunes." She strolled up the driveway ahead of Jessica.

"Let's take care of business, Satins." As lead singer, Chic urged the women into their customary places, Jessica to her right, Cindi and Rita adjacent. While Chic did not have Faye Schneider's musical training, she possessed an inborn talent for rhythm and staging, not to mention her nitty-gritty singing voice. No matter what the Satins thought of her otherwise, when it came to musical expertise they respected Chic.

With a bowlful of lemon sherbet, Angelita served as the evening's audience.

"Anytime you get tired, Angelita, just go upstairs," Rita said. Since the Xochi episode, she had become more solicitous of her daughter's needs.

"Don't you dare, kid," Chic cut in. "You can't skip out on us when we're in the middle of a song."

The little girl giggled, sitting cross-legged on the sofa.

Chic tapped her bare foot and gave the cue. "Let's do it, mujeres."

The housemates launched into an a capella version of "Under the Boardwalk," with their own contemporary twist to the lyrics. Their parodies had proven popular on the Promenade, yet Jessica preferred to concentrate on providing the Satins with fresher material. "Boca Loca" was among the songs on the rehearsal schedule, a tune Jessica had revived from the days when she and Cindi had dubbed themselves the Loca Mochas.

Cállate la boca
Me vas a volver loca

Ojos color de mocha
Quiéres que te toca

Ay, dáme tu locura
Y tu piel tan oscura
Dáme un beso en mi boca
Y te voy volver más loca

In step, in tune, the Satins moved sensuously while they sang together.

Tengo una boca loca
Bebé, una boca loca
Quiero amarte con mi boca loca
Ay, si, con mi boca loca

"Let's really feel it," Chic urged. "Put your bodies into the song, girlfriends. Act out those lyrics. Shimmy those shoulders and chichis—look seductive. Shake those sexy nalgas."

The Satins rolled their eyes, yet followed her instructions, clapping their hands, snapping their fingers, grooving with fancy footwork.

Ay dáme tu locura
Amor es la cura
Labios tan sabrosos
Pueden ser famosos

"I think I heard the doorbell." Cindi broke ranks at the end of the song.

"Who cares?" Chic was impatient. "We've got work to do."

Cindi was halfway to the locked screen door. "Hey, Rafi. Pues, mira nomás. You have our jackets!"

"Personal delivery," he announced, stepping inside. "Sorry to barge in," he added, noting Chic's irked expression.

When she saw the shimmering lavender creations draped over his arm, she broke into a grin. "Man, you sure don't have to apologize."

The Satins encircled Rafi like excited schoolgirls. He helped each one into her satin jacket and stepped back to get the full effect.

"What do you think?" Cindi asked, when they posed facing him.

"I'm really a genius, no question about it," he gushed. He guided the women to the full-length mirror by the door.

"Fabulosa," Jessica breathed.

"We look so shiny," Rita giggled.

"Oh, man." Chic thrust out a hip. "We're really goin' to cause a sensation."

"'One, singular sensation—'" Cindi sang, and the four of them cracked up.

His eyes gleaming, Rafi started to strut toward the door. "Wait, man," Chic demanded. "You *can't* leave. You've got to see our show."

9 Canta, No Llores

"She's avoiding me, no?" Rita wiped off the counter and handed Jessica a cup of espresso.

Jessica was noncommittal. She wished she had gone to the Novel Café instead. Old habits were hard to break.

"Dígame algo, Jessie."

She gulped the coffee and reluctantly put down the cup. "It's hard to avoid someone living in the same house."

"Ay, tú." Rita stared at her, one manicured hand on her hip. "You won't ever say anything negative about Chic."

"She's my friend, Rita. So are you." Jessica kept her voice low, trying not to attract anyone else's attention. "Anyway, you *know* how she is."

Rita wiped the counter with vigor, concentrating on a tenacious coffee stain. "Dos noches y entonces—poof! Adiós!"

"What else did you expect from Chic?"

"I have *feelings*, Jessie! Just 'cause she was hot for a couple of nights, I'm supposed to shrug it off and pretend it never happened?"

Jessica leaned one elbow on the counter. "Have you tried talking to her about it?"

"She hasn't been around much."

"Well, neither have you."

"Oh, so it's *my* fault since I went to visit my parents? That isn't fair, Jessie."

"Didn't mean it to sound that way. I'm sorry."

"Look, how can I talk to Chic when she's coming in late all the time? And last night—well, when she's Mama Satin, you can't approach her about anything but música."

Jessica sighed. In some ways, she could relate to Rita's frustration; on the other hand, she wished Rita would be realistic when it came to Chic Lozano. "Exactly what do you want from her? Have you really thought that out?"

Rita blinked, the thick mascara on her lashes glistening.

"Do you want a relationship with her? Do you want her to help you raise Angelita? Do you want to share the rest of your life with her? If that's what you want, I think you've picked the wrong woman. More than any of us, Chic wants to make it in music. *That's* her goal."

Rita turned her back to start another batch of coffee. Watching her, Jessica wondered if she had been overly blunt.

"Pues, you know her better than I do." Rita came back to the counter. "In all these years, she never paid much attention to me till she realized I could sing."

"Rita, look at who she was involved with last time: Roxanne Payne. The woman's in the music biz, for heaven's sake. Doesn't that say it all?"

"In other words, the only way *I* can help Chic's career is by singing with her, verdad?" Rita flicked her towel further along the counter. "She really doesn't want anything else from me."

Jessica reached over and touched her hand. "If it'll make you feel better, keep trying to talk to her. In the meantime, we really have to hang together as Satins this week. We can't have all this internal combustion going on. If Darryl Desmoines likes what she sees, we could even get a gig at her club."

"That'd be so cool, Jessie." Rita refilled the half-empty cup. "I could sure use some extra money."

"We all could." Jessica was relieved when another customer caught Rita's eye.

•

Since several mothers, though notably not Mrs. León, seemed enthused about the Cinco de Mayo party, Jessica left work in high spirits. Humming to herself, she rode her bike home. Her throat felt better, occasionally raspy, but no longer sore.

She left her bike in the garage and wandered into the backyard. Smudge, Chic's cat, greeted her, rubbing against her legs. Jessica picked her up and Smudge purred in appreciation. While Jessica cradled her, she heard the door of the rear house close. Berta Zepeda, clad in a mismatched cotton skirt and blouse, advanced with a wicker basket full of damp clothes under her arm. Her dark hair was in rollers, covered with a fraying scarf.

"Buenas tardes," Jessica called.

Berta barely nodded and proceeded to hang the clothes on the wobbly line behind the sycamore which served as a barrier of sorts between the two houses. "Angelita in your house," she told Jessica in heavily accented English.

"Bueno." Jessica smiled at her. She noticed Berta seemed quite preoccupied with her task.

Ever since she and Cindi had inherited the property, Jessica had tried being friendly to Berta, to no avail. No doubt Berta agreed with her husband as to the proximate evil incarnate in the four Chicanas. Perhaps she had even caught word of the Satins' antics at the recent parish fiesta. Regardless of Berta's opinions, Jessica felt some solidarity with her as a Mexicana, if nothing else.

"Berta, está Xochi con Angelita?"

"No. Xochi doing—tarea." Berta motioned with her head toward the back house.

Jessica wondered if Berta were purposely keeping the children apart. Never before had Xochi been instructed to do homework assignments directly after school. What was the reason for this new routine? Jessica hesitated briefly, then carried Smudge into the house.

"Angelita?"

In response, the child scampered into the kitchen. She attempted to hug Jessica which prompted Smudge to dash away.

"Why are you all by yourself, honey?"

"Berta said Xochi couldn't play with me." Angelita fidgeted with the ribboned ends of her braids, her eyes trailing the cat.

Jessica sighed. "Why don't we go for a walk by the beach?"

Angelita waited impatiently on the windowseat while Jessica changed into shorts, a T-shirt, and sneakers.

"Can we buy ice cream?"

"Only if we have it for dessert. I don't want to spoil your dinner." Jessica followed her downstairs. "We'll say 'hi' to your mom on the way, so she'll know where we're going."

"Hurry, Jessie," Angelita urged. She darted out the front door.

"Don't run. Wait." Jessica locked the door and jogged down the driveway. Taking Angelita's hand, she ambled with her to Hill Street.

Starbucks was crowded with late afternoon customers. In the doorway, Jessica waved to Rita and pointed westward. Looking harried, Rita nodded and blew her daughter a kiss.

"Did Berta say why Xochi couldn't play with you?"

"She has to do lots of homework."

Angelita seemed undisturbed by the loss of her playmate. Jessica wondered if the little girl had made any connection between the previous trouble with Xochi and this latest development. She noticed how the child clung to her more tightly while they approached the bike path.

"Jessie, why are these dirty, smelly people always by the beach?"

She sensed Angelita's combined fear and curiosity about the transient men and women who drifted throughout the beach city. She pondered whether her own uneasiness about them was obvious to the little girl.

"They don't have any place to live, Angelita."

"Are they poor?"

Jessica nodded. "They don't have houses, jobs, food or anything."

"They're scary."

"If I didn't take a bath, didn't comb my hair, didn't brush my teeth, and wore messy clothes, I'd be scary-looking, too."

"Yech." Angelita grimaced and quickly recovered. "You wouldn't scare *me*."

"Why not?"

"'Cause I *know* you, Jessie. I'd take you home and clean you up."

Jessica smiled at her perception. "I'll remember that."

They strolled along the fringes of the bike path, out of the way of leisurely cyclists and speeding roller-bladers.

"Can we go to the merry-go-round?"

"Don't have time." Jessica swung the child's hand in hers. "Did your mommy tell you about the faire on Saturday? There'll be music, carnival rides in the playground and other fun things for kids to do."

Angelita nodded with enthusiasm. "Can Xochi go with us?"

"Your mom will have to ask Berta about that." Jessica chose her words carefully. "Honey, you have to remember that sometimes people from Mexico don't like their kids being around anybody else. Berta and Efraín aren't used to the way we do things here. Lots of times, they don't even like how we live or behave."

"Xochi says they won't let her talk to Chic at all." Angelita's tone seemed baffled. "They think my mom does nasty things so they don't want Xochi to come inside our house any more."

"Your mom and Chic are fine women, Angelita. You know that." Jessica hoped she did not have to convince her. "So what did you say to Xochi?"

125

"I told her they're wrong. We all live together 'cause we like each other. We always have lots of fun. Why do they say stuff like that, Jessie?"

"Because they don't know any better. They're probably afraid Xochi will want to be like us when she grows up. That scares them."

"She can't even sing." Angelita laughed at the thought. "When she tries, it never sounds right."

Jessica smiled, amused that the little girl had derived a musical connotation from the conversation. "Maybe she needs to practice, huh?"

"Yeah, lots."

"Look, honey, you have other friends. Even if Xochi can't go to the faire with you on Saturday, there'll be lots of kids there, probably some from your school." Jessica tugged her gently and guided her to a cement embankment. "Let's take off our shoes and walk by the water for a while."

Moments later, Angelita played tag with the incoming tide. She squealed each time the cold water lapped her toes. Jessica smiled at watching her, relieved the child did not seem to mope about the lack of Xochi's companionship, yet saddened at the discrimination Angelita already faced. After several minutes, Jessica glanced at her watch and called to her.

"Come on. We have to buy the ice cream. What flavor?"

"Cherry Garcia!" Angelita dashed after Jessica toward the cement embankment. "The kind with chunky stuff in it."

"All right." Jessica sat and dried the child's feet with the old towel she had stashed in her daypack. "Put on your socks and shoes."

"I can tie the knots myself." Angelita bent over and demonstrated her proficiency.

"You make better bows than I do," Jessica marvelled.

"We brought dessert!" Angelita announced when she burst through the kitchen door. "Ice cream for everybody."

"Mind reader." Chic grinned, winking at Jessica. She stood by the crockpot, savoring the spicy stew. "Pretty damn good if I must say so myself."

"We all know you can cook, in more ways than one," Cindi remarked.

"So let's get on with the meal. We have to rehearse tonight."

"Angelita, why don't you set the table?" Cindi suggested. "Your mom's upstairs."

"I'll get Rita." Jessica called over her shoulder.

Rita stared through the casement window at the sycamore shading the bedroom she shared with her daughter. "What will I do if Berta and Efraín won't let Xochi take care of Angelita anymore after school?"

"I guess Angelita could hang out at Starbucks till your shift is over. I don't know, Rita." Jessica sighed. "Look, I could be jumping to conclusions. Maybe this has nothing to do with racism or homophobia or anything else. Maybe Xochi really did have a lot of homework—but maybe not. Whatever happened, it sounds like Berta and Efraín don't want Xochi spending much time with Angelita."

"Who would think these vecinos would be so mean to a little child? Angelita's skin isn't much darker than Xochi's." Rita muttered, using a wire brush to perk her curly hair. "How can these Mexicanos be racists?"

"Sometimes, Rita, our own treat us worse than anyone else."

Jessica arrived at Pacific Palms early Wednesday morning to finish decorating the classroom.

"Need any help?" Albert came in while she stood on a table, hanging red-white-and-green streamers from the overhead lights. Combined with the children's construction paper decorations, the streamers added a festive touch.

"Too late. I'm done." She leaped off. "What time is it?"

"About 7:45." He grinned, watching her bustle around. "Going all out, huh?"

"You bet." She grabbed her daypack and headed to the restroom. "Next time you see me, you won't even recognize me."

The children gaped when she greeted each one at the classroom door. In traditional sequin-decorated china poblana skirt, ruffled blouse and tooled boots, Jessica felt self-conscious, especially with the red silk roses Rita had lent her to pin behind each ear. She wore a pair of Tía Irene's silver filigree earrings from Taxco to complete the picture.

"What a lovely costume," said one of the mothers. "I'm just dying to meet your father, Jessica. He must be incredibly proud that you cherish your ethnic roots. I can't believe my little Denny can actually sing in Spanish, thanks to you."

"One song is only a beginning, Mrs. Bellingham." Jessica tried to keep from laughing at some of the well-meant comments of the liberal Westside mothers. "See you this afternoon."

Yolanda León seemed awed at Jessica's transformation. She glanced from her mother to Jessica, as if awaiting confirmation.

"Yes, it's me, Yolanda." Jessica bent to her level. "Happy Cinco de Mayo."

Abashed, the child hid her head in her mother's skirt.

Helen León patted Yolanda's pigtails. "I'm trying to rearrange my schedule to make it here in time for the party."

Jessica nodded and turned to greet another swarm of entering children.

By noon, children from other playrooms began congregating, joining Jessica's group seated in a semicircle on the carpeted floor. While other teachers supervised the restless children, Jessica rushed outdoors, hearing the distinctive rumble of her father's truck.

Guitar case in hand, Arturo Tamayo emerged from the El Camino, resplendent in black charro pants, boots, ruffled shirt, concho bolo tie, and a flashy black sombrero festooned with silver embroidery. Jessica admired his dashing figure.

"I have a handsome daddy." She gave him a sudden hug.

"Mi hermosita." He bowed and kissed her resoundingly.

Arm in arm, they entered the classroom. While the children clapped and squealed, Jessica introduced him to everyone assembled. "Children, this is my father, Señor Arturo Tamayo. When I was a little girl, he taught me many songs. Today we're going to sing some for you as soon as we tune our guitars."

Side by side, they adjusted the strings and strummed. Arturo's grin seemed permanent. Repeatedly, he nodded to the children seated at his feet and to their mothers lined against the opposite wall.

"Ahora, mija," he whispered. He tapped his boot, cueing "Mariquita."

Their voices soaring, the Tamayos launched into the rousing song. Making eye contact with the youngsters' upraised faces and the attentive expressions of their mothers, Jessica observed that, aside from Albert and a few children, she and her father were the darkest-skinned people in the room. Knowing she and Arturo were the focal points did not rattle her, however. To her, music broke all boundaries. Though she usually avoided traditional dress, she congratulated herself for wearing it for this performance. The little girls, especially, seemed entranced.

She and Arturo slid easily from one song to the next, their voices resounding in the hushed room. Jessica noticed Mrs. León, a latecomer, next to the classroom door. Her eyes seemed remote, frequently on her daughter. Yolanda's gaze bounced from Jessica to Arturo, her small, solemn mouth forming a half-smile. At the conclusion of their duets, Jessica and Arturo encouraged the children to join them in "Cielito Lindo." Even some of the mothers clapped and hummed along, everyone chiming in for the chorus.

Afterwards, children and parents alike surrounded the Tamayos. Jessica extricated herself from the congratulatory crowd to bring her father a glass of fruit punch. He took it gratefully as he stood beside her.

Kathleen Scott touched Jessica's shoulder. "Absolutely delightful. And Mr. Tamayo, my goodness! Obviously, like father, like daughter. You two ought to go professional."

"Gracias, Señora." Arturo took her compliments with his usual unpretentiousness. "We do sing for family and friends— you know, baptisms, first communions, weddings. I think Jessie was born singing," he added with a touch of pride.

Jessica blushed and darted aside to search for Yolanda. She found her with Mrs. León at the refreshment table.

"Jessica—gracias." Mrs. León took her hand in hers. "The other day—well, I apologize. I wasn't sure if I'd want to hear música Mexicana. It reminds me of—"

"I understand," Jessica said with a smile. She offered Yolanda a sliver of pan dulce. "And how about you? You looked like you really enjoyed yourself."

Yolanda nodded. "I like your pretty skirt," she said almost inaudibly.

Jessica extended the glittery fabric. "My abuelita made it when I was a teenager. I'm surprised it still fits." She turned to Mrs. León again. "Do you have time to meet my father?

"Of course."

Jessica thought she saw a glimmer of recognition cross Arturo's face when she made the introductions. He had been conversing with Albert, yet directed his full attention to the Leons. When Yolanda put a tentative hand on the neck of his guitar, Arturo asked if she would like to play with it. Shyly, the child agreed.

"Jessie was about your age when I started teaching her." He seated himself again, guiding the little girl toward him.

She glanced at her mother for permission. When Mrs. León gave her assent, Yolanda stood beside him. Arturo pointed out the strings and strummed each one. Before long, he had gained the attention of several other children. When they pressed too close, Yolanda retreated to her mother's side.

"Pues, mija, I have to get back to work." Mrs. León knelt to adjust the lacy collar of Yolanda's dress. "Dáme un besito."

Jessica walked with them to the door. "I'm really glad you came by. Yolanda, how about another piece of pan dulce?"

Mrs. León smiled and hurried to her car.

"She was married to Daniel León," Arturo revealed as he helped his daughter load her bike into the El Camino's bed.

"I don't think I knew him, Dad." Jessica climbed into the truck beside him.

"Daniel was probably closer to Vickie's age." He backed the truck out of the parking lot and headed toward Pico Boulevard. "The kid was muy interesado en música. He could do todo—dance, sing. Used to live en la calle Michigan, near Chic's abuelita. La Chica probably remembers him."

"How did he die?"

"I heard it was AIDS, mija."

Chic pulled a jumble of tank tops and panties from the combination washer-dryer the cousins had splurged on when they had inherited the house.

"Sure, I knew Danny León. A real heartbreaker." She spread her clothes atop the kitchen table and tried to untangle them. "What makes you ask about a dead guy?"

Jessica measured a cup of detergent and poured it into the washing machine. "Dad says he was married to the mother of one of my kids."

"Oh, yeah? What's her name?"

"Helen. Her daughter's Yolanda—the sad kid I told you

about." Jessica shoved her own load of clothes into the washer.

Chic uttered a low whistle. "La vida triste in a small-town barrio. Check with Rafi. He could fill you in."

Jessica stared at her. "Don't tell me Rafi was involved with Danny León?"

Chic shrugged. "All I know is, he used to make Danny's folklórico costumes."

During the Sapphonics' rehearsal break, Jessica kept the phone receiver close to her ear, listening to Rafi.

"Ay, Danny, Danny, Danny." He let out a long sigh. "After high school, he got a dance scholarship, then wound up in San Francisco for a while. He wasn't out to his family so he stayed there and danced with a couple of folklórico troupes. When he came back to L.A. to join Los Danzantes de la Playa, he got a lot of family pressure to get married. You know—Chicano only-son-syndrome."

"I can imagine," Jessica said quietly. "How'd he meet his wife?"

"At Priscilla Montelongo's sister's wedding. Helen was a career chick, muy professional, not into dating. But Danny—ay, Jess, he was tan guapito. Not a flaming queen at all—muy butch, all those fine dancer's muscles. I bet Vickie remembers him. Billie would kill for his eyelashes. Danny could charm the chones off anybody."

She did not care to ask for specific examples, and hoped Rafi realized that.

He continued, talking fast. "Next thing you know, he's married to Helen and she got pregnant like that." Rafi snapped his fingers.

Jessica closed her eyes, saying nothing.

"Danny couldn't keep living a lie, though. He finally came out to her. Helen loved him, and he broke her heart, Jess. They wound up getting divorced, and Danny helped support the little girl. He was crazy about her."

"And then he died," Jessica murmured.

"Yeah. A few months ago." Rafi's voice shook. "I made the suit they buried him in."

Jessica sat on the curb separating the YWCA building from its parking lot. Broodingly, she stared ahead, trying not to notice a couple of Chorus members necking in a nearby parked car.

"There you are." Cindi came along with a cup of tea for her.

"Thanks."

Cindi squatted next to her. "Remember, Rafi loves to gossip. Whatever he said might be puro chisme."

"He doesn't exaggerate with me," Jessica insisted. "Rafi told me what I needed to know. Cindi, I'm worried about Helen and Yolanda. They might be HIV-positive." Jessica sighed and put the cup beside her. "Helen's hot and cold—friendly one minute, aloof the next. She didn't volunteer that Yolanda's father's dead. Who knows what else she's keeping to herself?"

"What are you going to do now?"

"I *won't* report anything to Kathleen," Jessica said firmly. "All hell could break lose if anyone at the school found out the cause of Danny León's death. There's no way I'd want to make trouble for Helen and Yolanda. I just wanted to know for myself, so I can figure out how to deal with it."

"Jess, you get too involved." Cindi got to her feet. "If it's not Angelita, it's some other kid."

"*Somebody* has to care." Jessica gazed at her. "And don't tell me you don't care about Angelita. If you didn't, you wouldn't have gone to talk to Berta like you did tonight."

Cindi moved away from her. "Faye's calling us back in. Come on. You have a solo to rehearse."

When the cousins left the station wagon in the driveway, they discovered Chic stretched on the covered veranda swing,

133

Rita slouched on the top step. They shared a Miller Lite between them.

"The Sapphic Songbirds return." Chic raised herself on one elbow. "Rafi said he talked to you, Jess."

She nodded and slumped beside Rita. Cindi joined them on the step.

"From the looks of you," Chic remarked, "I take it Rafi gave you the lowdown."

"Yeah, damn it. I'm really fed up with gay Latinos who won't risk coming out to their families. Instead, they lead double lives—get married—and wind up hurting people anyway," Jessica said in disgust. "Look at us. We're open with *our* familias. Sure, it's cost us in some ways, but we haven't really hurt anyone by being ourselves, verdad?"

"You have a father who adores you. Not everyone's that lucky, Jessie." Rita offered her a sip of beer.

Jessica declined. "I *know* my situation's different. Even if Dad would probably like grandkids, he's never pressured Vickie *or* me to get married. I don't know what that would be like. I can't understand, though, how someone can live a lie and intentionally risk someone else's life."

"Happens all the time," Chic remarked. "Why do you think AIDS is making such an impact among la gente Latina? Macho types don't want to admit they go for guys, too. They cover up by having some pussy on the side. And macho men *have* to have kids. I hate all those lies, too, Jess. As usual, las mujeres are the ones getting shafted—in more ways than one."

"Women—and kids," Jessica added in a quivering voice. "Kids always wind up being everyone's low priority. And I'm damn sick of it." With a sob, she got up and hurried inside.

The other housemates stood outside her bedroom door, urging her to open it.

"Leave me alone," Jessica muttered. She lay face down on the futon, her heart aching for Yolanda and Helen León.

134

"Cuz, let's talk," Cindi coaxed. "I know you're remembering when you were a kid, how hurt you were when your mother went away. Come on, let us in. We want to help."

Shuddering, Jessica curled up, hiding her face in the sheets.

"You always listen to *us*, Jessie." Rita's voice sounded querulous. "We're your friends. We want to make sure you're all right."

"I just need to think." Jessica tried to sound firm, without much success.

"You heard what she said," Chic stated after a few moments. "She wants to get herself together. Give her some time."

Jessica listened to them whispering among themselves and then heard their footsteps retreating. Lying there, she cried for a long time before giving in to sleep.

She awoke to the click of the doorknob. She remained motionless, her senses alert. She was not surprised to hear Chic's voice.

"You okay, Jess?"

Jessica rolled on her back, hair matted against her face. "*Don't* try anything."

Chic spread her hands before her, is if to convince Jessica of her sincerity. "Look, I didn't expect you to be so shook up. I guess this pinche thing about the Leóns really got to you."

"Oh, damn it all, Chic." Jessica began to cry again. "Yolanda's a baby and look what she's faced already. What kind of world is this, anyway?"

"Ay, mi loquita." Chic knelt beside the futon, taking her friend into her arms.

Jessica sobbed harder, her head against Chic's shoulder. Through her tears, she heard the door's hinges creak. She saw a dim shape. In the threshold, Rita stood, her eyes intensely on them both.

135

10 In the Groove

Puffy-eyed, Jessica waited outside Rita's bedroom in the early morning hours. She moved aside quickly when Rita stepped out.

"Don't give me that phony triste look, Jessie. You must've had a blast with Chic all night."

"Wait, Rita—"

Ignoring her, Rita went into the adjacent bathroom and shut the door. Jessica sighed, feeling miserable. She paced the hardwood floor of the hallway for several moments. Unwilling to awaken anyone, she decided to be quiet and stationed herself outside the bathroom. She heard the shower in a while and knew Rita would take her time. Jessica hunkered down, determined to sit it out. A half hour later, Rita barely opened the door.

"I need to talk to you," Jessica whispered.

"What's the use? I'm not so stupid that I haven't figured out what's going on."

"Rita, will you please let me explain?" Jessica got to her feet, dusting off her jeans.

"Get in here, then," Rita said impatiently, holding her cotton robe around her. "Pero cállate. Don't let Angelita hear."

Jessica entered the steamy room. She grabbed a dry towel off the rack, placed it on the bathtub's rim, and situated herself there. "Chic was comforting me, that's *all*."

"Next thing you're going to say is she was mothering you, verdad?" Rita cast her a disdainful glance. She began applying make-up, using a lighter foundation to hide the circles beneath her round eyes. "Did she offer you her chichis tambien? We all know you grew up without your mother. Why shouldn't you try to find yourself a Mama Satin?"

Jessica winced at those stinging words. Taking a deep breath, she spoke softly. "You can think anything you want. All I'm going to say is this: Chic knew I was upset. She came to see if I was all right, and she stayed till I fell asleep."

Rita rinsed her hands, dried them, and began curling her eyelashes. Noting her coolness, Jessica felt sure her explanation had had no effect. Slowly, she got to her feet and was halfway out the door when Rita grabbed her arm.

"Wait, Jessie." Her eyes melted into apologies.

"You have a speck of mascara at that corner." Jessica pointed toward Rita's right eye.

Rita glanced into the mirror and carefully wiped it off. She studied herself while she spoke. "No sé porque I'm so jealous. That damn callejera isn't even worth it. She's getting her beauty sleep right now and both of us look like brujas." She turned to face Jessica. "Forgive me?"

Nodding, Jessica squeezed Rita's shoulder and hurried down the stairs.

She rode her bike a different way to work, uphill along Ashland, around Santa Monica College to Pico. The route was strenuous, though most of it wound through quiet residential neighborhoods where she could let her mind wander and not pay much attention to traffic.

Her thoughts continually swung from the Leóns back to Chic. How did she do it? How did Chic manage to detach herself from her emotions enough to exist, to bounce in and out of women's lives, their sensibilities, their beds? Such a capability had to require tremendous practice, Jessica reasoned. Yet how

137

much psychological wear and tear could a woman take without becoming hardened? She knew she herself did not possess enough distancing know-how to even attempt to imitate Chic Lozano's behavior. Jessica could not pull back far enough. Her head ached. She would have to make a pot of coffee as soon as she arrived at Pacific Palms. She hoped no one had eaten the leftover pan dulce; she counted on it for breakfast. Riding along, she determined, for her own peace of mind, to try to keep herself in check, not only with her housemates, but also in her future dealings with Yolanda and Helen León. She would not reveal to anyone what she had learned about Yolanda's father. Helen León had a right to her secrets. After all, Jessica had never revealed her lesbianism to anyone in the workplace either.

"You look like you had a rough night," Albert observed when he found her in the lunchroom.

"I was so high yesterday it took me a while to crash." Even at noontime, Jessica had to drink coffee to keep alert.

"Well, come on down, girl," he teased. "I like your daddy."

"Why wouldn't you? He's from your generation."

He chuckled. "He said besides doing the Promenade tomorrow, you and your friends will be at the multicultural faire this weekend. Ms. Tamayo, when were you going to let me in on that?"

She blushed. "You want to see four brown girls singing salsa-flavored rock? Albert, I thought you were into jazz."

"Sometimes, Jess," he said, shaking his head, "I can't figure you out."

Pedaling around the corner of Third Street, Jessica noticed Victoria's car perched tentatively at the top of the driveway, like a nervous insect preferring to be elsewhere.

"The Saab sister returns," she remarked, entering the

house through the front door.

Victoria glanced up from the dining room table. She and Cindi shared several clients and seemed to have been deep in discussion about them.

"Is that what *you* call me, or did Chic dream up that one?" Victoria turned to greet her.

"My creation, sis." Jessica laughed, giving her a hug.

Cindi winked and went into the kitchen to get Jessica a glass of water.

"You look awful, Jessie." Victoria touched her sister's warm cheek. "Ay, so sweaty. How can you stand riding your bike in this weather?"

"I need the exercise. Don't worry, I'm heading to the shower. I know you two are busy."

"We're going to do some closet reorganization," Cindi revealed when she handed Jessica the ice water. "It's not what you think," she added with a giggle.

Jessica smiled, noting her sister's irritation whenever they made frivolous comments about closets. Victoria continued to think it unlikely that both her sister and cousin were lesbians. She often commented to the rest of the Tamayos that Jessica and Cindi, the erstwhile Loca Mochas, had been merely trying to outdo each other as worldly twenty-one-year-olds by "claiming" to be lesbians. The "scheme" had backfired, Victoria persisted in advising the family, when both young women had wound up coming out of the closet simultaneously, instead of one at a time. Eventually, she assured the relatives, though a decade had passed, one or the other would give up "that lifestyle," as she called it. As if Victoria Tamayo led a traditional life herself, Jessica thought.

Victoria gestured toward the diagrams she had spread on the mahogany table. "Some of our clients prefer their closets to be color coordinated, like their wardrobes. I've sketched these out for us to follow. Cindi and I are working together to make these a reality."

"Is this a new phase—'Closets R Us'?" Jessica grinned,

taking a sip of the ice water.

"You're getting as bad as Chic. Well, I hope not *that* bad," Victoria glanced at her watch and began to gather her paraphernalia. "I have to go. The Bay Businesswomen's fund-raising dinner is tonight."

"Hey, next time, tell those mujeres to use the Satins as entertainment. We're locals, but not yokels." Jessica waited for them to groan appropriately. "By the way, Vickie, we're on the Promenade tomorrow."

"Sometimes, Jessie, you're so much like Dad it scares me." Victoria gave her sister a quick kiss and hurried out to the awaiting navy-blue Saab.

Cindi appraised her cousin. "You *do* look awful. You seem in better spirits, anyway."

Jessica shrugged. "I'm trying to cheer myself up. Every time I looked at Yolanda today, I wanted to cry. Have to realize I can't save the world."

"That's right. Keep reminding yourself." Cindi slid Jessica's portion of the daily mail across the table. "The latest issue of *La-LA Lesbian* is there, too. I was doing a condo by Sisterhood Bookstore so went in to pick up a copy."

"How's my review?"

"A couple of typos. That's the least of it." Cindi pointed to the fold-out magazine. "Check the cover. I made sure to keep it out of sight while Vickie was here."

Jessica grimaced at seeing a black-and-white photo of a slick-haired blonde in dominatrix regalia. "I can't believe it."

Cindi held it up. "We could always use that for a dartboard. Unless Rita would rather use your face. I hear she was pissed."

"We made up this morning."

"I hope so." Cindi tossed the magazine on the table. "We've got all these gigs to get through—all we need is for our harmony to be off. If that happens, we're all going to be dealing face to face with our resident dominatrix Chic Lozano. And she's the cause of all the mitote in the first place."

Jessica browsed through her mail, unwilling to make a comment. She suspected Cindi preferred to stay neutral and, at the moment, Jessica had no desire to change that.

"Since tomorrow night will probably be a little cool, we'll wear our purple jeans, high-tops, and purple tank tops under the jackets," Chic announced before they began rehearsing. "Mujeres, be sure to shave your underarms in case we get hot and have to take off our jackets."

"Ay. Tan grosera." Rita curled her lip. She sat on the piano bench, bare legs dangling.

"Rita, while we're getting ready, one of us could forget that."

"We have to really look sharp," Jessica remarked. "Remember Darryl Desmoines will be there checkin' us out."

"Right. We can't afford to blow it." Chic skimmed her checklist. "Next—the bookstore manager asks that we keep our audience from blocking the doorway. We'll be more in the center of the Promenade so people can sit on the curb or gather around us. Anything else to add?"

Cindi leaned forward. "If we take off our jackets, where are we going to put them?"

"Billie's offered to be our dresser. She'll be on the sidelines to hold the jackets, get us drinks, whatever. Mujeres, start collecting groupies so we don't have to ask our friends to give up their Friday nights. Chispas! There must be tons of chicks dyin' to wait on us hand and foot."

"De veras? You've probably alienated every lesbiana around here," Rita remarked.

Chic kept her cool, not about to be goaded before rehearsal. As if on reflex, Jessica and Cindi took their places beside her. Taking her time, Rita sashayed over. When Chic gave the cue, the Latin Satins provided harmony for her on "Bushwhacker."

Cold-hearted woman don't want me back
Turned me loose, she cut me slack
Sent me into the night so black
Just like that—whack, whack, whack
Turned me into a bushwhacker—whack, whack
Bushwhacker

With the latest issue of *Hot Wire* under her arm, Jessica padded down the attic stairs on her way to Cindi's room. She had borrowed the magazine and wanted to return it since Cindi had not finished reading it. Rounding the shadowy second-floor landing, she bumped into her cousin. They startled each other, and immediately Cindi held a cautioning finger to Jessica's lips.

"They're in the bathroom. Chic's really pissed. She's trying to keep her voice down, but once in a while you can catch it."

Imitating Cindi, Jessica pressed her ear to the adjoining wall.

"You keep fuckin' up and you're history, Rita. Comprendes, Mendes? The rest of us are committed to the group—you act like all you want to do is to sabotage everything. Your harmony, your rhythm, *and* your footwork were off tonight. What's your problem, huh? If you want out, say so. We'd have no problem switching into a trio."

"Cállate! I don't want out. I want *you* to treat me with respect. I want you to pay some *positive* attention to me." Rita sounded as if she were crying. "I've been going through all this shit with los vecinos over Angelita, and all you care about is the damn gigs."

"The 'damn' gigs mean as much to me as Angelita means to you, Rita. Get it? Who do you think started the Satins? Jess and Cindi were being wasted in that Sapphic Songbird chorus—"

The cousins exchanged wry glances.

"—'cause they'd gotten nowhere as the Loca Mochas. I sure noticed their talent. And I heard you at that Latina Lesbian Open Mike on the Eastside and remembered you from the old days. I worked my ass off to bring you all together. Do you think I'm goin' to let it go up in smoke 'cause you've had a bad week? Fuck that."

The cousins heard Rita sobbing. When Jessica sighed, Cindi lightly rubbed her cousin's back.

"Yeah, cry, cry, cry." Chic's voice was low. "Like I tell Jess—write a song about it."

The cousins strained to listen when someone turned on the water faucet.

"Here, put this washcloth on your face," Chic said a moment later without a trace of remorse. "Your ojos are going to be hinchados tomorrow."

"I hope my eyes *are* swollen so everyone can see what a bitch you are, Chic. You only care about yourelf. You *use* people."

"Uh, huh. Like you used Tremaine. Like you use Jess and Cindi and even Xochi to help you take care of your kid. Who's the ultimate user here, Rita?"

Both cousins winced at hearing the sudden slap.

Chic's voice was furious. "Don't you *ever* do a stupid thing like that to me again."

"Let go of me!"

"No! You're liable to slash me to shreds. I'm not letting go till you calm down."

"Maybe we better get in there," Jessica whispered quickly.

Cindi shook her head. "Chic can handle Rita. She won't hurt her."

"*Chic's* the one I'm worried about."

When Rita spoke again, she sounded plaintive. "Ay, Dios mio! Chic, you're bleeding."

"Shit. You and your damn fuckin' fingernails."

"She's probably scarred for life," Cindi muttered.

"I can't stand this." Jessica gave the bathroom door a hard knock. "You guys all right?"

"She slashed my face off, that's all," Chic retorted when Jessica swung open the door.

"Jesus." Jessica stared at the thin trickle of blood running parallel to Chic's left eye.

A chastened Rita sat on the bathtub rim, crying softly.

Cindi pushed past her cousin. "You could've poked her eye out. Rita, what the hell's the matter with you?"

"I'm so sorry, Chic," Rita sobbed. "Somebody please close the door."

Jessica shut it tightly behind her. "Let's all relax, okay?" She put down the toilet lid and gestured for Chic to sit there. "Does it sting?"

Chic nodded. "Take care of me, Jess."

"I will."

"I didn't mean to—" Rita stretched an arm toward Chic.

"Yes, you did." Chic gave her a wary glance. "Get the hell out, Rita. I've had enough."

"Come on," Cindi agreed, guiding Rita away.

Shrugging her off, Rita paused before Chic. She caressed her hair briefly, bending as if to kiss her. Abruptly, Chic moved her head away. When Rita began crying again, Cindi led her to the hallway.

"A day in the life of the Latin Satins," Chic muttered, while Jessica used a alcohol-dipped cotton swab to clean the scratch. "How bad is it?"

"Hairline. You're lucky she didn't dig her nails into you."

Chic grimaced. "Thanks for coming to the rescue."

"We should've burst in sooner. We heard most of it."

"You guys." Chic shook her head in exasperation.

"Keep still."

"Never thought I'd be a candidate for a battered woman's shelter."

"Chic, will you please be quiet?"

"If I stop talking, I'll start bawling." she murmured, as her face crumpled.

"Oh, Chic." Jessica knelt beside her, letting her friend bury her head against her. "It's going to be all right."

"How can you say that? Rita's a psycho, I'm scratched up, you're shook up about the Leóns—Cindi's the only one who has her head together and she only sings back-up. If we don't snap to it, we could blow our big chance."

"We'll be better than ever. You'll see."

"How are you surviving, Chic?" Cindi asked from the bathroom threshold a few minutes later.

"Así no más. Come in, Cindi."

Jessica moved aside to make room for her cousin. "How's Rita?"

"She told me to leave her alone. She's one scared woman."

"She ought to be," Chic said. She had regained her composure, a little worse for wear with the Band-Aid under her eye. "Look, we have to be ready for everything, mujeres. At the rate things are going, we might have to go trio."

Cindi sat on the tiled counter. "You sound serious."

"What else can I be? You and Jess wouldn't have any trouble handling back-up together. Instead of blending like you do now, one of you'd have to switch to Rita's harmony."

"We're flexible enough to do it," Jessica said quietly. "I hope we won't have to."

"Yeah." Cindi wiped smudges from the contours of the faucets. "And then there's the question of in-house turmoil."

"I'd move out," Chic stated flatly. "No point in making life miserable for you two."

Jessica straightened the towels on their racks. "Let's not get carried away. Rita could bounce back tomorrow. She hasn't said she wants out, anyway."

"If anyone wants her out, *I* do." Chic got up to inspect Jessica's expertise with the Band-Aid. She winced at seeing her reflection.

"Chic, come on." Cindi gave her a nudge with her bare foot.

"Think it over, mujeres. If she'd come at either of you, would you be so willing to forgive and forget?"

Cindi sighed. "She didn't *like* what you said."

"I think we ought to sleep on this," Jessica suggested.

"I told Chic we'd meet her at Urban Madness. No one knows where Rita is," Cindi added Friday evening while she warmed a couple of quesadillas in a frying pan for a quick dinner.

"At noon I phoned Starbucks." Jessica used a paper towel as an impromptu plate. "Ernie said Rita left early. She wasn't here when I tried reaching her. Hope Angelita's with her."

"I feel like throwing up," Cindi muttered. "Rita has the damn nerve to leave us in the lurch while she makes some kind of weird statement."

"We'll manage without her." Jessica gazed at her cousin across the table. "Better than she would without *us*."

The cousins harmonized in Cindi's station wagon on the way to downtown Santa Monica. Versatile singers, they knew all the Satins' parts including Chic's, and could easily switch if the need arose. They grabbed their jackets and left the car on Broadway, a few blocks east of the outdoor mall. In moments, they joined the Friday crowds leaving city parking structures en masse for the jammed sidewalks of the Promenade. The cousins elbowed through the throng in the direction of Urban Madness.

Chic met them at the doorway. "Rita's at Billie's. The trick is, getting her here. Billie has an hour to swing it. If not, we're

146

going trio." She led them into the music store. "I need help with this Band-Aid. There's no way I'm going to wear it tonight."

"Let me take a look," Jessica said, following her to the restroom.

Cindi started browsing. "I'll hang out in case Billie and Rita show."

"Go ahead. Tell me 'I told you so,'" Chic suggested when Jessica carefully peeled off the Band-Aid. "I never should've taken that cuerpito de uva to bed. What goes around comes around, verdad?"

"Shhh." Jessica lifted off the final edge.

"You're being too nice to me. What's the catch?"

"Loca, I want to sing at the Delta as much as you do. Where the Satins are concerned, I'm into cooperation. Haven't you noticed?"

Chic grimaced as Jessica dabbed at the scratch with alcohol from the store's first-aid kit. "You bet. You done?"

Jessica nodded.

Chic observed herself in the rectangular mirror, turning her head from side to side, checking each angle. "That shouldn't be too hard to cover. Thanks, Jess."

Chic dug into her leather bag and pulled out a little bottle of liquid make-up. She washed her hands, then dabbed on a speck of the flesh-colored hue, blending it in with her fingertips.

Jessica watched her transform herself into her public persona: a bit of blush to highlight her cheekbones, mascara and eyeliner to enlarge her eyes, red lipstick to emphasize her lush lips. No doubt about it, Chic Lozano, with her tawny skin and black moussed hair, was an eye-catcher, and she knew it.

"Want to use any of this stuff?"

Jessica wrinkled her nose. "My brown face is clean and my black hair's shiny. Nothing else for me to do."

"Suit yourself." Chic spritzed her short hair, slipped into her Latin Satins jacket and appraised herself. "Híjole. I'm a ringer for John Travolta in *Grease*."

Jessica smiled, pulling on her own jacket.

Chic stuck her bag in a locker outside the restroom and clicked the padlock shut. "Come on, chula. Let's party."

The three Satins strode from Urban Madness as if they owned the Third Street Promenade. With Chic in their midst, they moved in unison, swinging their shoulders and hips confidently. The strolling shoppers and queues of movie-goers seemed to part for the trio of purple-and-lavender clad Chicanas, their satin jackets glowing beneath the street lamps. Recognized by many, they approached a landscaped flowerbed in the center of the Promenade and paused.

Swiftly, Jessica scanned the gathering crowd, praying to catch a glimpse of Rita. Chic seemed intent on diverting Jessica's attention. She did a sudden dance step and wound up slightly ahead. Taking the unexpected cue, Jessica darted behind her, fingers in the back pockets of Chic's purple jeans. Cindi was at the rear, her hands lightly on Jessica's waist. Chic counted off softly, then they sang:

We're the Latin Satins/want to see us groove?
We're the Latin Satins/we'll get you in the mood
We're the Latin Satins/want to hear us sing?
We're the Latin Satins/we'll make you want to swing

We're the Latin Satins/we sing some golden oldies
We're the Latin Satins/our versions aren't moldy
We're the Latin Satins/we invite you to join in
We're the Latin Satins/but not before we're fin-ished!

Chic swung her hips enticingly and the Satins' voices rose and fell with the change in their lead singer's rhythm. Moving in a sensuous snake dance, they sang in a locomotive chant:

Lat-in Sat-ins, Lat-in Sat-ins, Lat-in Sat-ins

Chic's gritty voice led theirs into faster syncopation, repeating their collective name in varying tones and accents, then sliding into the introductory refrain:

We're the Latin Satins, and I'm Chic Lozano

She expanded her arms to encompass the others. Jessica and Cindi smiled and sang:

We're the Latin Satins, and I'm Jess Tamayo
We're the Latin Satins, and I'm Cindi Carbajal

They were about to burst into their first number when Rita dashed out of the crowd and hooked her arms around Cindi's hips.

We're the Latin Satins, and I'm Ri-ta So-lís.

With her wide-eyed expression and saucy body language, Rita elicited cheers and shrill whistles from the onlookers. Not missing a beat, the Satins got down to it.

11 Satins in the Spotlight

On the edge of one of the flower bed borders, the wide-mouthed Mason jar Angelita had decorated with purple glitter and scraps of lavender fabric sat chockful of dollar bills and miscellaneous change, tributes to the Latin Satins. Arturo, Rafi, Billie, and Rita's little girl maintained guard over the cache while the singers basked amidst gawkers and admirers. Jessica tossed smiles to her father and friends, Albert among them, whenever she had a chance.

"Yeah, we're all born and raised in Santa Monica," Chic said to a guy in an Izod shirt next to her. "Surprised? Well, yuppie-kins, how do you think this town got its name? Chicanos have been here a real long time, way before you foreigners took the place over."

The sandy-haired man looked perplexed. He had probably been hoping to pick up Chic and had not expected a local history lesson from the sultry Chicana.

A platinum blonde in a red spandex jumpsuit and matching stiletto heels elbowed him aside. "Chic!"

"Hey, Darryl." Chic gave her a slow grin.

The Satins simultaneously turned their heads when the glitzy woman approached. Her flawless skin seemed as white as her hair, her shrewd sapphire eyes trimmed with streaks of shadow.

"I'm Darryl Desmoines." She spread her arms before the

Satins, puckered her lips, and gave them the semblance of a collective kiss and hug. "An instant devotee! My darlings, your act really has legs—it keeps moving, it's eye-catching. Your voices are simply magnifique. And you're sensational—sepia and sexy." She feasted her eyes on them and gestured to Chic. "Let's talk."

Chic wore a triumphant expression while following her to a table outside the Congo Square coffeehouse.

"Quién es esa mujer?" Arturo whispered to his daughter.

"Darryl Desmoines owns the Delta, that club on Main Street," Jessica breathed, craning her neck to spy on Chic and the proprietor.

"Hey, Billie, don't tell me you do her makeup," Rafi joked, referring to the club owner's showy appearance.

Billie poked his shoulder. "Ay, cállate. Who cares what she looks like if she likes our Satins, no?"

Rafi laughed. "Heard through the grapevine she's opening another club in West Hollywood. Maybe *you* ought to audition for her, Tudy."

Arturo laughed and waved him off.

"Looks to me like the lady's ready to deal," Albert observed. He handed a grateful Angelita another chocolate chip cookie.

"Shouldn't we be in on that?" Rita said, nudging Jessica.

"Chic's been working on this for weeks," Jessica reminded her. "Let her have some glory while she lays the groundwork."

In a few minutes, the Satins huddled around the small outdoor table, listening to Darryl Desmoines outline her proposition. Rita squeezed herself to one side of Chic, often rubbing her bare arm against hers. Jessica sat beside Cindi and noticed Chic shift her chair once or twice. She seemed to want to divert attention from her annoyance at Rita's proximity.

"Chic tells me a couple of you also sing with the feminist chorus and you'll be out of town with them for a week." Darryl

Desmoines observed the Chicanas encircling her. "What would you think of doing a two-week gig in late June, after you come back?"

Jessica and Cindi nodded, too excited to speak. Baby-doll eyes widening, Rita squirmed in her chair.

"Fabulous. We'll have plenty of time to do publicity while you're gone. You'll work with the Chatelaines, the Delta's band. I'd like some original material for your debut. Since you perform around town a lot, we're going to need something quite smashing. Any problem with that?"

"Not a bit," Chic said easily, shooting Jessica a quick glance.

"I'm already working on our new material." Jessica hoped she sounded confident.

The Satins, their families and friends turned out to celebrate in the yellow Victorian on Third Street. Arturo and Cindi's parents made sure all had plenty to eat and drink. Rafi regaled everyone with tales of the jacket fittings, and Cindi's younger sister Mikki and her friend Lulu López plied Chic with questions about the Satins' future plans. Even Victoria showed up, though she did not stay long.

"Billie," Jessica began, pouring her another glass of Dos Equis. "I don't know how you did it, but you saved the day."

"Pues, I told la Rita she owed it to you and Cindi to show up." Billie grabbed a slice of lime from the kitchen counter and squeezed it into her beer. "I played on her guilt, mija, like the excellent recovering Catholic que soy."

"Thanks. Have to admit I was a little shaky about going on as a trio." Jessica stood by Billie while the others partied in the living room. The stereo blasted everything from Madonna to the Gipsy Kings.

"Ya lo sé. Pero you were maravillosas—even Rita. Esa mujer," Billie added, shaking her poufy black hair in consternation. "I told her to watch herself with Chic or she's liable to get kicked out of the Satins."

"Especially now," Jessica agreed. "We need to be solid, not chipping away at each other."

They turned when Rita swept in to replenish the supply of salsa for the others. "What's up with you two?"

"We're speaking of the devil," Billie responded with a hearty laugh. "Aren't you glad you came back tonight?"

Rita poured salsa from a hefty jar into a soup bowl, dipping one finger to catch an errant tomato chunk. "I'll be even gladder when I get to do a solo." She licked her finger. "You hear me, Jessie?"

"I'll see what I can do," Jessica murmured.

"Where *is* she?" Rita stood impatiently beside the station wagon the next afternoon while Jessica and Cindi loaded their Latin Satins outfits for their performance at the local multi-cultural faire.

"Didn't you hear Chic say she'll meet us there?" Jessica lay her jacket atop an old sheet in the rear of the station wagon.

Cindi quickly slid into the driver's seat. "Rita, don't act so surprised." Since the Sapphonics would perform earlier on the program, the cousins already wore their Chorus apparel of black trousers, tuxedo shirts, and red bow ties.

"Chic doesn't even want to be in the same car as me," Rita insisted.

"Quit exaggerating." Cindi dismissed her comment. "Chic always likes to drive herself in case she wants to leave early or stay late. Hurry. We still have to pick up Billie."

Pouting, Rita bounced into the back seat, gesturing for Angelita to join her. "Cindi, be honest. Don't you think you and me ought to do solos once in a while?"

"Shades of every group that ever existed." Cindi waited for Jessica to take a seat beside her. "I *like* doing back-up, Rita.

153

Who needs the pressure of being in the spotlight all the time?"

"You're not living up to your potential." Peeved, Rita crossed her arms and stared out the window while Cindi backed out of the driveway. "Jessie gets to sing solo with the Chorus, and once in a while with the Satins. Pero you and me—we're in the back seat in more ways than one."

"Rita, *I'm* driving right now. That's good enough for me."

Backstage at a Westside junior high school auditorium, the Sapphonics milled about, adjusting each other's bow ties, conversing in a low hum. The feminist chorus would be the closing act for the afternoon. Following an hour dinner break, the evening entertainment would recommence. The Satins were scheduled to perform at 8:30.

"What'd you think of this month's *La-LA Lesbian* cover?" Jody ambled next to the cousins. "Jess, how can you stand having a byline in that?"

"Less and less." Jessica shared her disgust. "Besides, who's even going to read a review buried at the back of the issue?"

"I think you ought to resign. Only say why."

"As if anyone would care."

"Like I told you, lots of dykes are unhappy about the format. Maybe we can hang out tonight and discuss it," Jody suggested. She pointed to the program she pulled from her back pocket. "Great line-up of acts. Andrea and I are stayin' for the whole show. She's in the audience somewhere."

"Actually, we have to hang loose." Cindi cracked her knuckles and rested one arm on Jody's shoulder. "Chic wants us to meet for dinner at the Thai place down the street."

Jody was incredulous. "There's international chow here!"

"When it comes to the Satins, we follow Chic's orders. Maybe we can get together later," Jessica added.

Faye Schneider stood in the wings, pitch pipe to her lips, awaiting the conclusion of a Caribbean dance troupe's performance. When the whirling, barefoot dancers bounded off to the rapid beat of conga drums, Faye signaled to the Sapphonics. They snapped to attention and filed on stage behind their conductor. Following the multicultural theme of the faire, they started off with Bernice Johnson Reagon's "Azanian Freedom Song," switching to Spanish for "La Andina" and "De Colores."

Faye turned to acknowledge the audience's applause. Waiting until it had subsided, she announced the next song. "As this faire demonstrates, those of us who identify with an ethnic or racial group experience more than one culture. Being lesbian or gay in this society also means being part of another culture. This next piece is a love song, written by Margie Adam, to a woman she once loved. Our soloist is Jessica Tamayo."

Smiling at hearing familiar voices cheering her, Jessica swallowed her fear and took her place at the microphone, her eyes on Faye's. At the count, she allowed her rich voice to bring life to the lesbian classic. Twenty-nine voices soon blended with hers to celebrate their own particular brand of diversity.

The majority of the audience applauded long and hard at the end of the Sapphonics' performance, yet Jessica noticed some people had left in the midst of her solo, including some with children in tow. At least, she reasoned, they had not caused an ugly scene to protest the inclusion of lesbian performers on the program. Taking her bows, Jessica rejoined the Sapphonics' ranks for their finale, Kay Weaver's "Take the Power."

"Rita, your voice ain't as strong as Jess's," Chic said flatly while they dined over steamed rice and phad thai. "You heard her just now. Could you top that?"

Rita glared at her. "I don't even like that honky song."

Jessica raised her brows. "Ay, tu."

"You know what I mean—it's a white chick's song. At least you put some corazón into it, Jessie." Rita swirled a mass of noodles with her fork. "I can do rhythm and blues, Chic. That's what I used to sing whenever I did an open mike."

"What's the harm in giving her a lead once in a while?" Cindi suggested, downing some Thai iced tea.

"*You* want one, too?" Chic gazed at her with narrowed eyes.

Cindi grinned. "What if I said yes?"

"I'll think it over." Chic blew them conciliatory kisses. "Eat up, mujeres. We have a show to do."

Midway through their act, the Satins switched from oldies parodies to Jessica's more recent compositions. A Latina lesbian contingent dominated the first rows and constantly shouted their enthusiasm for the Satins' choice of material. Throughout the performance, Chic had played to them, moving slinkily while flirting with the Satins. She had shed her Latin Satins' jacket and, in her tight purple jeans and tank top, she brushed herself against the other singers suggestively while they provided hip-swinging, shoulder-shaking back-up for her saucy antics. Chic grasped the mike and leaned toward the adoring Latinas in the audience, directing "Pocha Blues" to them.

My brother's brown but not a cholo
He wears Gap jeans and a bolo
He dresses downright snappy
He doesn't wear the khaki

He's got the pocho blues
Not in a gang, he's paid his dues
He's got the pocho blues
He doesn't bang, but still he'll lose

"Fuck los gavachos!" a male voice from the back yelled. "You tell them! We're not into gangs!"

Chic tossed Jessica a nod of approval as the Satins continued with another stanza. No doubt about it, those lyrics lit the emotions of many Latinos present.

My sister has an M.F.A.
In film from U.C.L.A.
She made a flick about Chicanos
Hollywood don't wanna us

She's got the pocha blues
She's smart, she's paid her dues
She's got the pocha blues
Not white, and so she'll lose

The Latinas in front joined in the ruckus. "Right on, Chica! Hollywood never gives us a chance."

When their set ended, the Satins stood at the edge of the stage, holding hands, hair and tank tops drenched with perspiration. They raised their arms in triumph and bowed together. The audience stomped their feet and bellowed, not wanting them to leave. In response, the Satins launched into their trademark theme and introduced themselves. Chic twirled the microphone, letting the applause ebb. "We'll be at the Delta on Main Street at the end of June. Hasta luego!"

Still hand in hand, the Satins darted backstage. Ecstatic, they jumped into each other's arms, holding and kissing each other repeatedly.

Their giddiness extended into Sunday morning. They had gone dancing at the Delta, surrounded by countless devotees, and stayed until the club closed. Billie had been a good sport and taken Angelita home with her to allow Rita the chance to celebrate.

The Satins lounged on Chic's rumpled bed, drinking coffee, feeding each other cinnamon rolls.

"I could make love to all of you right now," Chic vowed, lying amidst a pile of pillows, the sheet barely covering her. She seemed oblivious that her black hair stood in spiky tufts.

"Sin vergüenza," Cindi teased, throwing a handful of crumbs at her.

Chic laughed and ducked. "Nobody wants to take me up on it?"

"You'd rather make love to an audience," Jessica remarked, licking the sticky cinnamon from her fingers. "That was pretty obvious last night."

"Can you blame me? They *loved* us."

"I saw people walk out," Rita differed, stirring her coffee.

"They started that during my solo," Jessica said.

"Sure. The homophobes and the racists," Cindi reasoned. "You probably blew their minds with your solo and the Satins freaked them out with our Chicana commentary."

"Multicultural—we fit into that in more ways than one." Chic yawned and stretched. "Not that I like labels, but I sure dig scrambling anybody's sensibilities. Hell, we ought to do a lot of our dyke lyrics in the backyard sometime to make Efraín hightail it out of town."

Rita giggled, putting aside her cup and slumping beside Chic. "Promise? We can rehearse outside in short-shorts and halter tops since the weather's getting warmer."

"Sure, baby." Though Chic twirled one of Rita's curls around her finger, she spoke to Jessica. "Those new lyrics you dreamed up made quite an impact. Too much, Tamayo."

"I had a blast," Jessica admitted with a smile. "Listen, when you Satins feel like returning to reality, I want you to hear some of my latest stuff."

Rita ran enticing fingers along Chic's tawny shoulder.

"Después," Chic suggested, snuggling closer to Rita.

"They are both insane," Cindi muttered when she and Jessica left them alone.

"If it keeps Rita happy and cooperative, maybe there's a method to Chic's madness."

"Optimist." Cindi headed into the bathroom. "I'm taking a shower then heading to see the family. Mikki's probably bragging to Mom and Dad that we caused another escándalo last night. She said Lulu wants to feature us in the next issue of her 'zine."

"Yeah? We'll be written up in *Lulu's Labios*? What a trip."

"I thought so, too." Cindi laughed. "I'll be back in time for Chorus rehearsal. Want to come with me to see the folks?"

"No thanks. I'm going to work on the songs while I have the time." Jessica grabbed some towels from the hallway cabinet and went downstairs to use the other bathroom.

She flung open the attic's casement windows, allowing the ocean breeze to flow through. Jessica alternately strummed her guitar, plunked out melodies on the portable keyboard, and jotted notes on the composition sheets. Pencil in mouth, she concentrated on "Salsa Sex," a jumpy tune for Chic's distinctive voice, while striving to keep her mind off the bedroom activities on the second floor.

At the Delta, the Satins would work with a band. Keeping that in mind, Jessica was better able to concentrate on rhythm and tempo, tapping her pencil against the desk, imagining a drummer's interpretation of the tune. She immersed herself in sampling lyrics aloud, changing her mind, arguing with herself over the perfect choice of words and phrases.

Yawning, she eventually noticed sunlight filtering over her shoulder from one of the north-facing windows. She realized late morning had become late afternoon. She stood to stretch, the edges of her black Gipsy Kings T-shirt tickling her thighs. Moving to the west windows, she glimpsed a flotilla of sailboats drifting southward along Santa Monica Bay to their slips at Marina del Rey. Jessica wondered what it would be like to climb aboard one of those pretty boats and sail beyond the horizon.

Her stomach rumbled. She patted it soothingly and decided to search the kitchen for a likely meal. She had completely forgotten about eating while working. When she tiptoed downstairs, she heard no sounds on the second floor and suspected Chic and Rita were still in bed. She found a leftover enchilada in the refrigerator and popped it into the toaster oven.

Silence permeated the house. She looked out the kitchen window at the expansive backyard. Even the Zepedas seemed to be gone, probably visiting Berta's relatives on the Eastside. Jessica hoped they would stay away until she left for rehearsal.

She forked the enchilada onto a chipped plate, grabbed some iced tea, and went outside. She eased herself into a rusting lawn chair, poking her bare feet through the dry grass. She ate slowly, watching house finches and sparrows fluttering at the bird feeder.

"A songwriter at work," Chic called from the back porch. She wore a spaghetti-strapped tie-dyed camisole, her tawny legs in denim cut-offs. She strode languorously toward Jessica.

"You should talk."

Chic grinned and sat cross-legged on the grass. "Believe it or not, Rita left hours ago. I've been sleeping."

Jessica chewed the enchilada, absorbing that information.

"No comment?"

"Just this: I hope you know what you're doing."

"Ay, Jess. We had some fun together, like you and me did. What's wrong with that? Rita's a trip when she's having a good time. Too bad she had to go pick up Angelita. They had something planned with Billie."

"Next thing you're going to say is 'write her a solo.'"

"Mind reader."

"Jesus, Chic." Jessica shook her head and kept eating.

Chic pointed to the enchilada. "Any more of that left?"

"This is it."

"You pissed at me?"

"I think you're crazy." Jessica drank some tea, then put down her glass. It teetered a bit on the uneven ground and she bent to straighten it. As she did, Chic placed a hand over hers.

"Rita has a point about R&B. When I saw her at that open mike, she was damn good. Cindi even agrees on that. Otherwise, would I have bothered getting Rita into the Satins?"

Jessica shook her hand free. "You're asking *me* to follow your logic?"

"Ay, Jess." Chic edged closer. "Oh, I get it. Jealousy."

"In your dreams." Jessica looked at her directly. Without makeup, Chic appeared almost pale in the sycamore's shadow. "Rita used to sing 'You're No Good.' Remember that? Maybe she'd like to repeat it in the act. I'd vote for that."

Chic laughed. "You're cold, loca."

"I'm serious. We know she could handle that."

"She wants one of the new songs."

"No." Jessica got to her feet so abruptly, she jarred the glass; the spilled tea immediately absorbed itself in the parched earth.

"You're telling me 'no'?" Chic jumped up beside her. "Since when?"

"Since now. *I'm* the Satins' songwriter. When I write songs for this group, I write them for your voice, in your key, in your style. Damn it, Chic. You haven't even heard all the new material yet. None of it's R&B. And I'm not going to hand over one of *my* songs to let you make points with your lover."

"She *ain't* my lover," Chic retorted, her face inches from Jessica's.

"You could've fooled me."

"Chill out, will you? I'm only tryin' to keep the peace with my Satins."

"And getting some action while you're at it." Jessica did not back down. "You were the one ready to give her the axe when she took a swipe at you."

"Jess, listen to me. Let's get real, okay?" Chic placed a calming hand on her friend's tense shoulder. "On the Promenade, the crowd dug Rita. You saw that. I was ready to kill her when she showed up late. She won that crowd over with her cutesy stuff—shook her nalgita, batted her eyelashes, todo eso—"

"Like a Betty Boop cartoon."

161

Chic ignored that jab. "It's important that each Satin has her own stage personality. I'm the butch vamp, you're the romantic ballad singer, Cindi's the perky back-up, and Rita's little and sexy."

"What's your point?" Jessica appraised her, shrugging Chic's hand from her shoulder.

"You're makin' me forget since you're giving me the evil ojo." Chic's dark eyes glinted with repressed amusement. "Look, we need Rita to round out the group. Face it, she makes more of an impact than Cindi."

"Don't you dare put down my cousin," Jessica hissed.

"I'm not. Chispas! Cindi's real strong on back-up, but she has an easy-going personality. Rita has an edge."

"She's *on* the edge. She sure hasn't convinced *you*." Jessica whirled and hurried up the back steps.

She slammed the empty plate on the sink; it cracked in half. Disgusted, Jessica picked up the pieces gingerly and tossed them into the trash. Through the window, she saw Chic standing by the sycamore, arms crossed, head bent, as if weighing her next move.

Jessica glanced at the Coca-Cola clock. She had to get ready for the Sapphonics' rehearsal. Rather than wait for Cindi to return, she decided to walk to the Y.

She rushed upstairs to change. Leaving the house by the front door, she strode to Ocean Park Boulevard, unwilling to confront Chic again.

12 Like a Lesbian

"Mixed reviews, women," Faye Schneider announced. She ruffled the music sheets on her stand. "As you probably guessed, we raised some hackles at the multicultural faire, starting with our name 'Sapphonics' and winding up with the solo of 'Beautiful Soul.' Several people met me as I came offstage to express their 'disappointment' at our being included in the program—and especially at our choice of material."

Jessica felt Cindi's consoling hand on her arm.

"At least they appreciate a fine voice. They had no qualms about Jessica's delivery." Faye continued, "The lyrics, however, prompted many homophobic comments. I think the fact that we were performing before the dinner break intensified the matter. More children were in attendance then than later. I still think we made the correct decision to include the song. And to choose Jessica as soloist."

In support of Faye and Jessica, the Chorus broke into sustained applause.

One of the altos spoke up. "Faye, you said even our name was objected to?"

"That issue has been raised before. Even the mention of Sappho can cause a controversy these days."

"Dead poet, but still a dyke," the alto muttered.

Jody looked disgusted. "Did anyone actually approach *you*, Jess?"

Jessica shook her head. "No chance. I left right after to meet the Satins for dinner."

"*Our* lyrics are controversial, too, 'cause they have social *and* sexual implications," Cindi added.

"True, but the Satins came on after many families had already gone," Faye remarked. "Well, this experience serves to remind us why we came together in the first place. We're lesbian feminists who happen to be singers, too. Let's hope we won't lose any performing venues as a result."

The chorus members conversed among themselves until Faye tapped her baton for emphasis. "We can continue this discussion at break. We have the Northwest trip ahead. Focus, women. Let's warm up."

"Albert was probably in Saturday's audience with his grandkids." Jessica peeled the rind off an orange, wrapping the pieces in a paper towel. "And he saw us on the Promenade Friday night. He got an eyeful—and an earful."

"He's cool, right? I can't see Albert as a homophobe."

"I don't know, Cindi. I've never told him anything." Jessica broke the orange into pieces and offered her some. She munched the fruit, belatedly worrying about her co-worker's reaction. She had been too high after the performances to consider that. She wanted to talk more about it to Cindi and also to tell her about Chic's latest ploy. Rehearsal break was not the best time for either.

Jody poked Cindi with her elbow. "Don't look so down. All's not lost, dykettes. Jess's ballad caused at least one heart to flutter."

Jessica tossed her a skeptical look.

"Have I ever steered you wrong?" Not giving her a chance to answer, Jody pattered on. "My friend Andrea twisted my arm, bugging me for the scoop on you. Seems you had her floating when you sang 'Beautiful Soul.' When she saw you with the Satins, you sent her even further into orbit."

Cindi giggled. "Chic's usually the one women swoon over."

Her cousin grimaced. "I suppose you told your friend all about me."

"Yup—that you're single and you write the music column for *La-LA Lesbian*—she recognized your name right away," Jody added with considerable glee. "If you Satins hadn't flown after your set, I would've introduced you to Andrea on the spot."

"We went partying at the Delta," Cindi explained. "How come we've never met this friend of yours before?"

"She's only lived on the Westside a few months. Andrea's from my old stomping grounds, the San Gabriel Valley. She moved out here after her father died. Had a hard time dealing with that, plus switching jobs. All that kept her out of circulation."

Jessica nonchalantly ate slices of the orange.

"Catch her," Jody teased, pointing. "Ms. Cool, Calm and Collected. Acts like it's no big deal that Andrea's got a crush on her. Don't you have *any* questions about her, Jess?"

Jessica sighed. Cindi, Chic and everyone else, it seemed, wanted to lure her into the dating scene. This situation seemed too much like a set-up for Jessica's taste.

"If she's *that* terrific—"

"Her name's Andrea Romano."

Cindi squealed. "I know who *she* is—muy adorable, Jess. She was in my dream therapy group at Connexxus."

Jessica's skepticism intensified at that revelation. Unlike Cindi, she tended to be suspicious of lesbians who gravitated to any type of New Age activity.

"Andrea's my hiking buddy. You have to find out the rest yourself." Jody leaned a bit closer. "Want her phone number?"

Jessica swallowed the rest of the orange. "Wait a minute. Whoever said I wanted to meet her? If *she's* so interested in *me*, why should *I* phone *her*?"

"Don't be such a chicken," Cindi muttered.

For once, Jody disagreed. "Andrea *ought* to make the first move. Jess, is it okay if I give her your phone number?"

Jessica hesitated. "You guys know my schedule. I have a job plus a deadline for the Satins' new songs and all these Sapphonics rehearsals for the Northwest trip. When would I ever have time to meet this woman?"

Cindi mumbled something under her breath and stalked off; Jessica knew she had not heard the last from her.

Jody stayed steady. "I have to tell Andrea one thing or another. I promised."

"Tell her to write me a letter."

"You won't say anything to Chic and Rita about Jody's friend, I hope." After rehearsal, Jessica kept her eyes on wide Pico Boulevard while Cindi drove home.

"I can keep a secret." Cindi stopped at a red light. "Andrea's really cute, though. From what I remember, her father was sick when I knew her. Guess she's working on getting over that."

"Kind of like the widow who's interested in Dad. No wonder this Andrea liked my solo." Jessica tried to sound flippant. "Probably could relate to the lyrics."

"To your delivery, most likely. Give yourself some credit, cuz. Chic wouldn't have made you the ballad singer otherwise."

"Well, our fearless leader's willing to let Rita take a shot at a solo—preferably one of the new ones." Jessica turned to her. "I got the word before I left for rehearsal."

"Why does she always take me seriously when it comes to Rita? Remember when I joked about her solo at dinner?" Cindi revved the car forward.

"Sure. *I* turned Chic down flat. And I hope you back me on it, Cindi. Rita's not up to doing the new stuff."

"That's what I say."

•

166

Relieved that neither Chic nor Rita were home, Jessica went to bed right away. She found it difficult to surrender to sleep, her mind filled with Faye Schneider's remarks about the homophobes in Saturday's audience. She felt uneasy and wondered if she had been foolhardy to do the solo with the Sapphonics on the same program as the Satins' Chicana-flavored social commentary lyrics. Though the Satins performed regularly on the Promenade, none of her co-workers nor the mothers of the children had seemed to make the connection that the same Jessica Tamayo who sang Mexican folk songs at Pacific Palms also wrote for and performed with that up-front Chicana group. She wondered if she were truly that invisible or if everyone had merely ignored her after-work activities. She wrote music to express herself and sang for the sheer joy of it, whether the tunes were ranchera duets with her father, feminist anthems with the Sapphonics, or salsa rock with the Satins. Why should she worry about something she did so naturally?

The next morning, still in a reflective mood, she bought a croissant at the Boulangerie on Main Street and rode along the bike path bordering the Pacific, taking a circular route to work. She had not slept much, and the sea air invigorated her.

The ride took longer than anticipated. Arriving at the playschool, she darted into the restroom to freshen up, noting most of the children were already present. Albert waved to her, but she had no time for conversation.

While the children played outside, he joined her on the bench. "You sure do have talent," he said after a long moment.

"Thanks." She sensed his tentative manner. Facing him, she smiled. "Anything else?"

"Jess, if your daddy doesn't mind how you live your life, no reason why I should." Albert's voice grew gentler. "I've always gotten contradictory vibes from you—you're pretty and smart and without a man. I figured maybe you'd been burned. Didn't think there was more to it than that."

She gazed at him with fondness. "I never know how *anyone* will react, Albert, and I'm sorry I didn't confide in you. Being a lesbian is so much a part of me that I sometimes forget people don't know it automatically. In some ways, going into detail about it is like trying to explain why I call myself Chicana, instead of Mexican-American—why you say African-American instead of Negro. People either get it or not. I'm a Chicana lesbian, period. I can't separate either aspect anymore than I can stop singing."

"No need to explain anything to *me*, Jess. That's a honky game." He got up to settle a dispute between two of the children in his play group.

Each coming out was distinct, Jessica mused, fraught with stress and fear. She had begun to bond with Albert from their first meeting, and in his quiet way, he had defused what could have been a tense situation. She cherished his friendship.

She leaned back and closed her eyes, wishing she could cat-nap. When she heard Kathleen Scott call her, she quickly raised her head. The daycare director motioned for her to enter the private office.

"I need a word with you." Kathleen did not make eye contact and her voice sounded unnatural.

Jessica did not have to stare to sense trouble. "Yes?"

"When I hired you, Jessica," Kathleen began, leading the way into the office and shutting the door, "I remember you said besides writing songs, you performed and wrote occasional music reviews. What I didn't realize—because *you* failed to tell me—was that you sing with a—lesbian—vocal group and write for a—lesbian—newspaper." The edges of Kathleen's narrow lips twitched.

"Kathleen—"

"I'm not finished." She spoke rapidly. "Mrs. Romney happened to take Libby to that multicultural faire over the weekend. She was appalled at seeing you perform not once, but twice on the program, both times singing, to quote her, 'quite questionable lyrics.'"

"Kathleen—"

"I am *not* done." She kept her gaze focused on an unseen object over Jessica's shoulder. "Mrs. Romney phoned first thing this morning to inform me. Shortly afterwards I heard from another mother. It seems Mrs. Douglas is taking a sociology class and happens to be doing some research on women's issues. She picked up that—newspaper—at the feminist bookstore, also over the weekend, and saw your name and photo in it. As a result, both mothers have asked to meet with me."

Jessica kept clenched hands deep within her pockets. Trembling, she tried to keep her voice even, free of defensiveness. "I take it you have a problem with—all of this."

"To put it mildly, Jessica. Your behavior is unconscionable. How could you dare carry on like this while simultaneously working with children? You should have known better than to jeopardize your workplace—and yourself."

Jessica felt her temper rise. "Kathleen, why don't you tell it like it is? My being a singer-songwriter really isn't the problem. More than once you've complimented me on the music programs I've started for the kids. And my writing music reviews didn't bother you when you hired me. What's causing the difficulty, obviously, is the *lesbian* aspect. In the three years I've worked here, I've never taken you for a screaming homophobe. My mistake."

Kathleen's pale complexion colored considerably. "I am nothing of the kind! I only wish you'd been completely honest with me. All we need is for these mothers to pull their children out of Pacific Palms. That could have a domino effect on our enrollment."

"And put the place out of business? Like in that movie *The Children's Hour*—except *I'm* not white like Shirley MacLaine and Audrey Hepburn. I'm a brown dyke."

Kathleen's face became scarlet. "Don't you dare accuse me of racism."

"Accuse *you*? What do you think *you're* doing? You've said yourself I've been a role model for the handful of Latino kids enrolled. How dare you question my commitment to them or the others?" Jessica's words tumbled out in fury. "I bring music into the lives of *all* the children. Do you honestly think my hidden agenda is to harm them? Is that what you're *really* trying to say?

"Keep your voice down, please."

"If I have to raise my voice to prove my point, too bad. You *know* I come in every day, mind my business, do my job. Have any other parents ever complained about me? You know they haven't, Kathleen. But because one mother witnessed my performance at a—remember this, multicultural faire—and another curious mother picked up a lesbian newspaper and saw my name in it, all of a sudden I'm a threat to the kids? Maybe I ought to be talking to an attorney, not to *you*."

Kathleen exhaled slowly. "You are jumping to conclusions, Jessica. I am not making accusations. I told you about this situation because I want you to be aware of it. After I meet with both mothers, we'll discuss this in more detail. And, of course, the board of directors and other staff may have to be informed of it, too." Her voice suddenly sounded weary. "In the meantime, I think it's very important for you to go on with business as usual. I'm meeting both mothers tomorrow afternoon."

For the rest of that day, Jessica functioned automatically, unwilling to show her true emotions to Albert or anyone. Her mind filled with dizzying images of sensational headlines: LESBIAN BRAINWASHES TOTS WITH SAPPHIC LYRICS; DYKE DESTROYS WORKING MOMS' DREAMS. She recalled newspaper horror stories of the disrupted lives of daycare workers accused of child molestation; the possibility of that happening terrified her. Mentally, she played back scenes of her interactions with the children. Had she ever been overly affectionate? Could her past behavior ever be misconstrued as provocative or seductive?

She shuddered at those thoughts.

Prior to being interviewed for the Pacific Palms position, she had agonized about whether to be candid about her sexual orientation to Kathleen Scott. At the time, she had been involved with Trish who had counseled against disclosure. Jessica had taken that advice, eager to leave her office job and to at last use her love for music and her community college degree in early childhood education to work with children.

To Jessica's relief, the daycare director had been impressed additionally with her singing talent and her ideas about enhancing the children's daily activities with music. Kathleen had seemed delighted to offer her the position, making it possible to have a talented woman of color join the staff. Ever since, thriving in her job, Jessica had opted to remain in the confining, yet safe, territory of the closet. Her performances with two on-the-fringe vocal groups had seemed unlikely to come to the attention of Kathleen and the middle-to-upper-class mothers whose children attended Pacific Palms. She had figured that, to them, Chicanas, lesbians, and street performers were as invisible as the city's homeless. By afternoon's end, Jessica wondered if her decision to remain discreet about her personal life would cost her the job she loved.

"Jody just phoned." After dinner, Cindi found her cousin on the veranda steps. "She wanted to bug you about Andrea Romano again. I said I'd give you the message. You've sure been quiet tonight."

"Thinking about the new songs. I have to work on them some more before going to bed."

"And not a moment's thought about Andrea?"

Jessica sighed. "C.C., I've never even laid eyes on the woman."

"Aren't you a teensy bit curious?"

"Well, maybe a little." Jessica admitted with a half-smile. She had not spectulated about her so-called admirer since

Sunday night, yet she figured playing along with Cindi would be a smart move. If Cindi wanted to think Jody's friend were partially responsible for triggering the evening's silence, Jessica was not about to state otherwise. She did not want to discuss what really troubled her; she could not bring herself to reveal to any of her housemates the utter shamefulness of having her integrity and her devotion to children questioned.

"Gracias a Dios."

"Oh, stop." Jessica stood and brushed off her shorts. "Whether I'm curious or not, Cindi, this really isn't the best time to meet anyone."

Cindi offered an encouraging grin. "Why not take advantage of the momentum?"

"I have too much on my mind right now." Jessica moved to the door. "For one thing, I'd really like to blow this town."

"We'll be on our way to Seattle real soon. Maybe Andrea will give you something to look forward to when you get back."

Jessica sighed and went into the house.

She wished she had only Andrea Romano to think about, instead of worrying about the possibility of losing her job by the next afternoon. Her mind churning, she spread her music on her desk and endeavored to concentrate. Before long, the musical notes and penciled lyrics became blurs. She was unable to stop the pent-up tears, realizing with sudden clarity the fear Trish lived with daily.

"Can we bother you for a second, oh Satin Songwriter?" Chic's voice called from the second-floor landing.

Jessica swallowed a sob and wiped her eyes with her fingertips. She heard Chic and Rita giggling outside her door.

"Yoooo hoooo, mujer de las canciones."

Jessica felt her trembling lips twitch into a smile. She dimmed the light switch and opened the door.

"Are you guys tipsy?"

"We *did* have a little cerveza for dinner, but we're cold sober." Chic held Rita's hand as they entered. "Jess, que pasó? Estabas llorando?"

"A case of PMS." Jessica shrugged. "You know how it is."

"Still thinkin' about that Yolanda kid?" Chic's voice was uncommonly gentle. "Ah, Jess, you can't—"

"Pobrecita. You have cramps? I can make you some canela to drink, Jessie," Rita offered.

"I'm all right—really." She sniffled and sat on the edge of her futon. "What's going on?"

"Rita's agreed to sing 'You're No Good' when we do the Delta gig."

Jessica glanced at them alternately, wondering if there were a catch to this latest development.

"Ay, no me miras así, Jessie," Rita said, disturbed by her friend's incredulity. "It's true. I won't have time to learn a new song, con interpretation, choreography y todo. I'd rather do something I'm familiar with. Chic's going to help me work on it while you're finishing the other material."

"Well." Jessica felt a bit of relief. "Sounds fine to me."

"We just wanted to let you know," Chic added. "You can get back to work now."

"Okay, boss."

"I'm going to put Angelita to bed. Buenas noches."

"'Night, Rita." Jessica called after her.

Chic crossed her arms and leaned against the open door. "The blues are a bitch, huh? Don't work yourself to the bone, Jess. Call it a night."

"Maybe I will."

Chic studied her for a few seconds before coming over. She bent to kiss her friend's forehead. "See you tomorrow, loca."

Jessica nodded and watched her go.

13 Stop and Wish

"Yolanda, please move into the circle with the other children. Hurry now." Usually, Jessica was patient with the little girl's shyness and her preference for remaining apart from the others. On edge, she heard the sudden sharpness in her voice. Cringing, she immediately caught herself. "That's better. Yolanda, isn't it fun to sit next to Mindy and Allison?"

Yolanda kept her eyes downcast and shook her head.

Jessica gazed at the other assembled children. "Who'd like to play the tambourine today?"

When freckled Allison reached for the tambourine before Yolanda could make up her mind, the Chicanita looked about to cry.

"And who wants to play with Sally Seal?"

"I do! I do!" A chorus of small voices vied for the chance.

Jessica turned again to Yolanda. She sensed the child's desire to make music conflicting with her tendency to keep to herself. Yolanda's brown eyes seemed to silently beseech her teacher for an answer to the dilemma.

Jessica reached toward the little girl, handing her the cuddly puppet. "Here you go, Yolanda."

The child hesitated for a fraction of a second. Then she smiled slowly, her small fingers familiarizing themselves with the furry feel of the prized puppet.

"Put Sally Seal over your hand. That's right. Now let's all

sing "Sea Change, See Change." Seating herself in their midst, Jessica began to strum her guitar.

When I was little it used to be
You could walk a long way by the sea
And watch the waves roll in and crash
Where now there's styrofoam and trash

Whenever I'm there I stop and wish
Life was better for the fish
And the birds who live so free
Who can change that, only we

Yolanda kept the puppet on her small hand, swaying Sally to the beat of the tune. The child seemed to shed her timidity, losing herself in playing with the tiny sea mammal while the other children sang in unison.

Silky Sally Seal swims in the sea
Swims in the sea, swims in the sea
Eats the fish, her favorite dish
I have to tell her about my wish

Let's clean the water and the sand
Fix them always, make a plan
For healthy fish, birds and seals
Wouldn't that be a perfect deal?

Watching Yolanda, Jessica smiled. Her attention did not linger on the child, however. Her eyes wandered to the doorway, expecting to see a stern-faced Kathleen Scott beckon to her. All the while, she kept singing, wanting to vanish into the lyrics.

Silky Sally Seal swims in the sea
Swims in the sea, swims in the sea
Eats the fish, her favorite dish
Let's tell her all about my wish

.

175

When Albert led his youngsters into the playground a few minutes later, Jessica put aside her guitar and encouraged her class to join his. For a while, she sat with him on the bench, though soon grew fidgety and excused herself. Her heart hammered as she made her way toward Kathleen's office. Its door remained shut. She stood in the corridor for a dizzying moment, then decided not to wait any longer. She knocked on the door with more assertiveness than she felt.

When Kathleen opened it, she looked astonished. "Why, Jessica—we're in the middle of—"

"I want to speak with them myself," Jessica said, gazing beyond Kathleen to the two mothers seated stiffly in the office.

"Well, this really is most—"

Jessica felt a rush of adrenaline as she strode into the room with Kathleen following.

"Mrs. Romney, Mrs. Douglas—" Jessica paused before the perturbed women. She did not know either mother well because their children were in other play groups. She realized at once the women were both in their early thirties, close to her own age, yet totally unlike her. "I understand you came to meet with Kathleen because you have some some—concerns—about my outside activities."

"Jessica, this is highly—" Kathleen sputtered.

The noticeably pregnant Mrs. Romney leaned forward in her chair. Her blonde hair was French-braided, pulled back from her high forehead to reveal sky-blue eyes, a pug nose, and an unsmiling mouth. "As a matter of fact, I do," she said.

Mrs. Douglas, a sleek redhead in shiny exercise leotards and an oversized "I love Palm Springs" T-shirt, appeared as if she would have preferred to be in a gym doing aerobics rather than sequestered in Kathleen's office. She furtively glanced at her bracelet-like gold watch and seemed unsure about whether to comment or not.

"Jessica, I really think—" Kathleen began again.

"I want to know what their concerns are. Since I'm the one

at issue here, I do have that right," Jessica added, sweeping her eyes over the three women.

Mrs. Romney cut in. "Ms. Tamayo, I'll tell you what I'm concerned about: your honesty and your sense of propriety." The woman's creamy complexion took on a sudden flush. "My four-year-old daughter Libby has enjoyed the ethnic celebrations at this school. I'm glad about that because I want her to be able to get along with everyone. I took her to the multicultural faire to show her more about other people's music and customs. She tasted foods she's never had before and heard several different languages spoken and sung. While we were there, I *never* expected to see homosexuality flaunted on that stage. That was completely out of line; it had no place on the program. And I certainly did *not* expect to discover a teacher from Libby's school singing about loving another woman. I'm very upset over this, as any mother would be, under the circumstances."

Kathleen made a further attempt to control the flow of the conversation. "I really think we should—"

"Mrs. Romney, let me see if I understand you," Jessica said, turning her back to Kathleen and striving to stay calm despite her rising anger. "Your intention is to educate Libby about others. Well, lesbians and gays are part of the population. We're in schools, churches, in the military, in politics, and in singing groups, too. Sooner or later, Libby would find out we exist. She could even be watching TV someday, switch channels and find the Gay Pride Parade being broadcast."

"I *know* homosexuals exist. That doesn't mean I have to approve of them. No matter what they say, they are *not* a minority group. I don't want my little girl to know *anything* about them. I believe in the sanctity of the family and—"

"Peggy and I are most concerned about what our children are being exposed to here," Mrs. Douglas interrupted. "Before this weekend, Ms. Tamayo, I didn't know anything about you except your ethnic background. I'm not a bigot, mind you—I have a lovely Mexican housekeeper. I think you're wonderful salt-of-the-earth people with close family ties, and inviting your father to sing with you on Cinco de Mayo was delightful. That was a beautiful touch, and I thought how fortunate that the children could see a father and daughter sharing their talent. Then the other day, I walked into a bookstore and found your name and picture in a local publication. You know what I'm referring to. I was quite shocked. If I could find out something—personal—about you that easily, why couldn't anyone else, including the children? How would you be able to answer their questions about your—personal life?"

Jessica struggled to keep her voice steady. "All the children know that I'm a Chicana and I love music. I've told them about my ethnicity because I look different from them and I believe in combating stereotypes by confronting them firsthand. Aside from my ethnicity and my love of music, there's no need for the children to know anything else about me. I'm sure you realize preschoolers can be very self-absorbed, so I doubt if they think about me very much once they get home. Some of the more curious ones have asked if I'm married, if I have kids. I've simply said 'no.' What matters is, when I'm with them, I use music—sometimes Mexican music—to teach them about the environment and history. When I'm away from here, I sing with my father and in public as much as possible. I write music reviews, too. My sexual orientation is my business, no one else's. I prefer to keep my personal life separate, and I'm sure the other teachers feel the same way about maintaining their own privacy."

"The fact is, your privacy was compromised by no one other than yourself," Mrs. Romney reminded Jessica. "You chose to be in the limelight and to sing about an immoral subject."

"Love is not immoral," Jessica said in a firm voice.

"In my opinion, your behavior was unprofessional, Ms. Tamayo, and I, for one, don't want to see it repeated."

"Exactly what does that mean, Mrs. Romney?" Jessica

steeled herself to meet the woman's frigid gaze.

Kathleen abruptly positioned herself between Jessica and the women. "I believe it's time for you to return to your class, Jessica. Let's meet before you go home today."

Jessica hesitated, alternately looking at each woman. Kathleen was flustered, Mrs. Romney's face was taut, and Mrs. Douglas avoided any eye contact.

"All right, Kathleen. I just want all of you to know that bringing music into the children's lives is very important, very meaningful to me. I believe music can educate people and unite them. And I think it's made a definite difference here."

When no one responded, she slowly made her way to the door and closed it behind her.

Preoccupied, Jessica accompanied the uncommonly chatty Mrs. León to the parking lot at the end of the school day.

"After the Cinco de Mayo party," Mrs. León continued, "Yolanda wanted to listen to more música Mexicana. Can you imagine? I wound up going to a music store to buy her some tapes. What's the name of that place on the Promenade?"

"Urban Madness," Jessica said on reflex.

"They have such a huge variety," Mrs. León marveled. "I left Yolanda with her abuelita while I went there Friday night."

Jessica said nothing while pondering the significance of Mrs. León's statement; she felt too demoralized to respond.

Mrs. León clarified the issue. "Pues, I saw you singing with the Latin Satins. I had no idea you knew la Chica Lozano."

Jessica faced her with some defiance. "I've known Chic all my life."

"Like practically everyone who's grown up around here," Mrs. León added with a fleeting smile. "I hadn't seen her for a long time, but I'd heard she was singing around town. She's very good—all of you are."

"We really work at it," Jessica said, changing her tone. "Did you know Chic from the old neighborhood?"

"Her grandmother and my ex-husband's grandmother were amigas. May they rest in peace." Mrs. León seemed to prefer focusing on the Satins. "All four of you complement each other so well, Jessica. I think it was the first time I've seen a Chicana group on the Promenade."

"As far as I know, we're the only ones. We've been singing there for over a year, and we've been together for almost three."

"We need more entertainers like you."

Jessica nodded. Wishing she had the nerve to confide in Helen León about her troubles, she noticed Yolanda tug at her mother's handbag.

"Mommy—"

"Si, mija?"

"I played with Sally Seal today." Her brown eyes sparkled in the late afternoon sunlight.

"The hand puppet," Jessica explained. "Yolanda had Sally dancing her little heart out."

Mrs. León laughed. "Thanks to you, Jessica."

Jessica did not know what to say. In light of the week's disconcerting events and her recent meeting with the two mothers, she felt hypocritical.

"Before I forget—Yolanda has a doctor's appointment Friday. I'll be coming for her earlier."

"Oh." Jessica met her gaze questioningly.

Mrs. León averted her eyes and tugged at Yolanda's hand. Jessica watched them leave, then apprehensively returned to her empty classroom.

"It could have been worse." Kathleen observed Jessica from over her pastel-rimmed glasses when they were alone in the office. "At the end of the meeting, both mothers wanted to be sure we're all in accord."

"On what? Whether or not to fire me?" Jessica paced the narrow room, wanting to rip the nearest community service commendation from the wood-paneled wall.

"Jessica, there's no need to be negative about this." Kathleen remained seated, elbows on her desk. "Although I do have to mention that, due to your decision to burst into the meeting, Mrs. Romney thinks you have an 'attitude problem.'"

"That's probably the least of her opinions. She really doesn't like that I perform in public as an 'out' Chicana lesbian. She'd prefer that I sing to the kids and stay in the closet. Since I've done otherwise—behaved in an 'unprofessional' manner—no wonder she doesn't like my attitude. Believe me, it wasn't easy to keep my temper in line while I listened to her and Mrs. Douglas."

"I realize that. The fact is, I was attempting to do some damage control before you stormed in. Please bear in mind, Jessica, that neither of these mothers can be blamed for raising questions about your qualifications to care for preschoolers. Parents have plenty to worry about these days."

"I know, Kathleen. I read the newspaper."

The daycare director ignored Jessica's comment. "These mothers love their children and want the best for them. They're also aware of the need for diversity among our staff. I feel confident they'll both abide by the board's decision."

"In other words, it's up to the board to decide if my job's on the line?"

"Of course."

"And if I try to hang tight, this whole thing could blow up in my face and turn into a witch hunt?" Jessica stopped and stood before her. "I'll be on vacation when the board has its monthly meeting. Anything could happen. What if I get the axe while I'm gone? Will you leave a message on my phone machine or will I find out by registered mail?"

Kathleen got up and rounded her desk, moving nearer. "Listen to me, Jessica. I *want* you to continue working here. I've never said otherwise. You're wonderful with children. I've told you that many, many times. It's apparent to me every day.

We need more staff of your caliber. I only wish you'd been candid from the beginning, even though I can understand your—reluctance. Please have faith in the board. I doubt very much if any of the members will let you down."

Despite her inner turmoil, Jessica managed to finish two new songs and a large chunk of savvy lyrics for the Latin Satins that week. Most of the new material and some of the parodies seemed more cynical than usual, yet her musical compañeras had no qualms about that. In fact, the Satins—Chic, especially—liked the added satirical edge. The Satins did not realize she had channeled her fears and anger about her work situation into the music.

Jessica had decided not confide in her friends about her problems at work. She had hoped that the matter would blow over of its own accord and that eventually she would be able to laugh about it with the Satins. However, since meeting the two mothers face to face, she was less optimistic about the outcome. She worried that the board would disregard her attributes as a teacher and focus instead on the possible notoriety of her public performances. Sooner or later, she knew she would have to confide in someone about her dilemma, and her cousin Cindi seemed the most likely choice.

Once in a while—on long nights when she could not sleep and did not want to speculate further on the board's upcoming decision, on the impending upheaval of her life—Jessica wondered about Andrea Romano. She congratulated herself for not having taken the time to meet her so-called admirer, not while her stress level was sky-high and her employment situation nebulous. And after receiving no letter, she figured Andrea Romano had reevaluated the matter and had decided not to bother.

14   Even Homegirls Get
the Blues

"You doing your beach walk?"

At dawn, Jessica was startled to hear Chic's voice in the unlit living room. She lay sprawled on the sofa, covered with the granny-squared afghan her grandmother had made many years ago. Drowsily, Chic sat up, her black hair on end, rubbing her eyes and yawning.

"Couldn't sleep, Jess. Came down around 2:00. Can I go with you?"

Jessica nodded. "Well, hurry. Haven't got all day."

"Si, señorita." Chic aimed herself in the direction of the downstairs bathroom.

With impatience, Jessica stuck her hands in her sweat pants' pockets and paced the living room. She was annoyed that her morning privacy would be disturbed. For the past week, she had kept to herself as much as possible, using songwriting as an excuse. She stood by the front door, half-tempted to leave without Chic. Yet, she reasoned, perhaps her friend would provide a needed distraction. No doubt she had a story to tell.

Soon Chic emerged, unsuccessful in smoothing her hair.

"It's too cold for shorts, Chic."

"Homegirl, these are spandex." The tight bike shorts hugged her thighs. Over her head, Chic tugged on a faded red sweatshirt with the ribbing torn off its neck. She adjusted her slouch socks and tied the laces of her black hightops. "My femmy butch bod will warm up soon, loca."

"*You're* the loca," Jessica muttered, unlocking the door and heading outside. She shivered in her grey sweats and teal windbreaker, but Chic seemed unaffected, matching her long strides down the driveway.

"Let's go to the pier."

Jessica paused on the sidewalk. "We don't have time."

"I'll give you a ride to work when we get back." Chic glanced at her. "Humor me, Jess."

Jessica sighed. "What's your problem?"

"Thought you'd never ask."

"I take it Rita's wrapped up in it somehow." Jessica cast a swift look at Chic's pensive face.

The friends moved briskly to Ocean Park Boulevard, past fresh placas spray-painted on a brick wall, then westward to the Pacific.

"I love how you catch on," Chic answered dryly. "Have you realized me, Rita and the kid will have the house all to ourselves when you and Cindi take off with the Sapphic Songbirds? I'll be alone with them for *ten* days, Jess. Rita can hardly wait to play house—like Lucy, Ricky and Little Ricky. *I'm* ready to hide out at Rafi's."

"Fear of commitment strikes again, huh?" Jessica laughed. She had missed bantering with Chic.

"I'd *never* be committed to her—no way, José! I've only been trying to keep things smooth for our gig at the Delta. Rita actually thinks I'm *serious* about her."

"Can you blame her? You've been all over her."

"How do you know?" Chic raised her brows. "Been listening at the old bedroom door?"

"I'm not blind—or deaf either."

The air was cool and damp, though it did not disguise the urine smell emanating from a clump of bushes; someone had relieved himself recently. Down the hill, the friends passed the fading Jane Golden mural of the halycon days of the Santa Monica Pier, and on the opposite side of the street, the small wood-framed structure of the Ocean Park branch library. Someone lay sleeping near its steps.

Chic took on a brooding tone as they crossed Main. "Rita's reading a whole lot more into this than sex." She strode in unison with Jessica. "When you and I got it on that night—"

"That was a mutual decision, Chic. We gave each other a hand, un poco de mano a mano. Neither of us expected anything else from each other."

"Yeah." Chic walked faster. "Why can't Rita operate on that frequency?"

"Obviously, she doesn't want to. For one thing, she has Angelita and wants some security in their lives. For another, she and I are two different women."

"That's the understatement of the year." Chic scratched her head. "Maybe there's some truth to this 'dysfunctional family' shit."

"What?" Jessica turned to gaze at her as they drew closer to the beach.

"Rita comes from a big family—all her brothers and sisters are married. Her mom and dad are always there for her, even if Rita doesn't want to live with them. She wants her freedom, to a certain extent, anyway." Chic cleared her throat. "Then look at you. Tudy raised you and Vickie—all three of you're single. You didn't have your mother around, and neither did I. Tudy did the best he could, and so did mi abuelita. It's a fact that you and I have a definite hang-loose attitude compared to Rita."

"Chic, your grandmother gave you plenty of love and stability," Jessica said softly.

"Hell, yes. I don't know where I'd be if it hadn't been for her. Old man in jail, mi mamá dead. Poor Abuelita. She didn't know what the fuck to do with me most of the time. How do you think she felt when las madres del barrio would tell her I'd been diddlin' their hijitas and that's why I couldn't play with them any more?"

Jessica touched Chic's arm. "As far as I know, Dad never said anything like that to her."

Chic seemed curious. "Was Tudy wise to me?"

"I think so. He knew we spent lots of time together. He's always liked your spunk, Chic. And the fact that you love to sing."

"Plus I was safer than boys. I wouldn't get you pregnant," Chic added with the remnant of a grin.

"Maybe you have. My period's late."

Chic gave her a nudge. "Don't blame *me*. Hey, you're probably late 'cause you're jittery about your trip and the songs y todo. At least you won't have to worry about uptight audiences when you sing at that chorus festival. Wish *I* was going somewhere."

"You're going with me to the pier," Jessica joked.

"The highlight of the month, if you ask me." Chic yawned. On reflex, the friends crossed to the other side of the walkway on noticing several transients crouched by the side of a closed seafood restaurant. The unkempt men called out for "spare change." When the women did not answer and took quicker strides, one man yelled something incomprehensible after them.

Jessica and Chic were too streetwise to respond to the taunt. Many transients along the beach were mentally ill and best avoided.

"Does it ever bother you to see homeless white people?" Jessica turned to her friend when the men were far behind.

"No chance. What goes around comes around."

"Chic, those guys back there might've been Vietnam vets or laid off from their jobs. Don't be so hard line. When I first started noticing homeless folks around here, I couldn't believe that most of them were white."

"Don't matter to me, Jess. They all came to California thinkin' it was the land of plenty. It ain't anymore. So maybe they ought to go back where they came from. *They're* the foreigners."

Jessica sighed. For several minutes, she continued beside Chic in silence. She studied the flocks of Western gulls resting on the sand, south of the pier. Being with Chic, she felt a long-time affinity, whether they agreed or not. It bound them, much as instinct kept the gulls together, huddled and quiet.

The women drifted past the volleyball nets and children's swings and climbed a set of concrete steps. Beyond that was a ferris wheel and other carnival rides. They trod the planked walkway around the building that housed the restored carousel, and emerged on the pier. They strolled by closed video arcades, fish markets and garish souvenir stands.

Jessica's voice was low. "Want to go all the way out?"

Chic nodded. "Did I ever tell you the old man brought me here the day mi mamá died? He was drunk and blubbering." She pointed to one of the shooting galleries. "Somehow or other, he showed me how to aim a damn rifle at those fuckin' phony ducks. We blasted them for hours."

Jessica slowed her pace and touched her friend's arm. "Chic, is everything all right?"

"Had to get the hell out of that house." Chic looked at her through clouded eyes. "When you made that crack about being pregnant—all of a sudden I flashed on my mother. Don't ask me why. Never think about her anymore."

"I didn't mean to—"

Chic did not let her finish. "She died of eclampsia—'cause of no prenatal care. She got convulsions, went into a coma. The old man was never the same after that. Left me with Abuelita and went on the bender of his life. Then got mixed up with a bunch of losers and wound up in Folsom for armed robbery. Chico Lozano—stupid cholo. Stabbed to death before he even knew how to live."

Chic came to a halt; Jessica did likewise. She stood very close to her and did not interrupt.

"Damn it, Jess. None of them will ever see I'm going to make it, one way or another. Know what I mean?"

"Yes." Jessica touched her arm gently and guided her to the pier's steel railing. "I know exactly what you mean. Who the hell knows where *my* mother is?"

"*My* whole family's dead."

"I'm not." Jessica let her solacing fingers knead Chic's tense shoulder. "You've been mi hermana as far back as I can remember."

Chic's lips quivered. She blinked rapidly, hiding her emotions by moving behind Jessica. Tenderly, she brought her arms around her friend's waist. She stood very still and rested her chin on one of her compañera's shoulders.

Jessica stared at the outgoing fog, the haze of smog already smudging the horizon. She knew Chic craved her nearness, not words; she let Chic lean on her, expecting nothing in return.

Frothy white waves licked the pier's structural supports. A Western gull sailed overhead. Before too long, Chic let her hands slide downward into the pockets of Jessica's sweat pants.

"My hands are cold," she whispered.

On Saturday morning, Arturo Tamayo helped his daughter and niece unload their luggage from the El Camino to the curb outside one the terminals at Los Angeles International Airport. Their housemates had wished them well the previous evening, and gone their separate ways. Since the morning at the pier, Chic had, aside from rehearsals, spent less and less time at the house. Jessica and Cindi had been too excited preparing for their trip to Seattle to notice much else.

"Ándale, muchachas." Arturo rubbed his hands together in the morning chill. "Have a good time, eh?"

"Bye, Dad." Jessica hugged him tightly, inhaling his familiar scent. Not a frequent traveler, she felt a sudden pang at leaving him. "And thanks again for buying our plane tickets."

"Tío Tudy, you really saved the day for us."

"Pues, how many Tamayos have sung outside California? I'm proud of you two. Use the money you saved to enjoy yourselves."

Cindi hugged him, too. "Without being too obvious about it, can you check the house once in a while?"

"Cómo no," he assured her. "To make sure Efraín doesn't cause any more trouble, eh?"

"I think we're more concerned about Chic and Rita."

Arturo laughed. "Don't worry about anything. And send me a postcard."

On the flight to Seattle, Jessica gazed out the window at the fluffy coastal clouds. She hoped the change of scenery from arid southern California to the verdant Pacific Northwest would prove beneficial and ease her shattered nerves. She wanted to forget her daily realities, and could not imagine a better way to accomplish that than by spending a week singing with her Chorus pals and networking with other singers and songwriters from all over the country.

After the first eventful day of the Festival of Gay and Lesbian Choruses at the University of Washington campus, Jessica sat on the stone ledge surrounding a fountain not far from the campus library. Being suddenly thrust among scores of singers, songwriters and musicians had proved an overwhelming experience. She scanned the week's program, noting the rehearsal times for the women's choruses. Each would present its separate performance, and on the final evening, the assembled women's choruses would perform an original composition together.

Jessica waited while Cindi and Jody conversed with members of one of the San Francisco groups. Like Yolanda León, she found herself preferring to remain apart until she became accustomed to the heady environment. Jessica wondered how the little girl would fare during her absence; maybe Yolanda would have to get used to her teacher's permanent departure. With all her heart, Jessica hoped that would not be the case.

.

When Cindi and Jody caught up with her, they decided to splurge on a Chinese dinner in the nearby University district.

"Some hot ones in that Frisco chorus, huh? Makes me feel like Andrea, seeing all these women I might never meet." Jody rubbed a pair of balsa chopsticks together before plunging into her meal. "Speaking of Andrea, I hear she's nervous about writing to you."

Jessica slurped a bit of won ton soup and glanced at her across the table. "Oh, yeah—Andrea. Why?"

Cindi looked exasperated with her cousin while Jody was not about to drop the subject. "Believe it or not, Ms. Singer-Composer-Music Reviewer, if I didn't know you myself, *I'd* be intimidated, too."

"Jody, I'm the least threatening dyke I know," Jessica scoffed.

"Sometimes talented types seem unapproachable," Cindi remarked.

"I think that's what Andrea thinks," Jody said, munching an eggroll. "She's stumped about how to get to know you, Jess. She really likes what she's seen of you, thinks you're a fantastic performer. If the Satins had a cassette out, she'd be the first to buy it. She has it bad. Can't I just give her your phone number?"

"This isn't a good time," Jessica said calmly. "I thought I'd already made that clear. I haven't finished the new songs, Jody, and it doesn't look like I'll have much time to work on them this week. We have so many rehearsals for the finale."

Jody's eyes became more amused than annoyed. "It's going to be tough to crack your walls. Would you pass the sweet and sour shrimp?"

Jessica pushed the serving dish closer to her and went back to her soup. For several moments, Cindi watched her.

"We can work on the song we're writing together tonight. We have to hop to it anyway, cuz. The Delta gig's coming up and we still have to learn the stuff."

"Right. Mid-June's the absolute latest for that. Then we're booked for two weeks."

Jody sighed and swept a crumpled napkin across her mouth. "Which means you won't have time for Andrea till—"

"We're finished with our gig." Jessica wondered if she would be embroiled in a legal controversy by then, all the while collecting unemployment checks. "You guys, I don't get this whole deal. This kind of stuff never happens to *me*. How can Andrea tell whether I'm worth it? She really doesn't know *anything* about me."

Cindi poured Jessica another cup of tea. "Damn it, cuz, you'd better believe you're worth it. Just 'cause you don't flaunt your sex appeal like Chic doesn't mean you don't have any."

"It's sure about time someone noticed you," Jody agreed.

Shrugging, Jessica cracked open a fortune cookie. When she checked the message, she crumpled it against the bottle of soy sauce.

Jody quickly unfolded it. "It says 'Imagination is more important than knowledge.'"

The three of them looked at each other and burst out laughing. Despite her mirth, Jessica wondered if that fortune could possibly refer to Mrs. Romney's and Mrs. Douglas's homophobia as well.

Housing accommodations for the Sapphonics and other choruses were scattered throughout university dorms. In the room she shared with Cindi, Jessica lay quietly, waiting for sleep. She wondered if Andrea Romano would be so enthused to meet her if she were aware of Mrs. Douglas's and Mrs. Romney's concerns, of the possible notoriety involved. Yet, at the same time, she grew increasingly curious about her admirer. Jessica had been in those shoes a few times herself, hopelessly attracted to unattainable women. Not that she put herself in that category, but she understood Andrea's seeming frustration. Despite that and her own curiosity, she knew keeping her job and writing the new songs had to remain her top priorities.

"Jess, how come you're still awake? Does my book light bother you?" Cindi leaned on one elbow and put aside her paperback mystery. She studied her cousin in the single bed next to hers.

Recalling the day's observations, Jessica had a ready answer. "I've been thinking about how strange it is to be around so many white gay male choruses. That New York chorus is enormous! The men obviously have more financial backing than lesbians do. Then I look around and see how few people of color join any of these groups. Is that because fewer of us are out? Or is it due to the racism of white lesbians and gays?" She shrugged. "Plus I'm experiencing a weird combination of PMS and rapid-fire creative thoughts."

"Racism, cramps and lyrics coming together all at once?"

"Something like that." Jessica lay on her back and stared at the knotty pine ceiling. She was exhausted and wondered why the people upstairs were still moving around.

"I doubt if you can do anything about the racism angle this week. Maybe you can get a song out of it." Cindi leaned closer. "Didn't you just have your period?"

"It never came."

"Well, take a Midol, then write down the lyrics quick." Cindi yawned. "You're not having second thoughts about the ones we wrote tonight, I hope?"

"No. I think they're right on, Cindi. 'Domestic Hectic' has a social slant and a great beat. Your input really made the difference." She lay on her side, watching her cousin, debating about the timeliness of confiding in her at last. "How come you're not asleep?"

"I'm not used to being away from home." Cindi looked embarrassed to be homesick. "I can't believe I'm saying this, but I miss my homegirls—all that high drama between Chic and Rita. And I know what you mean about all the white gays and dykes here. We're definitely outnumbered. Maybe we could talk?"

Jessica smiled. "I'm not sure if a heavy discussion will make you sleepy."

"Actually, I thought ex-girl friends would be a better topic. Some of them were enough to put me to sleep then. They ought to do the same now. You go first."

Jessica felt too tired to engage in an in-depth revelation of her problems. Despite her fatigue, she took up Cindi's light-hearted challenge instead. "Give me a few minutes to refresh my memory. It's been *so* long."

Cindi giggled and punched her pillow into a lopsided marshmallow. She lay facing Jessica.

"C.C., let me just ask one thing first. Is Andrea Romano out of the closet?"

Her cousin was amazed. "You're finally getting interested?"

"Answer the question."

"According to Jody, Andrea's 'out' at work at the Women's Legal Center. She was in that dream therapy group 'cause she was having weird nightmares—like premonitions, I guess—about her dad's death. Jody says all that's been resolved and Andrea seems like she can face anything now. I liked her, Jess. You would, too."

Jessica did not look at Cindi while she spoke. "I asked 'cause I'm tired of meeting—and getting involved with—women either on the verge of coming out, or stuck in the closet. Whether they're white or of color, that type seems to be the only ones to go for me in a big way."

"'Cause you're compassionate. Anyone can see that."

"Yeah, right. From some of these lesbo wannabes, I get comments like 'Oh, Jessica. You're so safe to be with. When I'm ready to go all the way, I'd like it to be with someone like you.' What a copout."

"Not as bad as white women who go after us 'cause we're women of color and they have to prove they're not racists. I've had it with *them*."

"You're right—they're the worst. At the DeLovely DeDykeful show, one gavacha actually said to me, 'I bet your nipples are sooo remarkably brown—'"

Cindi laughed so hard she almost fell out of bed.

Jessica did not miss a beat. "—and I said, 'I *know* yours are too pink for me.' Chic was next to me and really got a kick out of my comeback."

Cindi raised herself into a sitting position, trying to catch her breath. "Who do these white chicks think they are, huh?" She grew serious at once. "Is that the problem, Jess? You're thinking Andrea's that type? Listen, she's not. She's Sicilian-American—almost as brown as us. In fact, she doesn't even refer to herself as 'white.' In the dream group, she called herself 'Mediterranean.'"

"Interesting." Jessica wanted to swerve away from the subject of Andrea Romano. "Okay. Now you tell me one."

Cindi leaned against the bed's plank headboard. "Well, let's see. Once I went out with this therapy junkie. And she says, 'I notice you use a lot of negative language. For instance, why do you refer to yourself as 'stubborn?' And I threw back: 'Cause it's true, and if you keep up this line of conversation, you're going to find out exactly *how* stubborn I am."

Jessica grinned at that. "What about the kind who thinks just 'cause I can write love songs I'm romantic to the core? That type isn't prepared if I cut it off 'cause I'm bored. I think Chic has that problem, too—especially nowadays."

"Ay, Jess. You and Chic are so fickle."

"Not really. Well, I'll speak for myself. After a lot of ego-deflating experiences—especially after Trish—and all the worries about safe sex, too, I've learned to get by on my own. It wasn't like this when we first came out, remember, Cindi? The world has changed so much since then, and so have I. I'm not as eager to get involved. Nowadays, I *know* what I love—music, kids—then women. I suppose lots of dykes would think my priorities are out of sync."

Cindi's eyelids seemed to droop; she lay down. "Cuz, who cares what they think? *I* think you're pretty smart to find another way to get by."

"You're probably the only one who feels that way." Jessica cleared her throat and faced her drowsy cousin. She spoke on impulse. "A mother whose daughter is enrolled at Pacific Palms went to the multicultural faire. She saw me do the solo with the Sapphonics. Cindi, I may not have a job when I get home."

"Huh?" Cindi sat up, immediately alert. "They *can't* fire you for that, Jess."

"Why not? Pacific Palms is privately owned. We're talking about preschoolers, remember? Can't have an 'out' dyke around innocent kids, can we? Who cares if I started a successful music program at the school? The board's supposed to meet on the issue this week."

"Dios mio! So that's why you've been so spaced out lately."

Jessica nodded. "Can you blame me?"

Cindi quickly left her bed to sit beside her, and Jessica snuggled close. Her cousin stroked her shoulders gently. "How can anyone think *anything* bad about you? That's unbelievable."

Jessica sniffled. "Promise you won't tell anybody—not even Chic?"

"How can you keep all this to yourself, Jess? You need *everyone's* support."

"Only if it gets worse. Promise me, Cindi."

Her cousin sighed. "I'll promise—for now."

"Remember, women," Faye Schneider advised the Sapphonics shortly before their evening performance. "Never mind that this audience will be friendly. Don't ever relax on stage. Stay on your toes. We've heard some excellent groups this week. Now we'll show these folks that southern California has marvelous singers, too."

"Let's hear it for Faye," one of the sopranos called while the Sapphonics congregated outside Meany Auditorium. "We wouldn't be here without her."

The chorus clapped spontaneously in honor of its conductor. Faye responded with a quick bow. She took Jessica's arm and walked with her on their way to the backstage entrance.

"Nervous?"

Jessica nodded. "I've never sung before an audience this size. I'm going to pretend I'm singing only for you, Faye."

"Be still my heart." Faye enveloped her in a bolstering hug.

Midway through the Sapphonics' performance, the spotlight caught Jessica in its unblinking glow while she glided to the microphone. She sensed the hushed audience's rapt attention and seized the moment. Taking the mike from its stand, she clutched it with both hands. Slowly, she licked her lips, raising the microphone to her mouth. Smiling, acting more confident than she felt, Jessica gazed at the shadowy audience and began to sing.

Far from home, she could almost forget the anxiety that plagued her. Channeling her deep-seated emotions into music, she faced the packed auditorium and sang with an intensity that elicited admiring murmurs throughout her performance, and lingering applause at its conclusion.

At the festival's end, the Sapphonics met for Sunday brunch at the Space Needle. Champagne glasses raised, they sat in the revolving restaurant, admiring the panoramic view of Puget Sound and basking in their first out-of-state performance.

"How many dykes will move to L.A. after seeing Jess do

her solo? Thousands!" Jody saluted her. "Andrea Romano, eat your heart out!"

Jessica glanced about in embarrassment while the Sapphonics whooped it up. "Jody, you don't have to broadcast that."

"Why not? The stage door sisters waited for *you*. You moved them in more ways than one, honey."

"They liked the Sapphonics, period."

"Be modest if you want. I won't keep my mouth shut about your Seattle debut." Jody chuckled. "I phoned Andrea and told her to get over her hangups. If she doesn't move fast, someone else will. You little old heartbreaker, you."

Jessica gazed at her in exasperation. Cindi winked and grabbed another piece of danish.

15   Brown Ladies

The cousins stayed in Seattle after the festival ended. Neither had been that far north and, with the money they had saved, they decided to play tourist. They sailed to Victoria, British Columbia on the Victoria Clipper, explored the quaint shops and the Royal British Columbia Museum. With their black hair and brown skin, both were amused by Canadians mistaking them for Native Americans, as if Chicanas were rare sights north of the U.S. border. In the days they spent together, Jessica felt relieved to continue sharing her worries with Cindi, yet in her fun-loving cousin's company, she was able to temporarily shelve them as well.

"Órale, mujeres," Chic yelled. Leaping, waving both arms, she did not fail to attract the cousins' attention when they emerged from the airline passenger ramp at LAX.

"Hey, loca." Jessica threw her flight bag on an empty chair and grabbed Chic. "How's la jefa? Really missed you."

"Me, too," Cindi said, burrowing into their midst.

"Yeah?" Chic kissed each one enthusiastically. "Chispas! Why didn't you at least phone once in a while? A postcard ain't enough when you're in that big casa all by your lonesome."

At her last remark, Jessica and Cindi pulled back.

"What?"

"Where's Rita?"

"With Tremaine." Chic grinned, seemingly thrilled to make that revelation. "The Ryot Garde got a recording contract. Tre and his rappers came back to L.A. to cut the album. And he wants 'his woman and his baby' back," she added, with a deeper voice and swagger.

"Are you kidding?"

"No way. Let's get goin'. Tengo tanto hambre. I'll clue you in while we eat."

The three friends bumped knees and munched hamburgers at a sunny outdoor café on the Venice Boardwalk. Cyclists and skaters zoomed by, mobile rainbows in fluorescent outfits. Jewelry and tie-dye vendors plied their artistry while destitute men and women panhandled among the beach crowds.

"Tremaine showed up like two days after you guys skipped," Chic revealed, smothering her hamburger with hickory sauce. "Rita wasn't back from work yet and I was boppin' around tryin' to change my clothes and split before she got home. Angelita was playin' out in front. All of a sudden, I heard this falsetto mitote. First thing I thought was, Xochi's at it again. I flew downstairs and out the door. And there's Brother Tremaine, big as life, kneeling on the grass, hugging Angelita like he couldn't believe he found her. She was crying up a storm and hanging onto him, too."

"Rita's friends told him where to look?" Jessica dipped a French fry into a puddle of Chic's hickory sauce.

"Right. So I said, 'Hey, Tre. Where've you been, man?' The brother said he just got off the road. Told me about the contract, even said he'd see what he could do for us. Hell, good thing I was smart enough to keep mi boca loca shut about Rita and me 'cause he wanted to see her right away. He stayed outside with Angelita while I phoned Starbucks."

Jessica raised her brows. "How did Rita take all this?"

"At first she was really freaked." Chic batted her eyes in an

199

outlandish imitation of Rita. "But she ain't stupid. She said to keep Angelita with me and to tell him to meet her at Starbucks. I think Rita figured he'd take Angelita and run."

"I hope you cooperated, Chic," Cindi cut in.

"You bet your chones I did. The man was like a cosmic bolt from el cielo." Chic signalled to the punk-haired waitress for another Corona. "I took Angelita to Urban Madness, rented some Disney flicks, and we came back to watch 'em. I've always liked *Dumbo*," she admitted with no trace of embarrassment. "When Rita didn't come back all night, I figured things'd gotten serious."

Jessica felt dizzy at the revelations. "Where are they now?"

"With Tre in a rented house a few blocks from here."

"How long will *that* last?" Cindi took another French fry. "Rita can't seem to make up her mind if she's gay, bi or straight."

Chic shrugged. "That's Rita for you. Shit, maybe she can work things out with Tre. All I know is—she's still singing with us, at least for our Delta gig. After that, quién sabe?"

Jessica was quiet. She already missed Angelita.

When Chic and Cindi invited her to a movie on the Promenade, Jessica opted for staying home, reorienting herself. Without Angelita, the Victorian seemed larger, emptier. No child's coloring books nor stray toys remained in the old house. The butterfly net and even the teddy bear cookie jar were gone from their usual places in the kitchen. Sighing, Jessica poured herself a glass of grape juice, took an aspirin from the bottle on the pantry shelf, downed it with the juice, and wandered back to the living room.

Her lower back ached, and not having menstruated in over a month added to her worries; the premenstrual symptoms in Seattle had been a false alarm. Although she realized her stress level remained high, she rarely had irregular periods.

Tomorrow, she promised herself, she would phone the women's clinic for an appointment, but only after she had met with Kathleen Scott. If she wound up jobless, she would be unable to afford a pelvic examination.

She felt tired, anxious, and more than a bit depressed. At the festival in Seattle, she had networked and solidified friendships with other singers and songwriters; she longed for that daily excitement. She still had the challenging assignment of finishing the Latin Satins' songs, yet how would she continue to cope with the uncertainty of her work situation?

Rubbing her lower back, Jessica flipped through the accumulated mail Chic had tossed in a haphazard pile on the piano bench. She separated hers from Cindi's, plucking out a letter-sized envelope with unfamiliar handwriting addressed to her. For several seconds, she stared at the rounded letters spelling her name, the triple-toned hummingbird rubber-stamped on the recycled paper, the return sticker reading "A. Romano" in the left-hand corner. She sank to Tía Irene's overstuffed sofa, carefully opened the envelope and spread the folded stationery on her lap.

Dear Jessica,
This may seem a bit unorthodox, but I am writing to tell you that I'd like to meet you. . . .

Swiftly, her eyes swallowed the introductory paragraph and the rest of the page made her pause.

"A few weeks ago I saw you at the Malibu Lagoon. I was near the Adamson House, photographing a night heron, and you were on the other side. Usually, I don't approach someone I don't know and I tried to work up my courage. Then I saw you going toward the highway bridge. I decided to meet you halfway. By the time I got there, you were gone.

Jessica's heart somersaulted. She conjured up her memory of the olive-skinned woman with the gilded brown hair, her appealing figure, the muscular curves of her legs. She felt dizzy as she read on.

I thought I had lost my only chance to meet you. In some ways, I felt ridiculous because I didn't even know if you were a lesbian. It's hard to tell sometimes by the way birders dress. Some look like dykes, but aren't! When Jody told me the Chorus would sing at the multicultural faire, I went to see her perform. She's a good friend, and I'd never taken the time to see her sing with the Chorus. And then—you were there, too! I thought, I'm getting another opportunity, but you vanished again. The way I see it now, if I don't go after things in life, I'd never know what could happen, and would always wonder, 'what if?' This time, I don't want to flub it. So here I am, Jessica, taking a chance."

With a sigh, Jessica leaned back. She recalled Andrea's intensity, her concentration, the fluid lines of her body. She also remembered fantasizing about making love with her, turning to Chic as a substitute lover.

"What if?" she repeated aloud. Did *she* dare take a chance, too? She glanced at the letter again.

Jody told me you made a hit in Seattle. I'm not surprised. She said you're involved with your music and I can understand that. She also said you like to birdwatch. I pretended to know nothing of this and didn't tell her I'd noticed you at the lagoon. Maybe I'll see you there this Saturday morning.

Jessica left the letter on the sofa. She drank half the glass of grape juice and paced the living room for a few minutes. She noticed which floorboards creaked, how many ceiling cracks had appeared since the last earthquake. She walked to the screen door and looked out. The grass was dryer; Chic had forgotten to water it. Everything seemed too silent, too still without Angelita playing in the yard.

She went into the bathroom and stared at herself in the mirror. Her eyes seemed bewildered beneath shaggy bangs. She pushed back her hair and looked at her narrow brown face with its thin nose and thick black brows. She half closed her eyes, making them sultry, licked her lips invitingly, the way she did when she sang. Then she contorted her face and stuck out her tongue.

She returned to the sofa and reread the letter twice. Andrea Romano sounded upfront. She had even included her phone number at the bottom. But could she fully understand Jessica's introverted personality, her need to be creative—and, in particular, her current dilemma?

Before her housemates returned, Jessica went to her attic bedroom and unpacked. She sorted the dirty laundry and stuffed it into a pillow case. She heaved the luggage into a corner of the attic beneath one of the eaves. She stayed on the window seat for hours, watching the moon shadowed by clouds, before creeping to the futon to sleep.

At dawn, she sat up, switched on the lamp, and reached for the stationery she had left on the bookcase beside her futon. She determined to put her doubts and worries aside and concentrate on preparing a message to Andrea. In some ways, she almost felt as if the woman were reaching out to her, daring her to respond. Tightly, Jessica held the Bic pen, willing the words to come.

"You're back!" Yolanda León let go of her mother's hand and hurtled across the parking lot to Jessica. The little girl grew more reticent as she approached, yet she wrapped ecstatic arms around her teacher's denim-clad legs.

Jessica untangled herself gently and knelt beside her locked bike to greet Yolanda. She was careful to refrain from touching the child.

"It's good to see you, Yolanda. Ten cuidado about running across the parking lot. There could've been a car coming."

"Jessica's right, mija." Mrs. León wore a navy-and-white pinstripe suit with a white, yellow and navy patterned scarf at her neckline. She smiled. "Yolanda's missed you so much."

"The kids were on my mind a lot, too," Jessica admitted.

Mrs. León adjusted one of the red bows in her daughter's hair. "Go inside with the other niños, mija. I'll see you más tarde."

Yolanda reluctantly did as she was told. Jessica fidgeted. She wanted to check and arrange the classroom before the other children arrived.

"I know you're in a hurry, Jessica, pero—"

At Mrs. León's serious tone, Jessica met her gaze questioningly.

"While you were gone, Mrs. Romney contacted some of the other mothers—about you."

Jessica felt an abrupt queasiness in the pit of her stomach.

Mrs. León reached over and grasped the younger woman's elbow, as if to bolster her. "They have no right to cause this trouble for you. You've worked miracles with Yolanda. Éstas gringas—always ready to shoot us down, verdad?"

Jessica sighed. "There's more than racism involved here."

"Ya lo sé. Mrs. Romney told everyone about the songs at the multicultural faire, and Mrs. Douglas brought a copy of the magazine to show us."

Jessica's knees weakened. Her mind whirled with a montage of the stark photo of the dominatrix on the cover of *La-LA Lesbian*, her romantic ballad with the Sapphonics, the confrontational lyrics of the Satins' tunes.

Mrs. León retained her grip on Jessica's elbow while her words tumbled out. "Eso no me importa. Haven't these mothers ever heard of artistic freedom? So much for their being patrons of the arts. And some of them even have husbands who are entertainment lawyers. You'd think they'd know better. I swear, if it weren't lesbians these women were after, it'd be someone or something else." Mrs. León looked at her directly. "Yolanda talks about you all the time, Jessica. She *loves* you.

And I want you to know *I'm* with you. It's made all the difference in the world for Yolanda and los otros niños de color to
have you here." She reached into her handbag and offered
Jessica a business card. "I'm the office manager at the Women's
Legal Center. I've already told Mrs. Romney I'll refer you to
one of our attorneys if she doesn't let up."

Jessica felt numb, yet she clutched the card within the palm
of her hand. "Thank you, Mrs. León. I really appreciate this."

"My name is Helen." She let go of Jessica's elbow and began to move away. "And I hope I won't have to see you in my
office."

Kathleen Scott averted her gaze in answer to Jessica's question. "The board hasn't been able to meet. One of the members
was called out of town on a family emergency, and since you
were away, too, the other members decided to postpone the
matter temporarily. The board won't be able to conduct business until the end of next week."

"You expect me to sweat it out in the meantime?" Jessica
kept her hands on her hips to keep them from shaking.
"Kathleen, I never thought you'd be a party to these delay
tactics."

The director rose and closed the office door. "Whether you
believe it or not, Jessica, I am appalled by this whole situation,
especially by the behavior of these mothers. They never
should've contacted other parents on their own accord. They
seemed reasonable enough when we spoke."

"What're you going to do about it?" Jessica struggled to
control her temper. "Either you tell them to lay off or *I* will."

"Please don't confront them again. That could turn into an
even uglier situation. You're too upset."

"How else can you expect me to react?" Jessica sighed and
clenched Helen León's business card tighter. "I still can't believe this is happening. I thought I was over being naive."

"Well, I think we've *both* been naive. No matter how

difficult this is for you, Jessica, please try to be a little more patient."

"Kathleen, I don't know how long I can keep doing that."

"It's a civil rights issue. You *know* that. Civil rights and— like Mrs. León says—freedom of expression," Albert concluded vehemently. He watched Jessica unlock her bike. "God damn heifer do-gooders. Shit, girl! They'll be after me next, tryin' to figure out what an old black man's doing around all these little white kids."

"Albert, take it easy." Jessica found it ironic to hear herself soothing him. "Mrs. León's in my corner, and considering where she works, I have some viable options. Thanks for hearing me out. I have to get home now."

"You be careful, Jess. I'm sorry you had to come back to this."

More depressed than ever, Jessica pedaled away. Riding home, she pondered how to maintain her sanity for another week. She tried to reassure herself she had found an unexpected ally in Helen León, yet her life had become too topsyturvy for that fact to hold the weight it deserved. Besides, she reasoned, if those mothers ever learned Helen's secret, she could become their next target. Jessica imagined clusters of power-suited mothers gathered around their BMW's and Volvos, gossiping and speculating about her and about Helen León. Arching over the handlebars, she rode faster.

When she turned the corner of Third and Hill, she spotted two figures on the Victorian's porch swing. Coming closer, she felt her tension slacken. She broke into a spontaneous smile.

"Jessie!" Angelita skipped down the driveway, followed by a stocky African-American man. The open jacket of his royal blue and black warm-up suit revealed a T-shirt proclaiming "White Men Can't Judge." His hair was cut in a trendy geometric style, and he grinned, watching Jessica jump off her bike and embrace his daughter.

"Oh, Angelita. You've grown inches in two weeks!"

The child giggled in Jessica's arms. "Look, my daddy's back."

"Yes. I see him." Jessica extended her hand. "Hi, Tremaine. What do you think of your beautiful daughter?"

Tremaine Walker took Jessica's hand in his large one. "Angelita's damn lucky she's had *you* looking out for her. Rita told me how much you've helped, Jessica. I want to thank you myself for taking care of our baby girl."

"I love this chulita." Jessica stood, keeping Angelita in her arms. "But I'm glad you're back. How's everything going?"

He bent to kiss Angelita. "Baby, do you think Jessie still keeps popsicles for you in her freezer?"

Jessica winked and nodded. "Here's the key to the back door. You can have a popsicle, Angelita, while your daddy and me catch up on things."

Angelita did not need a second invitation. She darted happily through the gate.

"What's the story, Tremaine?"

He paused, his brown eyes delving into hers. "I want Rita, Angelita and me to be a real family. When I left, I thought there was no way that would ever happen. Don't have to tell *you* Rita's history. I used to think I was a damn fool to fall for her—but I love that crazy woman. On the road—even before that—no one I ever met had Rita's heart, you know? I'm tired to hell of that fuckin' road scene. Thing is, now that I'm back, how do I know if I'm going to be enough for Rita?"

Jessica sighed. "You don't."

"Hoped you'd say somethin' more definite, Jessie."

"I'm being honest. Tre, I'm not sure if Rita *knows* what she wants, other than someone to love her and Angelita. It hasn't mattered to her so far if that someone was male or female."

He lit a cigarette. "You think my brain's fried for comin' back to her?"

207

Jessica shook her head. "I don't know. Rita's my friend, but she isn't always easy to be around."

He looked toward the house, observing his daughter with her beaded cornrowed hair, licking her popsicle on the veranda steps. "That baby girl makes it all worth it. Rita ever tell you we named her after the Roberta Flack tune?"

"Yes. 'Angelitos negros.'" She patted his arm. "You hang in there, Tre. I want it to work for all three of you."

"Thanks." He pulled out a leather wallet. "Listen, I want to give y'all a little somethin'. I owe you for taking in Rita and the baby."

"Tremaine, you don't have to do that." Jessica stared at the five one-hundred dollar bills he offered.

"You and Cindi gave Rita and Angelita a home while I was off rappin' with the brothers. She's grateful for that and so am I. Get some house repairs done with this." His dark eyes teased hers. "You want your yuppie neighbors to say their property values are gettin' shot to hell 'cause a bunch of Mexican chicks live next door?"

"Well, if you put it that way—" Jessica laughed and gave him a hug.

For the next few days, Jessica put her personal life on hold as much as possible. She was too nervous about lacking the inspiration to finish the Satins' tunes to confront Kathleen again; absorbing herself with creativity allowed her to cope. She went about her daily duties in a mental haze, and noticed the director and most of the mothers avoided her, too, a negative sign as far as Jessica could tell.

"Chic?" Jessica peered around the attic stairs when she heard someone on the second-floor landing.

"A sus ordenes." In her cowboy boots, a sleeveless black

shirt and a pair of tight white jeans, Chic clumped into view, recently arrived from work.

"I want you to listen to this."

Chic followed her into the bedroom, propped up the pillows and eased herself on Jessica's futon, keeping her boot-shod feet off the comforter.

Moving the portable keyboard to the edge of her desk, Jessica played an introductory salsa-flavored beat. She moved her hips slowly, warming to the song.

> *Girl, why'd you leave without a trace?*
> *Were you really hung up by my race?*
> *Making love in darkness was all right*
> *But morning showed me in a different light*
>
> *Well, I'm a brown lady*
> *Don't you know, a brown lady*
> *Yeah, I'm a brown lady*
> *And maybe much too shady*
>
> *When we danced you wanted more*
> *Held me close across the floor*
> *The lights were dim, you couldn't see*
> *How brown I am, you needed me*

Jessica's fingers flitted over the keys while she performed the rest of the song for Chic. She noticed her friend's booted feet moving to the danceable beat, her slender hands tapping the comforter in rhythm.

"All right, Jess!" Chic jumped off the futon and grabbed her in a full-bodied abrazo.

Jessica laughed and hugged her back, liking the way Chic seemed to fit her fine. "'Brown Lady' is yours."

"Top of my chart. Híjole! Let me see these lyrics." She let go of Jessica, moved to the desk, and quickly scanned the music sheet. "Yeah. These say a lot—tell those white chicks how we feel. Let's see the rest."

"This song started coming to me a while back. Have I made you crazy, waiting to see what I'd come up with next?"

Chic reached over to touch Jessica's cheek. "I tried to give you space, loca. Started gettin' frazzled 'cause I knew you had two more to do."

"Well, we shouldn't have any trouble learning these. We already know the other new tunes, plus the parodies we've gone over, Rita's solo, and my solo."

"You've done it, baby." Chic whirled toward the door. "Let's get Cindi. Phone Rita. We have to start rehearsing this tonight."

One hand on her hip, Rita stood in the living room, her eyes lustrous, her pouty lips half-smiling. Tossing Chic a carefree glance, she kept a hand on her hip and sang "You're No Good."

By Chic's satisfied expression, Jessica mused, she seemed to be listening to the most beautiful song ever written. Gliding together, the Satins backed Rita while she moved sensuously, her red-lacquered fingernails creating musical patterns in the air.

"What do you think?" She looked at them each in turn when she had finished.

"Quit smoking," Chic advised, glancing over Jessica's pile of music.

"Qué?"

"Rita, don't play dumb. Tre smokes and you've started. I can hear it in your voice." Chic took a sip of Coke. "Like Jess says, don't mess up your vocal instrument."

"You're so damn bossy. Tre *likes* the way I sing."

"Ay, mujeres!" Cindi clapped her hands. "Jeez, nothing's really changed between you two, whether you're living here or not, Rita."

"Esta bruja's always on my case." Rita cut her eyes at Chic. "It isn't like that with Tre and me."

Chic grinned, not a bit perturbed. "Atta girl, Rita. Keep your coraje. It makes your singing credible."

"Ay—see what I mean? Just listen to esa boca loca."

Chic winked at her and gestured for the others to take their places again. "We've got our work cut out for us, Satins. Let's shake to it."

16 Malibu Mania

Jessica rested her head against a scratched and graffiti-streaked window while the red and white RTD bus bumped along the Pacific Coast Highway, spewing dusky diesel smoke. She had situated herself a few seats behind the driver, hoping to catnap on the long ride. Aside from her and several sun-bleached teenagers with surfboards, the rest of the passengers were tired-looking Latinas on their way to work in hillside and beachfront homes in Topanga Canyon and Malibu. They spoke among themselves in Spanish, and while Jessica dozed or gazed out the dirty windows, she eavesdropped on their conversations. They were a seamless weave of Mexican dichos or memories of pueblitos, the foibles of husbands and children, the idiosyncrasies of employers. Although the mundaneness of the women's lives seemed to contrast with Jessica's, she recognized the parallels.

She had left the house on Third Street before anyone had awakened. Far into the night, the Satins had rehearsed; Chic and Cindi were no doubt still asleep. They had scheduled another rehearsal for late Saturday afternoon, to allow Rita some time with Tremaine and Angelita. Jessica planned to return before then.

At the Cross Creek Shopping Center, she grabbed her daypack and left the bus. Many of the Latinas also disembarked to meet their employers, who would drive them to luxury homes and back to the bus stop at the end of the day for the tedious return trip to the inner city. Watching the women fanning out, entering Mercedes sedans and Cherokee wagons, Jessica recalled the lyrics of "Domestic Hectic," the song she had co-written with Cindi in Seattle.

I come to clean your house
Quiet as a mouse
I see you when you're soused
Tu hombre's such a louse
You act like I'm not there
And I try not to stare
You act like I can't see
What's really happening

Domestic Hectic
What a life you live
Domestic Hectic
Tu vida such a sieve
Domestic Hectic
You want to have it all
Domestic Hectic
I see you have nada

The ocean air was cool. Jessica turned away from the departing Latinas and pulled on her blue sweatshirt. She headed across the parking lot to a small café and ordered coffee to go. While she waited, she took out her field guide and paged through it. She found an illustration of a black-crowned night heron and familiarized herself with the bird's appearance. Toting the coffee, she kept the field guide in hand, and ambled in the direction of the rolled-back fence under the highway.

Halfway across the parking lot, she noticed a shiny BMW reverse direction and back toward her. A grey-haired man with horn-rimmed glasses and a salmon polo shirt poked his head from the car's open window and gestured to her.

"Trabajo, señorita?"

"Excuse me?" Jessica put on her best blank face.

"Oh, perfect." He looked satisfied. "You speak English."

"Just like you." She realized at once sarcasm was lost on him.

"Want some daywork?"

"According to you," Jessica enunciated each word, "I would have no other reason for being in this parking lot."

"Look, my girl didn't show up and—"

"You mean, *sir*," she finished the sentence for him, "the woman who cleans your house decided to do something else today."

The man's face flushed slightly. "I pay well."

She smiled. Taking that for consent, the man leaned across the car and unlocked the door on the passenger side.

Jessica did not lose her smile. "Clean your own shit, mister."

The man gaped. She met his gaze unflinchingly until he accelerated quickly and drove across the parking lot.

Laughing to herself, she squeezed through the fence opening and hurried through the dank underworld beneath the highway bridge on her way to the lagoon, much as she sought creative paths to lead her beyond life's realities. In the past weeks, she had released much accumulated anger through songwriting, yet being able to express it directly, especially to a smug white man, felt exhilarating. He had seemed so complacent, so ready to assume she would be willing to change her plans to accommodate his needs. Her way of handling that encounter emphasized to Jessica the difference between her and the domestic workers on the bus earlier; few of them would have dared to speak to a white person with such defiance. Though she had the so-called advantages of U.S. citizenship and a better education, Jessica realized she was similarly dependent on the local middle-to-upper class for employment.

Stepping through the dampness beneath the bridge, she wondered if under other circumstances, she would possess enough courage to cross into another country for her livelihood, the way the domestic workers had. She broke through creative, cultural and sexual borders in her daily life as a Chicana lesbian; yet only recently had she been confronted with its economic consequences. That fact continued to frighten her, and her moment of levity faded.

She elbowed her way through the overgrown sagebrush and followed a path leading to one of the lagoon's inlets. Selecting a flat rock, she perched there and sipped the coffee, letting it warm her. The morning sun played hide-and-seek with the clouds; she hoped the sun proved the winner. She kept the field guide on her lap while removing her binoculars from their case. Soon she observed a large bird huddled on the uppermost branch of a jagged tree, its hooded eyes searching the overcast sky.

"It's a raptor."

Swiftly, Jessica glanced around. A small woman stood behind her, binoculars fixed on the bird.

"An immature peregrine falcon. Some were reintroduced into the wild and wound up in L.A. County. I hear there's even a pair downtown," she explained with a lilt in her voice. "Must be cold on that branch. Feathers all fluffed up."

Taken aback, Jessica studied the falcon once more. She wished the woman would put down the binoculars. She wanted to focus on *her*, not the peregrine. Yet she recalled Andrea Romano's unshaken concentration while birdwatching. Jessica was not surprised when the woman removed the lens cover from the camera hanging from her shoulder. Zoom already in place, she crept to the inlet's shore to photograph the falcon.

When Jessica had first glimpsed her across the lagoon, she had been unable to guess the woman's height. Up close, Andrea seemed about Rita's size, though her tomboyishness was the opposite of Rita's voluptuous figure. She wore loose-fitting jeans, a grey "Save Mono Lake" sweatshirt, and hiking boots, her lustrous brown hair partially covered by a visored cap dotted with enameled bird pins.

"Too bad I can't get closer. A canoe would sure be handy," Andrea said when she joined Jessica. Her chest was crisscrossed with both camera and binocular straps; the effect delineated her breasts. "I'm Andrea Romano."

"That's what I thought." Jessica rose, noticing she stood about a head taller than Andrea. "You already know who I am." She clasped Andrea's outstretched hand and liked the firmness of her grip.

Letting go, Andrea replaced the lens cover and squatted on the shoreline. On closer inspection, she proved to possess a simple beauty—sun-burnished skin, light brown eyes flecked with green, an incipient smile poised on appealing lips. She pushed back her cap.

"I wasn't sure you'd be here, Jessica."

She gazed into Andrea's candid eyes. "It was easier than answering your letter. And—I'm curious."

"Me, too." Her contagious smile sent shock waves through Jessica. "Jody says you've been doing lots of writing lately—songs, anyhow."

"No choice. The Satins are opening at the Delta end of next week."

"Jody told me that, too."

"I guess she's told you a lot about me."

"Oh, probably not everything."

Jessica smiled, liking her casual attitude.

"Well—there's a green heron by the first bridge. I saw it on the way over." Andrea stood, hoisting her equipment. "I'd like to get a shot of it while the sun's coming through."

Jessica suspected that was an invitation. She trailed behind Andrea, wondering if the woman felt as awkward as she did; so far she had not shown it. Jessica hoped birdwatching would continue to be a fitting subject for conversation; otherwise, she would be tongue-tied.

Andrea crouched at the bridge, supporting her zoom lens with one hand. In the filtering sunlight, the heron was motionless, identifiable by its black crest, chestnut face, neck and breast. The sleek bird remained partly camouflaged among the marsh reeds, its dark green wings blending into the tall grasses.

"Gorgeous colors," Andrea murmured, snapping a couple of photos. "Can you see it, Jessica?"

"Yes. It's so still."

"Fishing. Takes a lot of patience to catch a meal." She glanced at Jessica and grinned. "I have a lot in common with that bird—not that you're a meal." She broke into an embarrassed laugh. "God, how crass can I get?"

Jessica laughed, too, relieved Andrea had shown some trace of discomfort. While Jessica had no energy for playing games, she continued to question her reasons for being there. Leaning on the bridge's railing, she grew serious.

"Coming up the highway, I kept thinking: what is this going to be like, anyway? Can we call this a first date?"

"We're birdwatching. And we're only two of the birds we're watching."

Jessica liked that answer. "Fair enough."

Andrea adjusted her cap and moved on. "Let's see if the baby swallows are on the next bridge."

"What made you interested in—birds?" Jessica sat on the grainy sand, munching a granola bar. Not far away, tiny sanderlings raced along the shore, escaping the tumbling surf.

"I was a Girl Scout." Andrea held the camera carefully against her body and crouched beside her for the impromptu snack. "A long time later, when my dad was dying, I got into the habit of watching scrub jays from his hospital window. I remembered the names of some of the other birds—robins, starlings—but there were lots I couldn't identify. Right after he died, I signed up to do a bird count with Pomona Valley Audubon. I did it for the distraction—and I got hooked." She took the granola bar Jessica offered. "Thanks. Being interested in anything during that time was a blessing. Now I see birding as a made-to-order gift. It pulled me through."

"I'm sorry about your father," Jessica murmured. She noticed the peregrine remained above the water, surveying the area for unsuspecting prey.

"Maybe you feel about music the way I feel about birds."

"Guess it's my turn to share, huh?" Jessica glanced at her, aware of holding the woman's undivided attention at last.

"Only if you want to," Andrea said quietly. "I had a lot of expectations about meeting you. I'm not sure how *you* feel."

"I'm not either," Jessica admitted.

"Do you mind if I keep talking, then?"

Jessica nodded, not knowing what else to do.

"When I saw you with the Chorus and especially with the Satins, one of the first things I noticed was how vibrant you are when you sing. You looked like you were having a terrific time. Jody says you're kind of a loner, otherwise under wraps. That fascinates me. I'm seeing it myself right this minute, and I'm still fascinated. Creative people have that advantage—they sort of pop out and then pop in again."

Jessica felt abashed by Andrea's comments. She had not realized she could be read that easily.

"Does it bother you that I've said that?"

Jessica met her gaze again. "Sort of. I always feel like I'm wearing a mask, not showing my true self at all."

"Well, I'm the kind who likes to know the woman behind the mask. I'm glad we finally met—"

Jessica was about to ask why, when Andrea continued.

"—because I like you. Besides, you know less about birds than I do."

Amused, Jessica finished her granola bar. She stalked across the sand to throw the foil wrapper into a trash can. Morning had become early afternoon; she would have to leave soon. In the meantime, she resumed her place beside Andrea.

Surrounded by shallow water, she decided to take a figurative plunge.

"I hear you work at the Women's Legal Center. How well do you know Helen León?"

Andrea's clear eyes did not flinch at Jessica's sudden directness. "She's my boss." She rolled the foil wrapper tube-like in her fingers. "And Helen told me what's been going on with you."

"*Everything* about me, Andrea, is wrapped up in this—working with kids, performing my music, being lesbian. And to think a couple of freaked-out mothers and a probably terrified board of directors could take my job away—it makes me furious!"

Andrea studied Jessica's face. "How do your friends feel about it?"

"Cindi's the only one who knows. I haven't told the others."

Andrea looked surprised. "Why not?"

"I can't even believe I'm discussing this with *you*. The stigma of all this—it's shameful, disgusting. My integrity as a teacher is being questioned, Andrea, because I'm a lesbian. I wish no one had to know, not my friends, not my father or my sister." Jessica's voice almost broke. "Can you imagine what it's like to be assumed to be a danger to children? Andrea, it cuts me to the core. It's against everything I believe."

"I was speechless when Helen told me about it," Andrea responded. "One morning she put *La-LA Lesbian* on my desk. I felt embarrassed because of the raunchy cover. She didn't even comment on that; she wanted background on it. I told her what I knew. Then she filled me in about the situation at Pacific Palms. This happened while the Chorus was out of town."

Jessica leaned toward her, not wanting to miss a word.

"Helen understands how important singing is to you, maybe because Yolanda's father was an entertainer. She's ready to fight for you," Andrea said. "And that isn't easy for her. She's still dealing with her own problems."

"His death, I take it," Jessica suggested softly.

Andrea studied her. "How much do you know, Jessica?"

"I've been piecing it together."

Andrea continued looking at her closely, as if gauging how much to reveal. "Helen and Yolanda are HIV-negative so far. They have to be retested constantly. That's *not* common knowledge. And it really wears on Helen. At work, we try to be as supportive as possible. According to my co-workers, Helen was a paralegal at the center for a long time before she became office manager. She didn't have much of a personal life. And when she fell in love, she had no idea Daniel was gay."

Jessica sighed.

"It's taking her a while, but she's working through the anger and grief. Helen's a very strong woman. I wasn't sure what to think when she hired me—she has that cool side—but now I admire her so much. Her opinions count at the legal center. If you need it, Jessica, she'll make sure you have the best representation possible."

"I know." Jessica let her hand move tentatively to Andrea's jean-clad knee; the worn fabric felt warm, no doubt like the skin beneath it. "Bet you never thought we'd talk about this the first time we met."

Andrea edged nearer. "Don't keep all this inside anymore. Talk to Helen. Tell your friends. And please don't hesitate to keep confiding in me."

Jessica scrambled up Ocean Park Boulevard to Third Street. Andrea had continued birdwatching and photographing, seeming disappointed that Jessica could not stay for a pasta lunch at the Italian restaurant across the highway. Though she had used the afternoon rehearsal as an excuse to leave, Jessica had not mentioned her reliance on public transportation; she felt uncomfortable about asking Andrea for a ride back to Santa

Monica. Since she had not departed soon enough, she knew she would be late when her bus became delayed in beach traffic. That time had not been wasted, however; Jessica had daydreamed about Andrea all the way, recalling her snatches of humor, her candor, the way the afternoon sun glimmered, causing her eyes and skin to glow. She wished she would have been willing to meet Andrea sooner.

Out of breath, Jessica turned the corner of Third Street. She hoped Chic would not fume about her tardiness. She noticed her housemates congregated at the top of the driveway, Tremaine and Efraín among them. Immediately, she sensed trouble. She ran across the street.

"Get it through your head, Efraín," Cindi said firmly. "Tremaine is Angelita's father. He has my permission to park in this driveway."

Efrain's manner was belligerent. "No me gusta cómo estos negros cochinos—"

Cindi was almost in his face. "Your racist talk doesn't make points with me, Efraín. You have no right to tell Tremaine anything 'cause *you* don't own this place. Tremaine is *my* guest."

"What's going on?" Jessica called, panting from the uphill trek.

"This damn wetback's making a fuss about—"

"Tremaine!" Rita grabbed his arm. "I've told you not to use that word."

"I'm sorry, baby." Tremaine swung his gaze to Efraín. "I ain't goin' to let nobody push me around. Understand, hombre?"

Efraín stepped forward, fists clenched.

Chic pushed between them. "Hey, break it up. You're both overdosed on testosterone. You heard what Cindi said, Zepeda. Tremaine can park here. Get out and mind your own damn business."

Efraín glared at her menacingly. "Marimacha mugrosa. Hija de la chingada."

221

"Fuck you, too," Chic yelled at him.

Efraín muttered additional curses in Spanish and slammed through the gate leading to the back yard.

"What was all that about?" Jessica looked around at her knot of friends.

Rita sighed. "Tre parked here so he could take Angelita to the beach while we rehearse. Efraín saw him getting out of the car and—"

Tremaine cut in. "The man acted like I was about to burglarize the house."

Jessica shook her head and sighed. "Where's Angelita?"

"Watching cartoons." Cindi looked at her cousin with some relief. "She ran inside as soon as Tre stopped the car."

Tremaine lit a cigarette. "Rita says this is the dude who caused trouble before. You women goin' be all right when I take off?"

"Tre, we'll be fine." Chic patted his husky arm. "Leave it to me to handle that crazy S.O.B."

"I don't know, Chic. You're one hot-headed woman."

"That's the best kind, man."

"We have to get rid of Efraín somehow," Cindi muttered after Tremaine and Angelita left for the beach. "I'm tired of hassling with him."

"I am, too." Jessica followed her housemates into the kitchen. "The question is, *can* we get rid of him?"

"Even if he lives in back, he has no property rights," Cindi reminded her. "He doesn't own the house and has to pay us rent."

Rita took a Diet Coke from the refrigerator. "You'd think he'd want to get la familia out of here if he thinks they're surrounded by bad influences. Now Tre's included in that."

"With Efraín, it's really an economic issue." Jessica hung her daypack over a dining room chair. "How's he going to find a house to rent around here when he has four little kids?"

"That's *his* problem. *I'd* jack up his rent." Chic poured herself some ice water.

"Do you think that's legal?" Cindi glanced at Jessica.

"I don't know."

"It's probably *illegal* to have all the Zepeda clan living in that casita," Chic interjected.

"I think we'd better find out." Jessica wiped her sweaty forehead with the back of her hand. "If single-family residences aren't covered by rent control—"

"Then price the bastard the hell out of here. No great loss, if you ask me. Figure that out later," Chic suggested, leading the way into the living room. "In the meantime, let's subliminate our coraje into la música, mujeres. You okay, Rita?"

Her round eyes worried, she nodded and took her place beside Cindi.

Chic flipped through her notes. "How's this for timing? We'll start with 'Trace of Race.'"

Jessica turned to Rita, hoping the lyrics written with Angelita in mind would not upset her further.

Rita met her gaze. "I'm really glad you came up with this—*especially* now."

With a slow smile, Jessica nodded and fell into place between her and Cindi. Taking Chic's direction, the Satins formed a semi-circle around her. Her gritty voice evoked a challenging attitude.

Ain't just another pretty face
Flashin' diamonds, wearin' lace
People look, yeah, people gaze
Tryin' to figure out her case
She isn't white, she's in their haze
'cause she's got a trace of race

She's brown and black—that's her grace
Yeah, she's got a trace of race
She's brown and black—a change of pace
Yeah, she's got a trace of race

"We ought to put more emphasis on 'She's brown and black,'" Cindi suggested when they had run through the song once.

Her compañeras listened as she continued.

"I don't want to objectify anyone, but I think we'd make more of a visual impact if—I'm willing to volunteer—the morena Satins would sing that line. And las güeritas would sing 'and that's her grace,' and in the next line 'a change of pace.'"

"In other words, you and Jess do 'She's brown and black,' 'cause you're darker, and Rita and me do 'a change of pace' 'cause we're lighter." Chic shrugged. "That would definitely call attention to our own luscious shades of brown. Anybody mind?"

"It's a great idea," Jessica agreed. "Really visual."

"Might as well hit la gente over the head," Rita said. "Pero, since when am I light-skinned?"

"More than we are." Cindi gave her a teasing nudge.

The Satins rehearsed "Trace of Race," several more times before taking a breather.

"Jess, you've really covered lots of ground with these tunes." Chic held a glass of cold water against her perspiring brow. "Sounds like we're leaving the oldies parodies behind."

"Good move," Cindi interjected, slumping on the sofa.

"I think the time's right. If we're going to be doing club gigs, we need to face the competition." Jessica sat cross-legged on the living room floor. "Our strength is our material and our harmony. A certain lead singer can take some credit, too."

Chic grinned, saluting her with the glass.

"And I'm glad we're singing, not rapping," Rita said. "Nothing against Tre, but the Satins are more versatile than his group."

"Look who has the recording contract, though," Chic reminded her, signalling for her singers to get back to work. "Next item: 'Queer of the Year.' This one really ought to appeal to the masses, huh? Jess, I ought to make you sing it."

"I wrote it for *you*, Chic," Jessica insisted. She did not add that the lyrics evolved from her dealings with the two mothers and the possibility of being unemployed.

Chic blew her a kiss and sang:

I told my friends, I told my dad
Not the kind of news to make you glad
You don't like it, you think I'm bad
And you wonder why that makes me mad

I just got voted queer of the year
For righteous politics
Yeah, I'm queer of the year
For sex and other kicks
I'm L.A.'s queer of the year

Chic shook her shoulders, showing an up-front attitude.

A trendy honor to hang in my pad
A little funky, and kind of rad
Didn't figure you'd be such a cad
And make me lose that job I had

'cause I'm the queer of the year
Against office politics
Yeah, I'm queer of the year
For liking tits and clits
I'm reigning queer of the year

When Chic finished, she wrapped Jessica in a tight abrazo. "Loca, I've never known you to write lyrics like these."

"See what happens when you do a column for *La-LA Lesbian*? What's she going to come up with next?" Cindi laughed and joined in the communal hugfest.

Rita smiled at Jessica's seeming embarrassment. "Qué humilde. Say something, Jessie. Don't be humble. These lyrics are right on."

Deciding to take the momentum, Jessica at last faced her

friends. "Well, there's a lot I haven't told you about—"

Chic and Rita looked at her questioningly, their amusement subsiding at her serious tone. Cindi placed a steady hand on her cousin's arm, offering her quiet support.

"I've been outed at work," Jessica said softly. "And I may get fired."

17 Queer of the Year

Fury fired Chic's gaze. "How long did you think you could hold out on us?"

"Déjala," Rita said sharply. "You know how Jessie is. Pobrecita. She always keeps things to herself."

"Look, I don't want your anger or your pity. I *need* your support." Through her tears, Jessica observed her friends. "I don't know what's going to happen and—I'm scared. Keep wondering how I'm going to tell my dad—and Vickie. I've been praying all this would go away, but it hasn't."

Cindi gently rubbed Jessica's back. "It's going to be okay, Jess. I'm just glad you're finally letting it out."

"*You* knew about this, Cindi?" Chic glared at her.

"Yeah. I promised not to say anything. This affects Jess and it was up to her to decide whether to tell anyone or not."

"I'm sorry." Jessica tried to keep her voice firm. "It's not that I didn't want to say anything; I wasn't sure how. Besides, all of you have your own problems. I didn't want to weigh you down with mine, too."

"Hey, *I'm* the one who's sorry." Chic came over to kneel by her. "I hate it when you stuff your feelings, Jess. And you *know* how homophobia really pisses me off. And here I was, with no clue, puttin' pressure on you to finish the songs. Chispas!"

"The music kept me going, Chic. Honest. Now you know

why all these lyrics have more bite."

Chic smoothed back Jessica's hair, lightly touching her tear-stained cheek. "And with all this caca hanging over your head, you're still willing to get on stage with us. Tienes guts, loquita."

"I wrote these songs, I believe in them, and I'm going to perform them." Abruptly, Jessica stood and walked to the piano. She rearranged the numerous frames of family photos displayed on its top, gazing for long moments at the strong faces of her grandparents and their eldest offspring, Tía Irene. Jessica seemed to draw silent approval from them, and turned to face the Satins again.

"What I do away from my job is nobody's business, verdad? Don't all of you feel that way?"

"Absolutely," Chic agreed.

"No question," Cindi added.

"Seguro," Rita said.

"That's what's at stake here: my rights as a creative woman. No one has any complaints about how I do my job," she stated, regaining her composure. "They're opposed to what I do when I walk out of Pacific Palms Playschool and into my own life. That's *their* hangup. I can't let them jerk me around over that."

"Ay, Jessie." Rita's worried expression returned. "What if you get fired?"

"Then I'll sue. I'm a woman, a Chicana, a dyke—a triple threat minority."

"And 'Queer of the Year,'" Chic added.

"Columnist for *La-LA Lesbian*," Cindi tacked on.

Rita seemed annoyed with their joking. "This isn't funny, carnalas. How are the kids' mothers treating you, Jessie?"

"I think some of them are nervous about bringing up the subject. Everyone seems to want to stay out of my way. The mothers making the mitote don't even have kids in my room."

"That's so unfair." Rita slipped a consoling arm around Jessica. "Yo sé más que nadie that you're the kind of woman kids *ought* to be around. Qué locura that they're trying to make you into some kind of weirdo. I trust you with Angelita's life, Jessie. Hasn't *anyone* spoken up for you?"

"Helen León's in my corner, and Albert, of course. Helen's even willing to have the Women's Legal Center represent me. Andrea told me more about that today."

"Andrea?" Cindi's curiosity was sparked.

"I met her at the Malibu Lagoon. That's why I was late getting home."

Chic leaned forward. "I think I get the picture, but it's still a little hazy. How about some fine tuning?"

Rita looked puzzled. "Quién es Andrea?"

"You really had us in the dark." Chic sat on the veranda steps, a bottle of Corona set between her long legs.

"I told you I'm sorry." Jessica bit into a burrito of carnitas. She took her time chewing the spicy concoction.

"Cuz, you don't have to keep apologizing. I know it isn't an easy thing to talk about. If you want, I'll be there when you tell Tío Tudy and Vickie. You *do* have to tell them, you know." Cindi handed her a napkin. "Don't give her such a hard time, Chic."

"I'm her friend, remember?" Chic still wore a miffed expression. "She lets *me* use her for a sounding board, but *she* holds out."

Jessica swallowed the last bit of carnitas. "Do we have to talk about this all night?"

"No. I'll cool it." Chic relented and took a swig of beer.

Cindi undid the elastic band holding her ponytail in place. She released her black hair, her fingers massaging her scalp, spreading her thick strands past her shoulders. "Before we change the subject, I suggest saving the money Tremaine gave us. I sure don't want to pay it to Efraín to fix things up around here. You might need that money for legal fees."

Jessica sighed and said nothing.

"Well, since Rita left I guess rehearsal's officially over." Cindi got to her feet and headed to the screen door. "I have to phone a client about a closet."

"Don't let her talk you into going back in," Chic called. Cindi made a face and left.

Chic cast Jessica a tentative glance. "Cindi made some good points. Can't hurt to take her advice."

Jessica wiped her mouth and hands on the napkin.

"Would you rather talk about the lagoon chick?"

Jessica felt exhausted. "I'm talked out."

"Keeping her for a fantasy, Jess?"

"You'll meet Andrea at the Delta. I invited her." Jessica picked up her plate and rose.

"Wait, loca. Don't be pissed at me."

"For a change, I need *you* for backup. Chic, please. I have to know you're behind me."

"How can you even doubt that?" Chic stood beside her. "I'm with you *all* the way on this. You're a Satin, babe. The thing is—"

"What?"

"I have to tell Darryl about this shit—in case word gets out."

"You don't think she'd—"

"Darryl doesn't back away from controversy. And neither do the Satins."

"Urban Madness. Chic speaking."

"Uh, do you have a Latin Satins' cassette in stock? I've been calling all over town and—"

Chic paused for a second. "Jess, is that you?"

Jessica quit pinching her nose and laughed into the receiver. "How'd you know?"

"You talk like that whenever you're around an open can of cat food. What's the matter?" Chic did not even try to hide her concern. "Are you all right? Where're you callin' from?"

230

"Work." Jessica spoke quietly into the phone in the teachers' lounge. "Everything's copasetic for the time being. Listen, Helen León invited me for dinner. What time were we planning to rehearse?"

"About eight. Rita has a nails appointment at Billie's, and Cindi has a piano lesson. You'll be here on time, I hope."

"Sure. I figured I ought to get to know Helen better, especially nowadays. Did you talk to Darryl?"

"Went over last night. She thinks those metiche mothers are assholes and that you're an Amazon. See, some lipstick lesbians are top notch, Jess."

"I suppose. Catch you later."

"Quiéres un vaso de vino?" Helen studied the menu at the seafood restaurant off Main Street. A converted warehouse, the eating establishment boasted brick walls and a high wooden ceiling decorated with fishing nets and anchors.

"I'd rather have a beer."

"Pura Mexicana." Helen smiled briefly. "Jessica, how are you coping?"

"I'm not into 12-step," she admitted, "but I'm trying to take things one day at a time. Plus I have to get my energy into high gear for our show Friday." Jessica paused when the lanky red-haired waitress arrived.

"Hi, I'm Cheryl." The young woman did a double take on spotting her. "Oh my God! Aren't you one of the Latin Satins?"

Jessica nodded, somewhat embarrassed by Cheryl's exuberance.

"Wow! I see you on the Promenade all the time," she added in her Valley-tinged accent. "It's a kick to see women performing. You're so out there."

"Thanks." Jessica beamed, deciding she enjoyed the novelty of being recognized. "We'll be opening down the street at the Delta this weekend."

"Terrific! I'll make it a point to be there." Cheryl's smile did not quit. "What can I get for you in the meantime?"

"I'll have a Moosehead."

"Fumé blanc," Helen replied. She waited until the waitress left. "Another fan, eh?" Her hands played with the fresh carnation in its slender vase atop their table. "I'm glad to hear you and Andrea met. Está muy interesada en ti."

Jessica sighed, keeping her eyes on the menu. "Helen, I don't know if this is the best time for me to be thinking about—well, it isn't that I don't like Andrea—I *do*."

"You have so much else to occupy you now. She realizes that." Helen continued fingering the carnation. "Andrea's my right hand in the office—a bright, aware woman. I'm not here to tout her, mind you. She's enthused about seeing the Latin Satins at the club, and I may go with her Friday. I'm wondering, though, if performing this weekend is wise, considering—"

"We've signed for a two-week gig. Chic's already talked to the club owner about the playschool mitote." Jessica pushed a straying strand from her cheek. "Helen, I'd be insane by now if I didn't have the performances to think about."

"I know. Pero you're giving the mothers and the board more ammunition at the same time. Don't you think the board will want to do some investigating—find out for themselves exactly what kind of music you perform? Y what about local reviews of your debut at the Delta?"

"I've sung all over town, with the Satins and the Sapphonics. It isn't my fault that no one's caught on sooner. Neither group has been exactly undercover," Jessica added with a trace of annoyance. "And the Satins have worked our asses off to land this gig. Helen, we need all the publicity we can get."

"Ya lo sé," Helen murmured. "Even so, Jessica, I can't help feeling anxious about this. Do you know if you're going to be called before the board?"

"Kathleen hasn't mentioned that," Jesssica said, her shoulders slumping, "and I'm trying not to think about it."

"You have to be realistic." Helen had another question. "Have you talked to your father yet?"

"Not a chance," Jessica looked away. "I don't want to break his heart."

"He deserves to know, mujer." With impatience, Helen surveyed her. "How's he feel about the Satins?"

"Dad's too much a caballero to tell us he doesn't totally dig our act. He catches us on the Promenade whenever he can."

Jessica leaned back to allow the waitress to serve the beer and wine, and to take a respite from Helen's interrogation. While she liked having Yolanda's mother as an ally, she had not expected that direct line of questioning.

When Cheryl took their dinner orders and departed, Jessica and Helen clicked their glasses together. "To the best daycare teacher in this city."

"You may be one of the few who thinks so, Helen."

"Not true. Thanks to you, Yolanda's becoming a happy child again." Her eyes flitting to the restaurant's entrance, Helen tasted the wine. "Is that someone you know?"

Jessica whirled in the direction of Helen's gaze. In a dusty rose silk suit, pearl-grey blouse and complementary scarf, Victoria looked stunning, awaiting a table. "My sister."

"Qué linda. She's been staring at us since she walked in."

"Probably thinks you're my date."

"Ay, Dios." Helen allowed herself a smile. "Pues, ask her to join us."

Amused, Jessica put down her glass and rounded the table. "Hey, Saab sister."

"Cállate," Victoria shushed her. "Who's that you're with?"

"Helen León, the mother of one of my kids."

Victoria looked skeptical. "Jessica, what kind of caper are you up to?"

"Caper?" Jessica laughed. "She invited *me* for dinner. Look, it's not what you think, Vic."

Victoria feigned ignorance.

233

"You can join us if you like."

Victoria glanced around, ascertaining if anyone had overheard her sister's comments. "I'm waiting for a client."

"Have a drink with us in the meantime. Helen's cool—more your type than mine."

Victoria Tamayo and Helen León appraised each other, Jessica noted, as if recognizing each other's own reflection. Both were Chicana upwardly mobile professionals, commonly referred to as "Chuppies," well-dressed, perfectly coifed and groomed women, a definite contrast to Jessica in her blunt-cut hair, fuschia Hawaiian shirt and white jeans.

Helen smiled while studying the Tamayo sisters. "What do you think of the Latin Satins' upcoming engagement, Victoria?"

A hint of displeasure creased Victoria's otherwise smooth brow. She tapped the stem of her glass of Sauvignon Blanc with the tip of one polished fingernail. "Oh, you know about that? I thought you were in the habit of keeping the Satins separate from work, Jessica."

"Helen's seen us on the Promenade," Jessica said casually.

Victoria adjusted one of her pearl stud earrings. "By now, I suppose half the town has. Helen, Jessica seems to have inherited our father's musical ability. Neither of them are content to sing in the shower."

Jessica cast an amused glance at Helen. She was long accustomed to her sister's putdowns, her preference for personal discretion.

Helen did not grab Victoria's bait. "With talent like that, they *ought* to flaunt it. Your father charmed everyone on Cinco de Mayo. It was brilliant of Jessica to invite him to perform with her at the school."

Daintily, Victoria dabbed her lips with the cloth napkin. "I hadn't realized you'd dragged Dad along."

"He loved it."

Looking uncomfortable, Victoria let her brown eyes wander to the restaurant's door. Seeing no one she recognized, she checked her designer watch and sighed.

"Stood up, sis?" Jessica began to eat her spinach salad.

"I'll wait a few more minutes."

"If your client doesn't show, why don't you have dinner with us?" Helen suggested.

"Sure, Vickie. After all, you have to eat something."

Eventually, Victoria's client arrived. As her sister rose to leave the table, Jessica spoke to her softly.

"Can you stop by the house later? I need to talk to you."

Distracted, Victoria nodded, acknowledged Helen, and left to meet the stylish woman across the room.

"Good. The sooner you tell her, the better. Do I come across as *that* restrained, Jessica?" Helen carefully removed the scallops and shrimp from the seafood brochette skewers.

"Sometimes."

"Ay, Dios. Todo el tiempo Daniel encouraged me to 'loosen up.'" She bit into a piece of shrimp. "I guess Andrea told you about him."

"My dad did first. He knew Daniel as a kid." Jessica kept her voice low. "I'm sorry, Helen."

She poked a slice of pineapple with her fork. "In some ways, losing him made me stronger. It's strange how that happens, verdad? I've learned to see how—no matter whether one happens to be Chicana, gay, HIV-positive—no le hace—any kind of difference scares people."

"I'm more aware of that every day—at work, even in my own backyard."

"Jessica, I know you're a fine woman, an outstanding teacher—and now, a trusted friend. I'm going to help you through this."

.

"Tre says he's willing to be a character witness for you, Jessie—if things get that bad," Rita announced while the Satins took a rehearsal break that evening. "I told him, 'Honey, don't think esas gavachas are going to be impressed by a black rapper's opinion.' That didn't faze him. He thinks you're the greatest, Jessie. He's even wondering if you could do some tunes for Ryot Garde."

Jessica smiled tiredly. "Tell Tre I dig having him on my side."

"You're exclusively the Satins' songwriter," Chic cut in. "Deal?"

"If I wind up without a job, Chic," Jessica replied with firmness, "I won't hesitate to write songs for other groups."

"We'll handle that if we have to." Chic did not want to get bogged down in speculation. "Right now, we have our own gig to think about."

All business, she moved to the center of the living room. "Next on the bill is 'Woman, Not Your Girl.' Cindi, Jess—let's get the beat right this time on your duet. Rita, stand over here by me for back-up. Mujeres, show some attitude, some defiance. Remember how you hated working in offices. Believe the words. Don't let 'em drag."

Tap, tap, tap I'm typing
While you're in there griping
Hey, man, quit your hyping
Stop your stereotyping

40 hours in a grinding whirl
Hey, I'm a woman, not your girl
Phones and fax, their wires curl
Around a woman, not your girl

The cousins stood side by side, faces close.

You treat me like an extension
Electronic high-tech invention

But I have my own intentions
And creative interventions

40 hours of heels and pearls
Yes, I'm a woman, not your girl
Can't wait to give these clothes a hurl
'Cause I'm a woman, not your girl

Chic gave them the high sign to show her satisfaction. She signalled Jessica and Cindi to continue on center stage for their second duet "Saab Sister." Taking on sassy tones, they alternated the lines:

Hey, girl, is that a yuppie?
No, it can't be, she's too dark
What kind of car does she park?
Too far to see the trademark

Hey, girl, she's not a yuppie
Her skin's naturally brown
Watch her roll her window down
While she's driving into town

Hey, girl, she's a Chuppie
And she's in a brand new Saab
She's in a hurry to her job
Driving faster thru the mob

Chic and Rita joined in for the chorus:

She's a Chuppie
Chicana, upwardly
Mobile, professional
What a Chuppie

A great job, a new Saab
Chuppie Saab sister
Chuppie Saab Sister
My own Chuppie Saab Sister

237

"And I suppose that's the comedy relief on your program," Victoria remarked, peering through the screen door. "I am *not* amused."

"Vickie, it's not really about *you*—you just inspired it," Jessica insisted, strolling over to let her in.

"We're burlando a little, giving las career chicks a razz," Chic added, trying not to laugh aloud at Victoria's irked expression. "Hey, Vic, the Satins are *really* proud of you. You've made it in that big, bad world out there. Look at you—a glamorous Chicana with a dynamite cuerpito. Ooooh, baby."

"You expect me to believe that line of drivel? Eres tan mentirosa, Chic." Victoria arched a brow, brushing off the sofa before seating herself. "And everybody *knows* I own a Saab."

"'Saab' rhymes with lots of words," Cindi cut in. "BMW, Mercedes and Porsche don't. Jess had to keep that in mind."

"Hmm." Victoria seemed unconvinced. She crossed her legs, one high-heeled foot swinging in annoyance.

"Quiéres una taza de té o algo?" Rita offered. "We all could use a warm drink for our throats."

"Come on, Victoria. Admit you're damn flattered to be the inspiration for a song," Chic urged, slumping on the sofa beside her.

"I wouldn't admit anything to *you*."

Chic grinned slyly. "Did you know I used to have un crush gigante on you? When I was una chamaquita mugrosa, I used to check you out and say to myself—"

"Am I supposed to be charmed? Well, I'm not." Victoria rose and disappeared into the kitchen. "Jessica, can you come here?"

Jessica gave Chic a mock karate chop on her arm and reluctantly followed her sister.

"I can't believe you're going to sing that—ridicule me—in public. How do you think that makes me feel?" Victoria leaned against the refrigerator, seeming deflated. Rita put the tea kettle on before scurrying away.

Jessica took on a placating tone. "Vickie, you heard what Cindi said. Anyway, you aren't the only person in the world who drives a Saab."

"You've been calling me 'Saab Sister' for weeks. I never imagined—"

"The title came first—honest—before I ever dreamed up the lyrics. Please don't be mad, Vic." Jessica spread her hands in exasperation. "Jeez, I had to come up with all these songs in a few weeks. That hasn't been easy, especially with all this other shit going on."

"What're you talking about?" Victoria moved aside when Jessica removed a lemon from the refrigerator.

"My job's on the line. I might be unemployed by Friday afternoon."

"And that's why I had dinner with Helen León," Jessica concluded, her wet eyes holding her sister's.

The tea cup sat untouched before Victoria. She had removed her jacket, draping it behind the scarred kitchen chair. "Sooner or later, you had to fall off the tightrope."

Jessica frowned. "What kind of reaction is *that*?"

"You know how I feel about your 'lifestyle' and about your decision to sing with the Satins all over creation. You're like Dad—impractical, never thinking ahead. Have you told him anything yet?"

Jessica shook her head.

"I'm having my monthly dinner with him Wednesday night. Can you make it?"

"No way. Tomorrow, Wednesday and Thursday we're rehearsing with the band at the club from 5:00 on. I don't even know what time I'll get home."

"Maybe I should tell him myself," Victoria suggested.

239

"Oh, God." Jessica's stomach turned. "*I'd* rather do it."

"When, Jessica? If I tell him, it'll be less emotional for him—and for you, too."

"But—"

"Do you have any better ideas?" Victoria gripped the rim of the table tightly. "You're involved in a horrible situation, Jessica. And you can't exactly take time off your job to go explain all this to Dad. Why give Kathleen any more to complain about?" Victoria shook her head and finally picked up the tea cup. "I hope you can see now that Trish gave you excellent advice about staying in the closet."

"Oh, no, she *didn't*." For the first time, Jessica raised her voice. "Trish's afraid to be herself. Don't you dare throw her in my face."

"She knew how difficult it can be to work with children and be out of the closet. *That's* what I meant." Victoria stood and crossed her brown arms in their clingy silk blouse; several delicate gold bracelets slid to one wrist as she did so. "At this point, it doesn't matter *what* I think. You're my sister and you're in trouble. I know Cindi, Chic and Rita are giving you a lot of emotional support; they're powerless otherwise. Not so with me."

Jessica looked on questioningly as Victoria continued. "I can get you better legal representation than anyone at the Women's Legal Center. I know plenty of high-powered women lawyers in this town. 'Vestiges by Victoria' chooses their courtroom wardrobes, after all. And, I know for a fact that those liberal bleeding-heart types would love to defend a Chicana lesbian—particularly if they know she's *my* little sister. All I'd have to do is say those words."

18   Doin' It At The Delta

Chic and Cindi met Jessica on the second-floor landing while she was on her way to bed.

"How'd Victoria take it?"

"She's fighting mad. Big sister on the rampage." Jessica sighed with some relief. "Oh, she threw in that she doesn't like my 'lifestyle.' If she has to, though, she's ready to fight for me. For all her high-falutin' ways, Vickie's a woman I can count on."

"I'm in lust," Chic uttered breathlessly. "Those plum lips, those ojitos de india, those sexy cinnamon legs."

"That's her pantyhose shade, mensa. I'm way darker than Vickie," Jessica added with pride.

"Let me have my fantasy, loca. I'm a sucker for chicks in short skirts and high heels." Chic blew them kisses and backed into her bedroom, shutting the door behind her.

"She'll make love with Manuela tonight," Cindi remarked, gesturing with her fingers.

"Good old reliable Manuela." Jessica sat on the bottom attic step. "C.C., I think Vickie's going to tell Dad."

"Uh, oh." Cindi nestled beside her. "How do you feel about *that?*"

"I don't like it, but I don't want to tell him over the phone either." Jessica looked at her cousin. "Won't be able to see him till Saturday. By then, I could be fired."

Cindi held her cousin close for several moments, and Jessica sensed her empathy, her familial support.

"No matter what happens, Jess—remember this: We're partners, in this house, in the Satins—for always."

Tuesday afternoon, while Jessica straightened up her classroom, Kathleen paused in the doorway. At seeing her, Jessica tried to remain calm.

"The board is meeting Friday morning at ten o'clock."

Jessica lay the Sally Seal puppet on a shelf. "Will I have a chance to state my case?"

"This isn't a trial, Jessica."

"It feels like one."

Kathleen remained by the door. "The board will simply discuss the propriety of your outside activities."

"Kathleen, *that's* a trial."

"I wish you'd be less pessimistic about this." She seemed intent on soothing Jessica. "As you've said yourself, no one has ever complained about your capacity on the job. My goodness, anyone can see you have an innate rapport with children."

"And what I do away from here is inconsequential? If that were true, why would the board even have to meet about this? Who's being naive now, Kathleen?" Jessica brushed past her on her way out of the building.

"Friday, Albert," she said in a clipped voice while she unlocked her bike. "Man, you really have to win the lottery. We could quit this jive place and start our own. You'd still hire me?"

"In a second." He stood by the fence, watching her. "You got to put this place out of your mind, girl, as much as you can. How are the rehearsals going?"

"We're meeting the band tonight. Cuttin' it pretty close, if

242

you ask me." She adjusted her daypack over her shoulders. "They've had our music since the weekend, but were busy with other gigs. Makes me nervous."

"Yeah. Like you have nothing else to worry about, huh?"

Waving, she mounted her bike and rode out of the parking lot.

Chic and Jessica walked through a couple of numbers with the Chatelaines while they awaited the other Satins' arrival. A quintet of frizzy blondes, the Chatelaines—Carole, Caryn, Carla, Chris and Cathryn—were a local product, Westside lesbians who appreciated the salsa-flavored rock rhythms of the four Chicanas.

"As you can hear, we've played around with your music, thrown in additional riffs. Check this," Carla suggested, crouching over her Fender bass and elaborating on some lines of "Brown Lady." Jessica and Chic grinned at each other, admiring Carla's hard-driving improvisation.

"Hey, Carla, I dig your moves," Chic teased, winking at her. "Maybe we can rehearse sometime in private, huh?"

"Darryl really likes your style," Carole cut in. "You're originals—not copycats like some of the other groups we've backed. Believe me, it's a pleasure to work with you women. We're ready to rock 'n' roll. Where's your other two?"

"Right here," Cindi called, entering the club's back door with Rita behind. "Sorry we're late. I couldn't remember which turn to make at Rita's." She slid a scrap of paper into Jessica's hand. "Un mensaje from the answering machine, cuz."

Jessica stuck the note in her jeans' pocket.

"Hi, Andrea. I'm calling from the Delta," Jessica spoke softly into the receiver at rehearsal break. "Cindi told me you phoned earlier."

"I thought about you all weekend. Helen told me you're holding up. I wanted to hear that myself." Andrea's voice sounded warm, like her sun-burnished skin. "What's it like to sing with a band?"

"Fabulous. I'm used to singing while playing my own accompaniment on acoustic guitar. Haven't had any trouble letting the Chatelaines take over. Chic's flirting with all five of them—she's already got them in the palm of her hand." Jessica laughed, glancing at Chic schmoozing with Carla.

"I've heard she's a player."

"Chic Lozano? My rockin' sistah, my lifelong amiga? Andrea, she's really a pussycat," Jessica insisted. "And very curious about you, by the way."

"*You're* the Satin *I* want to get to know. Remember that."

Jessica thought it best to change the subject. "Listen, will you tell Helen the board's going to meet Friday morning?"

"It must be awful knowing it's the same day as your opening."

"Yeah." Jessica tried to sound optimistic "The bad comes with the good. See you Friday, Andrea. Chic's glaring at me. We're ready to start."

That week, Jessica lived for the evening rehearsals at the Delta. Anticipation for the two-week gig ran high among the Satins and the Chatelaines. They collaborated well together, their musical know-how fusing and coalescing into a distinct blend. Cindi had begun a light-hearted flirtation with Cathryn, the Chatelaines' quiet-spoken drummer. Cathryn's blonde ringlets almost covered her small face, yet her pale grey eyes were startling, almost ethereal. No wonder, Jessica thought, her cousin had been smitten. She smiled when watching them at break, drinking mineral water and whispering together.

Meanwhile, Chic could not seem to make up her mind whether she preferred Carla, the inventive bass player, or Carole, the talkative lead guitarist and band organizer. She bounded between the two; both women seemed amused to share her affections. On her best behavior, Rita spent her breaks on the phone with Tremaine and Angelita.

Friday morning, Jessica awoke with a painful right-sided headache. Stress, she thought, or maybe her period was finally about to start. In all the tension over her job and completing the songs, she had never gotten around to making a doctor's appointment. On her way to work, she rode her bike slowly, hoping the exercise would lessen the headache. She wondered if she were making her last trip to Pacific Palms Playschool.

At noon, Kathleen beckoned her into the office. Jessica remained by the door, too agitated to be seated.

"Well?" Her voice wobbled on that one word.

"The board acknowledges that during your employment you've been an excellent teacher, with an extraordinary record—"

"But?"

"Jessica, let me finish," Kathleen said irritably. "Your contract is up for renewal at the end of July. The matter will be continued until then."

"That's ridiculous!" she uttered in disgust. "Why can't they reach a decision now? Do they enjoy making me squirm?"

"They're trying to be fair." Kathleen kept her hands together primly. "Jessica, can't you see, it's the nature of the situation. You're an 'avowed lesbian.' You're out of the closet. You perform in public. And you work with children."

"And never the twain shall meet? You know as well as I do that when I'm with the kids, I'm their teacher, nothing else." Jessica leaned against the door, her anger rising. "What's the board think anyway? That I'm going to recruit kids to pose for Gay Pride posters? Kathleen, this is so asinine! On Cinco de Mayo, I was everyone's darling. Now I'm the dyke outlaw."

She clutched the doorknob for support while she stated her intent. "I want to talk to the board members myself. Will you arrange that?"

Kathleen's mouth opened in astonishment. "If you insist—"

Jessica's voice was emphatic. "I have a right to defend myself. Yes, I insist on it."

"I'll add it to the agenda, then." Kathleen jotted a note in her calendar book. "You'll have a month to change your mind."

Commiserating, Albert offered to take care of her end-of-the-day chores. Jessica rode home, feeling sick at heart, her head still aching. On the kitchen table, she left a note for her housemates, explaining the board's delay in reaching a decision. Listless and depressed, she crept upstairs to take a nap before the evening's performance. She fell asleep immediately.

When she awoke a couple of hours later, she discovered her long overdue period had started.

"Decision postponed. And now the Red River Valley's flooding," she muttered to herself.

Groggily, she pulled on a cotton robe and poked her way from the attic to take a shower, only to find Cindi had gone to use the bathroom downstairs and Chic had commandeered the second-floor one. Frazzled, Jessica pounded on its door.

"Hurry up, Chic! My damn period's started!"

"Chispas!" The door opened quickly. "You don't have to get ballistic about it." Chic wrapped herself in a turquoise bath sheet. "Want your privacy?"

"Damn right." Jessica pushed her aside and slammed the door behind her. She pulled a box of tampons from the cabinet under the sink and sank on the toilet seat, fighting back tears.

"Cindi and me saw your note," Chic said through the door. "We're with you, Jess—the Satins, Vickie, Helen León—

everybody you know. Those daycare shitheads don't know their asses from their elbows. Damn bureaucrats! Nothing's going to happen to you. We won't let it. Comprendes, Mendes?"

Jessica nodded, without speaking.

"Did you hear me, Jess?"

"Yeah," she murmured.

"Good. It's a damn shame you're on the rag tonight, but hey—la sangre's a creative source. Hmm. Not a bad idea for a tune. 'Babe, don't think of it as blood; it's the source, your creative flood.'"

Despite herself, Jessica laughed at the impromptu lyrics.

"That's my Jess—laughin' and goin' with the flow."

"How many tampons will fit in a Latin Satins jacket pocket?"

"Is that a riddle?" Cindi joked.

"As many as you want," Chic supplied. "You can stick some in mine, if it makes you feel better. Chispas! You hemorrhaging or what?" Her eyes bulged at the handful Jessica jammed into the pocket of her lavender jacket.

"Two months' worth of sangre all at once. I may have to hang onto the mike for dear life. I'm kind of light-headed."

"Cuz, we're all jittery. And you're still in shock from this afternoon," Cindi soothed her as they got into the station wagon. For once, Chic decided to accompany them in Cindi's car.

"Jess is goin' to be sensational tonight," Chic vowed from the front passenger seat. "Listen, let's blot out that pinche daycare board. We've all worked our nalgas off for this gig. And we want it to go perfectamente."

"Believe me, so do I," Jessica said, easing herself into the back seat. "Tonight that's the only important thing."

•

Backstage at the Delta, Jessica made a quick trip to the bathroom, only to discover her bleeding had not diminished.

"You look pale, Jessie," Rita said when her friend emerged from the toilet.

"Quite a trick for a Chicana, verdad?" She allowed Rita to guide her into the small dressing room.

"Cindi told me about the board. Pendejos! It's a crime for them to keep you hanging on like that. Ay, Jessie—I don't see how you can stand it."

"It's getting harder, Rita."

"Pues, sí. Siéntate, chula," Rita said with affection. "I want to put a little blush on you."

Jessica eyed her warily. "Do I really look *that* pale?"

"See for yourself." She pointed to the lighted mirror.

Catching a glimpse, Jessica relented. "Only a speck, Rita. Don't make me into a payaso."

"I know what I'm doing. Be still."

"Get ready, mujeres," Chic whispered while Darryl Desmoines began introducing the Chatelaines.

The Latin Satins congregated around Chic, each smashing in lavender jackets, purple tank tops, plum velvet jeans, purple suede high-tops.

Darryl Desmoines' voice caught the excitement of the awaiting audience. "Tonight the Delta presents one of the most magnifique acts to originate from the Westside—Sapphic Santa Monica sisters—lush Latina lesbians—the Latin Satins!"

To a drum roll plus selected guitar riffs, the Satins danced out, holding hands, forming a semi-circle with their backs to the audience. Their shiny lavender jackets sporting their collective name captured the spotlight. One at a time, each Satin whirled, taking her place before the two awaiting microphones. Chic pulled hers from its stand and nodded to the Chatelaines. She gazed at the packed house before growling the introductory lyrics of "Bushwhacker":

Cold-hearted woman don't want me back
Turned me loose, she cut me slack
Sent me into the night so black
Just like that—whack, whack, whack

Chic sliced the air with swipes of her long fingers. The audience roared its approval.

Made me into a bushwhacker—whack, whack
Bushwhacker

As Chic graphically demonstrated the lyrics, lesbians in the crowd—no doubt the majority—screamed at the double entendre.

Now I go where I don't have to pack
Travel here and there, leave no track
Find a woman who won't give me flack
Just like that—snuggle in her sack

"Come to me, Chic," someone yelled.
"I want you in *my* sack, baby," another voice shouted.

'Cause I'm a bushwhacker—whack, whack
Bushwhacker

"Ay, yi, yi! You can whack my bush anytime!" A voice with a Southwestern twang invited.

Finishing the song, Chic winked at the stomping, carousing audience. Slowly, she removed her jacket. A shrill series of whistles accompanied that action. Cindi took the jacket, draping it over a nearby chair.

"Gracias for the come-ons, mujeres," Chic said, her slim fingers outlining her damp tank top. "We'll talk después, eh? In the meantime, vamos a cantar otra vez." She tapped out the beat for "Brown Lady."

Baby, why'd you leave without a trace
Were you really hung up by my race?

Making love in darkness was all right
But morning showed me in a different light

Doing back-up with Cindi and Rita, Jessica forgot about her bodily discomfort, her swerving emotions, too absorbed in the visual dynamics of watching Chic making collective love to the receptive Chicana lesbians seated directly before her. Jessica recognized many familiar faces: Toni Dorado, Alicia Orozco, Marti Villanueva, Monica Tovar, Adriana Carranza, Jen Avila, Pat Ramos, Veronica Melendez and René Talamantes. All of them cheered and teased their homegirl, Chic Lozano, showering her with amor Chicana. Behind them Rafi danced in his seat, while Billie Otero raucously egged on the Satins' lead singer.

"I want to neck with you in the balcony of the Criterion, Chic!"

Tawny face illuminated with pleasure, Chic sang:

Well, I'm a brown lady, don't you know,
A smooth brown lady
Yeah, a sexy brown lady
And maybe much too shady

Concluding, Chic rehooked the mike and backed away, allowing Jessica and Cindi access for "Woman, Not Your Girl." Chic wiped her brow and joined Rita at the other mike. The cousins alternated lines, Chic and Rita sliding in for the chorus.

While you're dealing on the phone
I'm writing songs in my head alone
You try to work me right down to the bone
But I'm composing rhythmic tones

40 hours of skirts and curls
Hey, I'm a woman, not your girl
Can't wait to give this place a twirl
'Cause I'm a woman, not your girl

Remaining at the mike, the cousins took their cue for "Domestic Hectic." Interspersed with the original tunes, the Satins did a few goldies parodies, including Rita's rhythm and blues take of "You're No Good." Chic returned to the mike for "Boca Loca."

Cállate la boca
Me vas a volver loca
Ojos color de mocha
Quiéres que te toca

"You can touch me toda la noche, Chica!"
Grinning, Chic licked her lips for the next stanza and held the mike closer to her mouth.

Ay, dáme tu locura
Y tu piel tan oscura
Dáme un beso en mi boca
Y te voy volver más loca

"Make love to me, Chiquita!"

Showered with adulation, the Satins wrapped up their first set with "Latin Satins Theme," and after introducing themselves, boogied off-stage.

Giggling among themselves, they discovered the narrow hallway between the dressing room and bathroom had already become jam-packed with friends and fans. Soon Jessica and Cindi were surrounded by proud, though abashed, family members. Arturo hugged and kissed Jessica, while Victoria awaited her turn.

"Hermosita, estoy muy orgulloso," Arturo whispered into his daughter's ear. "Helen León's at the table with us y Cindi's familia también. Vickie me dijo todo. I don't want you to worry about anything, hija. Things will work out, eh? Keep singing your heart out tonight. Promise me?"

"I love you, Dad," she murmured. "I just couldn't—"

"Jessie, nobody in this family has an easy time explaining anything to each other."

Victoria leaned over to kiss her sister's cheek. "Are you actually wearing blush? I can't believe it!"

"Rita insisted on it." Jessica struggled to make herself heard amid the hubbub. "Vickie, thanks for talking to Dad. I wasn't sure if it was a good idea, but—"

"Once in a while, little sister, you *do* have to let your family take care of you."

Jessica kissed her and edged through the well-wishers on her way to the backstage bathroom. Despite her euphoria about the performance and her father's positive attitude, she felt physically and emotionally depleted from the varied stimulations in her life. She needed some moments alone to regain her equilibrium, to prepare for the Satins' second set. She used the toilet and freshened up. At the mirror, she confronted her tired eyes and wondered again what Andrea Romano saw in her. Jessica had glimpsed her with Jody among the crowd outside.

When she emerged from the bathroom, she noticed the friends and family members had returned to their seats. Andrea stood alone by the opposite wall.

"Hi, Jessica." She wore a peach ribbed pullover and pleated ivory slacks, the soft colors accentuating her olive skin.

"Hi." Jessica approached, admiring again her unadorned beauty. "I needed to cool off. It's hot under those lights."

"You lit a fire under the audience, too. The new songs are so dynamic," Andrea raved. "They seem a lot more personal, not a bit like the parodies."

"You think so?" Jessica glimpsed Chic at the end of the corridor in a spirited conversation with René and Veronica. "Mostly, I write with Chic in mind—the songs show my perception of her more than anything else—you know, her upfront personality, her anger, her raunchiness, her sense of humor. I show myself some in my solo. You'll see in the next set. Are you staying?"

"I wouldn't miss it," Andrea promised.

Before Jessica had a chance to respond, Chic interrupted. Her friends had left, and striding over, she wore a towel around her neck. Her moussed hair still dripped with perspiration. She shot Andrea a bold once-over, though focused her attention on Jessica.

"Hey, songwriter—buenas noticias. René T. wants to do a video of the Satins. She's even talkin' documentary. La Tejana could tape us during the next two weeks. No objections, I hope."

"Not at all." Jessica grinned at her. "Maybe things are really starting to fall into place, Chic."

"Quién sabe, loca? I can't see any problem with a little creative collaboration. René has a good eye—sure can make us look even better." Chic appraised Andrea again. "You must be the Lady of the Lake. Or should I say, the Lesbo of the Lagoon?"

Andrea was ready for her. "I'd prefer that to 'butch birder.'" She extended her hand to Chic. "I'm Andrea Romano."

"A straight shooter from the lip, so to speak." Chic gripped her hand and offered her a slow smile.

"And strictly Sicilian," Andrea added.

"Ay—tortellini and tits. Plenty of pasta and petting. The kind of menu Jess craves." Chic nipped, then kissed Jessica's shoulder. "Don't start partying yet, loca. We *do* have another set tonight." She swung her hips and two-stepped into the dressing room.

Though Jessica felt embarrassed by Chic's actions, she realized the Satins' leader had aptly demonstrated their bonds of friendship, ethnicity and talent. Chic never wasted an opportunity to proclaim those strong connections, especially to someone expressing an interest in any one of the Satins.

Andrea raised her brows. "You *do* like pasta, I hope?"

With a laugh, Jessica nodded. "And Mama Satin has spoken. She thinks you're—"

"Never mind Chic. What do *you* think, Jessica?"

She studied Andrea's direct gaze. Those green-tinged eyes had drifted slowly to Jessica's mouth. She decided not to let Andrea distract her.

"I'm going to talk to the board myself next month. My contract is up for renewal then."

Andrea stepped closer. "How does that feel to you?"

"I'm scared, of course. At the same time, I know that I'm the only one who can really speak for myself. I *have* to do it, Andrea."

"You'll discuss it with Helen first?"

"No question." Jessica sighed and leaned against the corridor. "You know what I'd like right this very minute?"

Andrea's feathery lashes nearly hid her eyes and her pink lips were mere inches away. "I think I do."

Jessica felt captivated by her nearness. "So kiss me," she whispered.

They both smiled at that. Whatever shyness existed between them began to fade. Jessica leaned toward her, and their mouths touched in an exploratory smooch. Andrea brought a gentle hand to the back of Jessica's warm neck. She held her firmly, reaching for her. They kissed again, deeper, longer.

"Andrea—"

"Hmm?"

"Wait for me—after the set."

"Like a night owl."

The Satins opened their second set with "Queer of the Year." Chic paraded the stage, her voice taunting.

You thought I'd grovel, thought I'd cower
From where you sit in that ivory tower
You think you've made it, but your life is sour
Look, I'm into gay/lesbian power

'Cause I've been voted queer of the year
For community politics
Yeah, I'm queer of the year
For taking gibes and licks
I'm proud to be queer of the year

Someone screamed, "You ain't too queer for me, Chic!"

Mike in hand, Chic sang and swaggered, eventually stopping to gaze into the audience. "How many queers here tonight?"

The Delta exploded into pandemonium, foot stomping, shouts of "Queer Power," cat calls and wolf whistles.

"That's what I thought." Chic nodded. "Y cuantos son de color?"

The audience response was deafening. Billie, in a low-cut sequined cocktail dress, stood and issued a shrill chola whistle, causing Rafi to laughingly cover his ears. Around them, the other Latinas yelled "Lesbiana Power."

"Bueno." Chic paused and swung the mike. "The next ones, mi gente, son para ustedes." She signalled to the Chatelaines for "Trace of Race," while the Satins provided backup. To fuel the audience further, Chic directed her gritty voice into "Salsa Sex."

Are you tired of white chicks
Blue eyes and vapid licks
Fed up with limp dicks
All those gavacho tricks
Yeah, they're all so sick

Pues ven conmigo, chica
Por un taste de salsa sex
Ah, sí, my blend of salsa sex
Sabor Chicana con salsa sex

The Chicana lesbians went wild, their long-withheld sentiments expressed in Chic's lowdown voice.

Fed up with lines so slick
You say, "Oh, what a prick!"
Mujer, I'll wet your wick
Go down slow and get a lick
Trust me, I ain't no trick

"Ay, mi corazón! Dáme tu boca, Chic!"

Porque conmigo, chica
You'll taste la salsa sex
Ay, bebé, un taste de salsa sex
Sabor Chicana con salsa sex

Without missing a beat, Jessica and Cindi took a turn with "Saab Sister," which prompted giggles and murmurs of recognition from the Chicana contingent. Jessica hoped Victoria would take that in stride and be able to laugh at herself.

"I want to reintroduce Jessica Tamayo," Chic announced on her return to the mike. "Don't be fooled 'cause she's the quiet Satin. Jess puts her feelings into songs. She wrote all the new material we've done tonight, including the next one, 'Niños.' Here she is—the Satins' songwriter, hermana de mi alma—Jessica Tamayo!"

Acoustic guitar strapped to her shoulder, Jessica nodded to the cheering audience. She stood alone at the microphone, feeling her emotions rise. Strumming the strings, accompanied by Cindi at the keyboard, Jessica faced the crowded room and began to sing.

Niños sitting in a circle there
I watch them playing and I swear
They're the future, but so unaware
Of how folks hurt them and don't care

Niños look at me with hopeful eyes
Creen que I'm smart, they think I'm wise

256

Pero tengo doubts and lots of sighs
Por este mundo, they don't realize

She noticed the stillness of the audience. She wondered if they sensed her intense conviction through the words she sang. She glimpsed Andrea, who quietly nodded to her. She saw her family sitting together with Helen León, Vickie's attentiveness, her father's look of pride. Fortified by their presence, knowing she would gain strength from their support in the weeks ahead, Jessica allowed her voice to soar amid the audience's sudden silence, revealing her hopes, her dreams.

Niños don't hate, they're color-blind
They have amigos, they don't mind
Skin color, looks and other kinds
Of people because friendship binds

Closing her eyes, she sang for Angelita, for Yolanda, for Xochi, for all the children she worked and played with daily—and for herself.

Niños are the future, they're our hope
Remember that and learn to cope
Within their eyes we see the scope
Of tomorrow; niños are our hope

Niños don't hate, they're color-blind
They have amigos, they don't mind
Skin color, looks and other kinds
Of people because friendship binds

Tee Corinne

Terri de la Peña is the Chicana daughter of a Mexican immigrant mother and a Mexican-American father. She is a native of Santa Monica, California, where her father's family has lived since the early 1800s. She has been awarded the Chicano Literary Prize twice from the University of California at Irvine, and has taught fiction in workshops on the West Coast. She is the author of *Margins,* and her short stories have appeared in numerous anthologies.

OTHER LESBIAN TITLES FROM SEAL PRESS

MARGINS by Terri de la Peña. $10.95, 1-878067-19-2. One of the first lesbian novels by a Chicana author, *Margins* is an insightful story about family relationships, recovery from loss, creativity and love.

ALMA ROSE by Edith Forbes. $10.95, 1-878067-33-8. A brillant novel filled with unforgettable characters and the vibrant spirit of the West, *Alma Rose* is a warm, funny and endearing tale of life and love off the beaten track.

OUT OF TIME by Paula Martinac. $9.95, 0-931188-91-1. *Winner of the 1990 Lambda Literary Award for Best Lesbian Fiction, Out of Time* is a delightful and thoughtful novel about lesbian history and the power of memory.

HOME MOVIES by Paula Martinac. $10.95, 1-878067-32-X. This timely and evocative story charts the emotional terrain of losing a loved one to AIDS and the intricacies of personal and family relationships.

LOVERS' CHOICE by Becky Birtha. $10.95, 1-878067-41-9. Provocative stories charting the course of women's lives by a noted African-American lesbian feminist writer.

CEREMONIES OF THE HEART: *Celebrating Lesbian Unions* by Becky Butler. $14.95, 0-931188-92-X. An anthology of twenty-five personal accounts of ceremonies of commitment, from the momentous decision to the day of celebration.

GAUDÍ AFTERNOON by Barbara Wilson. $9.95, 1-878067-89-X *Winner of the 1990 Lambda Literary Award for Best Lesbian Mystery and the British Crime Writers Association's '92 Award.* Amidst the dream-like architecture of Barcelona, this high-spirited comic thriller introduces amateur sleuth Cassandra Reilly as she chases people of all genders and motives.

GIRLS, VISIONS AND EVERYTHING by Sarah Schulman. $9.95, 0-931188-38-5. A spirited romp through Manhattan's Lower East Side featuring lesbian-at-large Lila Futuransky. By the author of *People in Trouble, After Delores* and *Empathy*.

SEAL PRESS, founded in 1976 to provide a forum for women writers and feminist issues, has many other titles in stock: fiction, self-help books, anthologies and international literature. Any of the books above may be ordered from us at 3131 Western Ave., Suite 410, Seattle WA 98121 (please include 15% of total book order for shipping and handling). Write us for a free catalog.